Acclaim for Kathleen Fuller

"Return to Birch Creek for another delightful Amish Mail-Order Bride Novel by Kathleen Fuller. *Love in Plain Sight* combines Fuller's engaging style with a strong plot and compelling characters who will steal your heart. Don't miss this 'must read' story that's sure to remain a lifetime favorite."

—Debby Giusti, *USA Today* and *Publishers Weekly* bestselling author of *Smugglers in Amish Country*

"Kathleen Fuller's emotional and evocative writing draws readers into her complex stories and keeps them cheering for her endearing characters even after the final page."

—Patricia Davids, *USA Today* bestselling author

"Katharine Miller has everything she ever wants, until she realizes what she's gotten. *Love in Plain Sight* is Kathleen Fuller at her best. She shines the spotlight on an unlikely heroine who runs away to find herself . . . and discovers what true love looks like."

—Suzanne Woods Fisher, bestselling author of *Mending Fences*

"Fuller continues her Amish Mail-Order Brides of Birch Creek series (following *A Double Dose of Love*) with the pleasing story of Margaret, the youngest of four sisters who visits Birch Creek, Ohio, to stay with her aunt and uncle to avoid the temptations of *Englischer* life . . . This charming outing, filled as it is with forgiveness, redemption, and new beginnings, will delight Fuller's fans."

—*Publishers Weekly* on *Matched and Married*

"This is a cute story of two sets of twins learning to grow up and be adults on their own terms and finding love along the way. It is another start of a great series."

—*Parkersburg News and Sentinel* on *A Double Dose of Love*

"Fuller (*The Innkeeper's Bride*) launches her Amish Mail-Order Brides series with the sweet story of love blooming between two pairs of twins . . . Faith and forgiveness form the backbone of this story, and the vulnerable sibling relationships are sure to tug at readers' heartstrings. This innocent romance is a treat."

—*Publishers Weekly* on *A Double Dose of Love*

"Fuller cements her reputation [as] a top practitioner of Amish fiction with this moving, perceptive collection."

—*Publishers Weekly* on *Amish Generations*

"Fuller brings us compelling characters who stay in our hearts long after we've read the book. It's always a treat to dive into one of her novels."

—Beth Wiseman, bestselling author of *Hearts in Harmony*, on *The Innkeeper's Bride*

"A beautiful Amish romance with plenty of twists and turns and a completely satisfying, happy ending. Kathleen Fuller is a gifted storyteller."

—Jennifer Beckstrand, author of *Home on Huckleberry Hill*, on *The Innkeeper's Bride*

"I always enjoy a Kathleen Fuller book, especially her Amish stories. *The Innkeeper's Bride* did not disappoint! From the moment Selah and Levi meet each other to the last scene in the book, this was a story that tugged at my emotions. The story deals with several heavy issues such as mental illness and family conflicts, while still maintaining humor and couples falling in love, both old and new. When Selah finds work at the inn Levi is starting up with his family, they clash on everything but realize they have feelings for each other. My heart hurt for Selah as she held her secrets close and pushed everyone away. But in the end, God's grace and love, along with some misguided Birch Creek matchmakers stirring up mischief, brings them together. Weddings at a beautiful country inn? What's not to love? Readers of Amish fiction will enjoy this winter-time story of redemption and hope set against the backdrop of a beautiful inn that brings people together."

—Lenora Worth, author of *Their Amish Reunion*

"A warm romance that will tug at the hearts of readers, this is a new favorite."

—*The Parkersburg News and Sentinel* on *The Teacher's Bride*

"Fuller's appealing Amish romance deals with some serious issues, including depression, yet it also offers funny and endearing moments."

—*Booklist* on *The Teacher's Bride*

"Kathleen Fuller's *The Teacher's Bride* is a heartwarming story of unexpected romance woven with fun and engaging characters who come to life on every page. Once you open the book, you won't put it down until you've reached the end."

—Amy Clipston, bestselling author of *A Seat by the Hearth*

"Kathleen Fuller's characters leap off the page with subtle power as she uses both wit and wisdom to entertain! Refreshingly honest and charming, Kathy's writing reflects a master's touch when it comes to intricate plotting and a satisfying and inspirational ending full of good cheer!"

—Kelly Long, national bestselling author, on *The Teacher's Bride*

"Kathleen Fuller is a master storyteller, and fans will absolutely fall in love with Ruby and Christian in *The Teacher's Bride*."

—Ruth Reid, bestselling author of *A Miracle of Hope*

"*The Teacher's Bride* features characters who know what it's like to be different, to not fit in. What they don't know is that's what makes them so loveable. Kathleen Fuller has written a sweet, oftentimes humorous, romance that reminds readers that the perfect match might be right in front of their noses. She handles the difficult topic of depression with a deft touch. Readers of Amish fiction won't want to miss this delightful story."

—Kelly Irvin, bestselling author of the Every Amish Season series

"Kathleen Fuller is a talented and gifted author, and she doesn't disappoint in *The Teacher's Bride*. The story will captivate you from the first page to the last with Ruby, Christian, and other engaging characters. You'll laugh, gasp, and wonder what will happen next. You won't want to miss reading this heartwarming Amish story of mishaps, faith, love, forgiveness, and friendship."

—Molly Jebber, speaker and award-winning author of *Grace's Forgiveness* and the Amish Keepsake Pocket Quilt series

"Enthusiasts of Fuller's sweet Amish romances will savor this new anthology."

—*Library Journal* on *An Amish Family*

"These four sweet stories are full of hope and promise along with misunderstandings and reconciliation. True love does prevail, but not without prayer, introspection, and humility. A must-read for fans of Amish romance."

—*RT Book Reviews*, 4 stars, on *An Amish Family*

"The incredibly engaging Amish Letters series continues with a third story of perseverance and devotion, making it difficult to put down . . . Fuller skillfully knits together the lives within a changing, faithful community that has suffered its share of challenges."

—*RT Book Reviews*, 4 1/2 stars, on *Words from the Heart*

"Fuller's inspirational tale portrays complex characters facing real-world problems and finding love where they least expected or wanted it to be."

—*Booklist*, starred review, on *A Reluctant Bride*

"Fuller has an amazing capacity for creating damaged characters and giving insights into their brokenness. One of the better voices in the Amish fiction genre."

—*CBA Retailers + Resources* on *A Reluctant Bride*

"This promising series debut from Fuller is edgier than most Amish novels, dealing with difficult and dark issues and featuring well-drawn characters who are tougher than the usual gentle souls found in this genre. Recommended for Amish fiction fans who might like a different flavor."

—*Library Journal* on *A Reluctant Bride*

"Sadie and Aden's love is both sweet and hard-won, and Aden's patience is touching as he wrestles not only with Sadie's dilemma, but his own abusive past. Birch Creek is weighed down by the Troyer family's dark secrets, and readers will be interested to see how secondary characters' lives unfold as the series continues."

—*RT Book Reviews*, 4 stars, on *A Reluctant Bride*

"Kathleen Fuller's *A Reluctant Bride* tells the story of two Amish families whose lives have collided through tragedy. Sadie Schrock's stoic resolve will touch and inspire Fuller's fans, as will the story's concluding triumph of redemption."

—Suzanne Woods Fisher, bestselling author of *Mending Fences*

"Kathleen Fuller's *A Reluctant Bride* is a beautiful story of faith, hope, and second chances. Her characters and descriptions are captivating, bringing the story to life with the turn of every page."

—Amy Clipston, bestselling author of *A Seat by the Hearth*

"The latest offering in the Middlefield Family series is a sweet love story with perfectly crafted characters. Fuller's Amish novels are written with the utmost respect for their way of living. Readers are given a glimpse of what it is like to live the simple life."

—*RT Book Reviews*, 4 stars, on *Letters to Katie*

"Fuller's second Amish series entry is a sweet romance with a strong sense of place that will attract readers of Wanda Brunstetter and Cindy Woodsmall."

—*Library Journal* on *Faithful to Laura*

"Well-drawn characters and a homespun feel will make this Amish romance a sure bet for fans of Beverly Lewis and Jerry S. Eicher."

—*Library Journal* on *Treasuring Emma*

"*Treasuring Emma* is a heartwarming story filled with real-life situations and well-developed characters. I rooted for Emma and Adam until the very last page. Fans of Amish fiction and those seeking an endearing romance will enjoy this love story. Highly recommended."

—Beth Wiseman, bestselling author of *Hearts in Harmony*

"*Treasuring Emma* is a charming, emotionally layered story of the value of friendship in love and discovering the truth of the heart. A true treasure of a read!"

—Kelly Long, national bestselling author

LOVE IN
Plain Sight

Other Books by Kathleen Fuller

The Amish Mail-Order Bride Novels

A Double Dose of Love

Matched and Married

Love in Plain Sight

The Amish Brides of Birch Creek Novels

The Teacher's Bride

The Farmer's Bride

The Innkeeper's Bride

The Amish Letters Novels

Written in Love

The Promise of a Letter

Words from the Heart

The Amish of Birch Creek Novels

A Reluctant Bride

An Unbroken Heart

A Love Made New

The Middlefield Amish Novels

A Faith of Her Own

The Middlefield Family Novels

Treasuring Emma

Faithful to Laura

Letters to Katie

The Hearts of Middlefield Novels

A Man of His Word

An Honest Love

A Hand to Hold

The Maple Falls Romance Novels

Hooked on You

Much Ado About a Latte

Sold on Love (Available August 2022)

Story Collections

An Amish Family

Amish Generations

Stories

A Miracle for Miriam included in *An Amish Christmas*

A Place of His Own included in *An Amish Gathering*

What the Heart Sees included in *An Amish Love*

A Perfect Match included in *An Amish Wedding*

Flowers for Rachael included in *An Amish Garden*

A Gift for Anne Marie included in *An Amish Second Christmas*

A Heart Full of Love included in *An Amish Cradle*

A Bid for Love included in *An Amish Market*

A Quiet Love included in *An Amish Harvest*

Building Faith included in *An Amish Home*

Lakeside Love included in *An Amish Summer*

The Treasured Book included in *An Amish Heirloom*

What Love Built included in *An Amish Homecoming*

A Chance to Remember included in *An Amish Reunion*
Melting Hearts included in *An Amish Christmas Bakery*
Reeling in Love included in *An Amish Picnic*
Wreathed in Love included in *An Amish Christmas Wedding*

LOVE IN *Plain Sight*

AN AMISH MAIL-ORDER BRIDE NOVEL

KATHLEEN FULLER

ZONDERVAN®

ZONDERVAN

Love in Plain Sight

Requests for information should be addressed to:

Zondervan, *3900 Sparks Dr. SE, Grand Rapids, Michigan 49546*

Library of Congress Cataloging-in-Publication Data

Names: Fuller, Kathleen, author.
Title: Love in plain sight / Kathleen Fuller.
Description: Grand Rapids, Michigan : Zondervan, [2022] | Series: An Amish mail-order bride novel ; [3] | Summary: "She has a secret she's determined to keep. He's just as determined to get to know her. These two strong wills clash in beautiful romantic sparks in this Amish rom-com"-- Provided by publisher.
Identifiers: LCCN 2021052439 (print) | LCCN 2021052440 (ebook) | ISBN 9780310358992 (paperback) | ISBN 9780310359524 (epub) | ISBN 9780310359531 (downloadable audio)
Subjects: LCGFT: Novels.
Classification: LCC PS3606.U553 L67 2022 (print) | LCC PS3606.U553 (ebook) | DDC 813/.6--dc23/eng/20211029
LC record available at https://lccn.loc.gov/2021052439
LC ebook record available at https://lccn.loc.gov/2021052440

Publisher's Note: This novel is a work of fiction. Names, characters, places, and incidents are either products of the author's imagination or used fictitiously. All characters are fictional, and any similarity to people living or dead is purely coincidental.

Printed in the United States of America

22 23 24 25 26 LSC 10 9 8 7 6 5 4 3 2 1

To James. I love you.

Glossary

ab im kopp: crazy in the head
ach: oh
appeditlich: delicious
boppli: baby
bruder: brother
bu/buwe: boy/boys
daed: dad
danki: thank you
Deitsch: Amish language
dochder: daughter
dummkopf: stupid
familye: family
frau: wife
geh: go
grosskinner: grandchildren
grossmutter: grandmother
grossvatter: grandfather
gut: good

Glossary

Gute morgen: good morning
Gute nacht: good night
haus: house
kaffee: coffee
kapp: white hat worn by Amish women
kinn/kinner: child/children
lieb: love
maedel/maed: young woman/young women
mamm: mom
mann: man
mei: my
mutter: mother
nee: no
nix: nothing
Ordnung: written and unwritten rules in an Amish district
sohn: son
vatter: father
ya: yes
yer: your

Prologue

"C'mon, Katharine. I said I was sorry."

Katharine Miller leaned against the bathroom door and closed her eyes. How many times had Simeon said those exact same words? More than she could count. More than she wanted to think about.

"Katharine. Please let me come in."

A shiver traveled through her, and again, like several times before, his sudden gentle tone chopped at her resolve.

"I shouldn't have lost *mei* temper," he continued, his deep voice barely muffled by the oak door between them.

No, he shouldn't have.

"I promise I'll do better. Let me prove it to you."

His last plea almost had her opening the door, but she held firm. He'd made these promises before, and for a while he kept them, becoming the nice, caring man she had fallen for when he asked her out on a date after a Sunday singing less than four months ago.

"Katharine . . . can you forgive me?"

A thump sounded against the door, as if he was leaning against it. She closed her eyes and stayed as still as possible. Normally when he asked for forgiveness, she gave it. Her Amish faith required it. But this time, she couldn't respond. When he pounded his fist against the other side of the door, she flinched, knowing she had to answer before he became incensed again. "I—I'll be right out."

"Make it quick," he said, sounding less remorseful and more demanding. "I don't want to be late for supper at the Schroeders' like we were last time."

Even though it hurt to do so, she pressed her lips together. Their tardiness to his best friend's monthly Saturday afternoon barbecue had been due to another one of their fights. She couldn't remember what started that argument, and he had hit her on the shoulder on the way to Galen and Elsie's house. But this was the first time he'd slapped her across the face.

"I'll be waiting outside," he finally said, his tone now edged with frustration. "Be out in five minutes."

He didn't have to add anything else to that order. When she heard him walk away, she hurried to the bathroom mirror and nearly cried at the sight of blood on the corner of her mouth. Quickly she pulled herself together. Her tears would anger him further, and he was plenty mad as it was, despite his attempts at making her believe he was apologetic. She washed her face, then carefully patted her skin dry. Her complexion, always prone to breakouts, was now constantly covered with acne. One more thing for Simeon to complain about.

She stared at her reflection, her lips trembling, and this time she couldn't steady her emotions. "I can't do this anymore," she whispered, fighting to keep her composure. But she didn't have a choice. In their small district in Hulett, Wyoming, potential spouses were scarce, and when Simeon had showed interest in her, she hadn't only been surprised, she'd been beyond grateful. Even though she was twenty-one and not an old maid by any means, her constant battles with her weight and complexion made her assume she'd never marry—and more than anything, she wanted to get married and have a family. But she had to be realistic. There were far prettier single women in Hulett. Why would any man want her?

But Simeon, a handsome, muscular blacksmith who'd had all the women's attention at one time or another, inexplicably pursued her. After their first date, he wanted to spend every minute with her, showering her with compliments and devotion. What woman wouldn't be thankful to have a man like him? And when he asked her to marry him two months after they started dating, she thought God had answered her prayer.

But the closer they came to their wedding date, the more he had changed. Now he was barely a remnant of the man she'd fallen in love with . . . and was set to marry in less than a month.

Oh no. She was doing exactly what she shouldn't be right now—wasting time. She hung the towel back on the hook and rushed out of the bathroom. Her parents were out with friends this afternoon, leaving her and Simeon alone in the house. If her mother and father had been there, they wouldn't have gotten into a fight. He was always on his best behavior when anyone else was around. But when they were alone . . .

She ran out of the house and jumped into the buggy, not an easy feat since she had gained more than forty pounds this year on top of the thirty she already needed to lose. The buggy's cover did little to mask the heat of the hot desert sun, and she immediately broke out in a sweat.

Simeon gave her look of disgust. "You need to *geh* on a diet," he said, lightly tapping the horse's back with the reins.

So much for being sorry. It wasn't lost on her that he often treated his horse better than he treated her. "I am on a diet."

"Then why do you keep getting fatter?" He glared at her, his thick black brows becoming a single line over his deep-set, dark brown eyes that used to make her swoon every time she looked into them. Now all she felt was fear.

"I-I don't know," she mumbled. But she did know. Each morning she promised to stick to her diet, and by the end of the day, she failed. This past month she had given up entirely, the urge to eat becoming more overwhelming the closer they came to their wedding day. There was no reason to talk to him about it, or about anything else important to her. He wouldn't understand, or even try to.

He turned the corner and guided his buggy down the Schroeders' road. Her stomach turned, and she stared at her lap, sweat dripping down the sides of her face as they continued on the short drive. She glanced at his profile, remembering when his chiseled jaw and full mouth made her heart race. How could a man with such a beautiful outside be so horrible inside?

At least she would have a reprieve at the Schroeders', not only because they would be around other people but because Galen's wife, Elsie, was one of Katharine's friends. One of the few she had left since Simeon monopolized all of her time outside of her job making baskets and her chores at home.

When they arrived at the Schroeders', Simeon parked the buggy and turned to Katharine. "Not a word about what happened today. Do you understand?"

She nodded. "*Ya*."

His eyes switched from hard to endearing, almost loving. He cupped her cheek with his palm, and she fought not to pull away. "I love you, Katharine. That's why I get so angry. I care about you so much, and I just want what's best for you. But when you get rebellious, I have to intervene. That's *mei* God-given duty. We both know that."

Her fingernails pressed into her palm. Earlier today his idea of her being rebellious was not being ready when he came to pick her up. Last week she was late for their date because she had helped her mother bake apple pies to take to a store to sell. Whenever she didn't do or say exactly what he wanted, she was "rebelling."

"Do you forgive me?"

She paused, feeling his fingers tighten slightly on her cheek. "*Ya*," she finally managed to say. "I forgive you."

He removed his hand. She didn't miss him wiping his palm on his pants before getting out of the buggy. The way he could switch his emotions on and off confused her. *Lord, am I wrong when I don't do everything he says and I don't perfectly follow his schedule? I don't want to rebel or disappoint you. But I'm miserable, Lord. And I'm sorry, but lately I haven't felt anything for Simeon. I thought I loved him, and he loved me. But now I'm not sure of anything.*

"Katharine!"

She hurried out of the buggy, then turned around and grabbed the basket that held an extra apple pie she and her mother had baked to bring to the Schroeders'. It was one of the first baskets she'd made when she started weaving them four years ago. Since then she had developed a good business selling them out of her and her parents' home, and she had a large nest egg built up, one that Simeon knew about. She wished she'd never told him about the money.

By the time she headed for the house, Simeon was already talking to Galen, who was standing in front of a black gas grill. The lid was open, and large puffs of smoke floated in the air. As she passed by the two men and headed for the house, Simeon's eyes narrowed at her for a split second before he grinned and turned to talk to Galen again.

Was this how their marriage would be for the rest of their lives? Him running hot and cold, physically abusing her and pleading for forgiveness afterward? And what about any children the Lord might bless them with? Would he treat them the same way?

She schooled her features and walked into Elsie's kitchen. Her friend was at the counter preparing a large salad. She barely glanced at Katharine and smiled, her cheeks plump and cute during her eighth month of pregnancy. "Hi," she said, turning her focus back to the carrot she was chopping.

"Hi, Elsie. I brought apple pie. Where should I put it?"

"There is fine." She gestured to the table, which wasn't set for the meal. Although it was hot outside, the Schroeders had a shaded patio, and there was a pleasant breeze in the air. As long as it wasn't raining or snowing, they usually ate outside for lunch since the winters in Wyoming were long and everyone took advantage of nice weather whenever they could.

Katharine took the pie out of the basket and set it next to a bowl of homemade potato chips, keeping the plastic wrap on until they were ready for dessert. Then she walked over to Elsie. "Can I help you with anything?"

"I'm almost done here." She scraped the small pieces of chopped carrot on top of a bed of lettuce, cucumbers, grape tomatoes, and red onion. As she picked up the tongs to toss the salad, she looked at Katharine and continued talking. "I've got a pitcher of lemonade on the counter—" Her eyes widened and she dropped the tongs. "Katharine, you're bleeding!"

Katharine touched the corner of her mouth and felt the blood. Oh no. She went to the table and grabbed a napkin from the holder and pressed it against the wound. "It's *nix*," she said. Elsie's shock had disappeared, now replaced with concern.

Elsie waddled over to her. "Let me see."

Reluctantly she removed the napkin, wincing at Elsie's livid expression. "Did Simeon do that to you?"

Katharine started to shake her head. It had become a habit to make excuses for the marks he left behind—the pinched bruise on her upper arm that her mother had noticed last month because it was too hot to wear a long-sleeved dress. The dent in her shin when he had kicked her "accidentally" because she was walking too slow on their tour of the property he bought where he planned to build their house. At least last month, when he punched her shoulder, he hadn't left a mark. This time he'd left one she couldn't cover up.

Elsie folded her lips inward. "Never mind, you don't have to tell me. I know he did. Katharine, why do you stay with him?"

She fought back tears again and glanced out the back kitchen window where Simeon and Galen were in full view. The warning look he gave her before she walked inside helped keep her emotionless. "I love him," she said, trying to convince herself even more than Elsie.

Elsie didn't say anything for a long moment, and Katharine thought she had dropped the subject. Then she frowned. "Come with me," she said, heading out of the kitchen.

Puzzled, Katharine followed her to her bedroom. Elsie went to one of the bedside tables and opened the drawer. She fished around for a few seconds before pulling out a letter, then she gestured for Katharine to sit down on the bed next to her. "My cousin Amy in Montana sent this to me a month ago. When I read it, I thought of you. Read the third paragraph." She handed the letter to Katharine:

Mother told me the funniest thing the other day, Elsie. There's a small settlement in Ohio near Holmes County—I think she said the name was Birch Creek. My Aunt Clara found out from her sister Lucy, who had talked to an old friend in Shipshe who has a third cousin in Millersburg who had seen an ad in the paper advertising for brides for the bachelors in the district. Can you believe that? A town so desperate for women that they have to advertise in the paper. If I wasn't already married, I might be tempted to go there myself. Aunt Clara tried to convince her daughter Frannie to go, only to find out Frannie had been dating her now fiancé for over three years. Aunt Clara is over the moon, of course. She was so sure Frannie would never get married . . .

Katharine continued to read the next few sentences about Frannie's upcoming wedding, then stopped. "What does this have to do with me?"

Elsie awkwardly shifted her pregnant body on the bed and faced her. "You need to leave Hulett."

"What?"

"Simeon is *nee gut*. I'm afraid if you marry him . . ." Her voice sounded thick. "You're not safe, Katharine."

After a long pause, Katharine said, "I know." She'd never admitted that out loud, but now that she had, a new fear kicked in. Elsie was right, she couldn't marry Simeon. But he wouldn't let her go that easily. The one time she expressed doubts about their relationship and told him she needed some time to think things over, he exploded. "Why are you hurting me?" he'd shouted. "How can you be so cruel?" She'd been so startled by his reaction she reassured him that she wasn't breaking up with him. And that occurred when he was still treating her well. If she left him now, his reaction would be so much worse.

"I don't know what to do," she said to Elsie. "I can't break up with him. He won't allow that. And won't people question my arrival in Birch Creek?"

"That's why this is a perfect opportunity for you. There have to be plenty of women in Birch Creek by now, searching for a husband. If you went there, everyone would think you're looking for one too."

"But I'm not."

"You don't have to tell anyone the real reason you're there."

Katharine got up from the bed. The idea of being free from Simeon, even for a little while, gave her a tiny bit of hope. She turned around. "But what about *mei* parents? I can't tell them the truth. They won't believe me anyway. They think Simeon is perfect." And he was when he was around them. So much so that they were more excited about her engagement than she was.

"Oh, Katharine," *Mamm* had said with tears in her eyes as Simeon stood next to her. "God has blessed you with a wonderful *mann*!" Then she glanced at her father, who looked just as pleased. Three years ago he worked for a commercial roofing company and had fallen off one of the buildings, breaking his back. He hadn't been able to work since. His recovery had been long and hard on both of her parents, and her marrying Simeon made them happy. How could she destroy their happiness, especially when the last three years had been so difficult?

Elsie tapped her finger against her chin. "I'll figure something out for you to say. I can come up with a story to cover for you."

"I can't ask you to do that."

"You're not asking. I'm doing this because I refuse to stand by and watch you be abused." She pushed herself up from the bed and went to Katharine, grabbing her hands. "When I moved to Hulett after marrying Galen, he was eager to introduce me to his best friend, telling me what a great guy he is, that he would do anything for anyone. Simeon was there for him when his father died, so I understand *mei* husband's loyalty. But I knew a man like Simeon once."

"You did?"

Elsie nodded. "*Mei* cousin almost married him. A friend helped her escape. She's happily married to a *gut* man who treats her well. I want that for you too."

Katharine didn't know what to say. Could she leave Hulett and travel over a thousand miles without telling anyone? What would her parents do? What would Simeon do?

There was another, deeper thought that she couldn't share with Elsie. What if Simeon was her only chance at marriage and a family? There were still moments when he was nice to her. Even sweet, like the time he brought her flowers when she had a cold. Her mother had been impressed by that, and so had Katharine. Perhaps he would change after the wedding, and she would have the husband she had prayed so hard for.

"Give it some thought, at least." Elsie hugged her. "We better join Galen and Simeon before he gets suspicious."

"Does Galen ever get suspicious?"

"*Nee*." She half smiled. "He's so sweet and trusting. I'm sure that's why Simeon is friends with him."

For the rest of the afternoon, Katharine kept quiet as she mulled over what Elsie said. To her friend's credit, Elsie hadn't given any hint to either man that they were discussing Simeon and Katharine's relationship. In fact, she placed an extra helping of roasted potatoes, Simeon's favorite, on his plate. When he glanced at the pile of potatoes, he looked at Katharine. "You should take cooking lessons from Elsie," he said, his smile as genuine as she'd ever seen it.

"Katharine's a *gut* cook," Galen said, cutting into his steak. "That cherry cobbler she made for lunch after church last week was delicious."

"You're right. She does make good desserts." Simeon continued to smile as he stabbed his fork into a potato. "But there's *nix* wrong with learning new things."

Galen nodded, shoving a big bite of steak into his mouth. He was a hearty eater and had some extra weight on him too, but she doubted Simeon ever commented on it.

She met Simeon's gaze. The smile was still there, and now he was directing it at her. She couldn't help but give him a tiny smile back.

After picking at her slice of apple pie, she decided that she couldn't go through with Elsie's plan. She wasn't a good liar, and she detested deception. She didn't want her parents to worry about her either. She was an only child, and while her father was fully recovered, she wanted to be here to help them if they needed her. She also didn't want to put Elsie in a bad situation. If Simeon ever found out she had helped Katharine leave him . . .

She couldn't bring herself to think about that. Later she'd tell Elsie thank you, but that she would handle Simeon. Surely after they were married and the house was built, he wouldn't be so stressed. Then things would go back to normal in their relationship.

During the ride home from the Schroeders', Simeon said, "You didn't eat much today."

Katharine stared straight ahead. "I wanted to stick to *mei* diet." That was partially true, but she couldn't tell him the other reason she had lost her appetite, or that she had spent even one second thinking about leaving him.

"What were you and Elsie talking about earlier?"

She stilled. "When? We talked about a lot of things today."

"I saw the two of you coming out of her bedroom. I was in the bathroom washing up." He turned to her, a cool expression on his face. "I heard you talking, but I couldn't make out what you were saying."

"Just *maedel* talk," she said, unable to look at him. "And *boppli* talk. She's due in three weeks."

He didn't say anything for a long moment. When he pulled into her driveway, the lights were on in the house. Whew, her parents were back from their visit. She didn't have to worry about him getting mad or doing anything else since he knew they were nearby. Normally she would invite him inside, mostly because he expected the invitation, not because she wanted him there. Eager to get away from him, she grabbed the pie carrier. "See you tom—"

He seized her hand, squeezing it tight, the carrier falling out of her grasp. "I don't believe you."

She looked at her hand. The tips of her fingers were turning purple. "You're hurting me," she said, trying to pull out of his grip.

He held fast, then increased the pressure until she winced. "You're lying to me," he said through gritted teeth, twisting her wrist. "You know I don't like lies. What were you two talking about? Were you talking about me?"

Pain shot up her arm, and she scrambled to think of a response. "I'm going on a trip," she cried out.

"Where? Why am I only hearing this now?"

"I just decided. *Ow*! Simeon, you're going to break *mei* wrist!" After ten years of being a blacksmith, he was strong enough to do so.

He let her go but didn't move away. "We're getting married in a month. Why would you take a trip now?"

God, please help me. Then the words came to her, as if she had been thinking about this plan for months instead of hearing about it from Elsie. "I have a friend in Montana. Her name is Frannie. We've been writing to each other for years. She invited me to visit her next week."

"You never said anything about this friend before."

"I haven't?" How she managed to sound lighthearted, she had no idea. "I thought I did.

"I would have remembered if you had."

That was true. Simeon didn't forget a thing. "I'm sorry. I should have."

"Write her back and tell her you can't *geh*."

Panic set in. "But I want to see her. I won't be able to visit after our wedding." She moved closer to him, keeping her gaze downcast. "Please?" She nearly choked on the next words. "I'll do anything you ask if you allow me to *geh*."

His suspicious expression disappeared, replaced by a satisfied smile that turned her stomach rancid. He moved closer to her, until his face was inches from hers. "Anything?"

Gulping, she nodded. "Anything," she whispered.

Simeon sat back, his mouth forming a smirk. "How long will you be gone?"

"A week." *Or forever.* Right now she didn't care. Elsie was right, she had to get away from him.

"I can take a week off work. I'll *geh* with you."

"*Nee*!" When his eyes narrowed, she added, "What about the house? It's not finished yet. You do want it to be finished before the wedding, *ya*?"

Slowly, he nodded. Paused. Then said, "Five days. You will be back in five days."

Intense relief flowed through her, and she almost dropped her facade. "I will. I promise." And because she knew from experience how to mollify him, she bowed her head. "I'm sorry. I should have talked to you about this before."

"*Ya*. You should have." He picked up her hand, still sore from his grip, and kissed the top of it, as if that made everything good between them. "I love you, Katharine. Everything I say and do is because I love you."

There it was again, the softness in his voice, the tenderness in his eyes, the gentleness of his touch as he lightly held the hand he had nearly damaged minutes before. These were the moments that gave her hope that if she could somehow keep from upsetting him, everything would work out. They would be happy. *I would be happy*.

"And I forgive you for not telling me about your trip." His lips pressed together before he said, "Just don't *ever* keep me in the dark about anything else again, or you will regret it."

Just like that, her hope vanished. "I won't."

"And?"

"I—I love you."

He let go of her hand and gave her a satisfied smile. "*Gut. Gut*. Tell your parents I'll see them tomorrow for supper."

She nodded quickly, thankful he didn't want to see them now. She picked up the pie carrier from the buggy floor and climbed out, ignoring the urge to run to the house and raise his suspicions and ire again. With a calm she didn't feel, she walked up the driveway, then opened the front door.

Her parents were in the living room, both of them taking their usual late Saturday afternoon naps, a habit formed after *Daed*'s accident. A wave of relief hit her that she didn't have to deliver Simeon's message or explain her afternoon to them. She tiptoed to the stairs, made her way to her bedroom, went inside, and silently closed the door. Then she collapsed onto the bed.

Thank you, Lord. There was no way she could have made up the pen pal idea or convinced Simeon that she could visit her nonexistent "friend" without God's help.

Then she sat up. She had lied, and God wouldn't be happy about that. *Please understand. I'm desperate.* She bowed her head and asked for forgiveness for the lie she told Simeon—and the one she was going to tell her parents later tonight.

In spite of her fervent prayer, when she opened her eyes, doubt began to set in. *Am I doing the right thing?*

A sharp ache shot through her hand, and she looked at it. The skin wasn't crimson anymore, but still pink and painful. He would have broken her hand if she hadn't been able to appease him. She was sure of that.

She touched one of her pudgy fingers. Her parents had been only a few feet away inside the house when he contorted her wrist. What would he do to her the next time she made a mistake when they were alone? Slap her face again? Break her arm? *Or something worse?*

Her doubt fled. She had no choice . . . She had to go to Birch Creek. She didn't have a plan. She didn't even know if she was doing the right thing. All she knew was that she had to leave Hulett and Simeon behind . . . or she might not survive.

Chapter 1

A YEAR LATER

"You're cute, you know that?"

Ezra Bontrager paused, his axe hovering in the air. He glanced at Charity Raber, the overly thin young woman who had been following him around Stoll's Inn grounds for the past hour. Levi had warned him two weeks ago when he took the job as the inn's handyman that many of the guests here were answering the bride ad in the paper—an ad that was placed over a year ago but was still causing trouble in the community. Since then three of his brothers had gotten married, and one was engaged to marry this fall. Birch Creek was running out of bachelors, and now there was no shortage of bachelorettes. Whoever put that ad in the paper had no idea what they had wrought.

He set the axe next to the stump, letting the piece of wood he was about to split fall over. "Uh, that's nice of you to say, Charity, but I'm kind of busy right now."

"Need any help?"

That was the fourth time she'd asked him since he'd checked the dripping faucet in the guest room that she shared with another husband-seeking woman. That repair was easy since all he had to do was turn the water completely off, tighten the faucet, then turn the water back on again. When he left the room, she followed him down the staircase, out the front door to the mailbox he still needed to fix after a car clipped it two days ago, then back up the driveway to the woodpile, maintaining a steady stream of chatter the whole time. When he grabbed the axe, he figured she'd get the hint that he didn't have time to chat. Unfortunately, she didn't.

"*Nee*. I don't need any help." He fought for patience. Normally he was a good-natured guy, but there was only so much banal monologuing he could take. "Don't you have some plans for today?"

"*Ya*," she said, nodding. Her bright-red hair peeked out from underneath her white *kapp*. The *kapp* was shaped like a heart and different from the round ones the women in Ohio wore. "But that's not until later this afternoon." She tilted her head at him, her freckled face breaking into a smile. "You're cute, you know that?"

Oh brother. Not only was she repeating herself, she was also getting close to his last nerve. "Look, Charity, I'm really . . ." He spied Katharine Miller walking into the Stolls' barn. "I forgot I have to do something," he said, hurrying away from her. When she started to follow him again, he held up his hand. "It's something I have to do by myself."

"Okay," she said, doubt creeping into her pale-blue eyes. "I'll wait outside then." She batted her almost transparent eyelashes. "Don't be long."

He figured she was trying to be flirty, but she'd only accomplished getting further on his nerves.

Ezra rushed into the barn, heading to the back where he figured Katharine would be. He didn't know her very well, and she kept to herself most of the time. Odd since every other woman who had answered the advertisement had been on the prowl for a husband, with the exception of his brothers' wives. But for the most part, women who came here either went home disappointed or married someone in a nearby district. They didn't stay unless they'd married a Bontrager.

Sure enough, she was in a small space in the back of the barn where she had set up her basket weaving business. She was just sitting down in the chair in front of the table when Ezra skidded to a stop in front of her.

Glancing up, she frowned but didn't say anything. They hadn't interacted with each other before he took the job at Stoll's Inn two weeks ago, but he did remember when she first came to church. His young and *extremely* immature brother Jesse had mumbled a crack about her weight, and after cuffing him on the head, Ezra turned to take a look at her. Sure, she carried some extra weight, and he could even see the red acne on her face from his seat near the front of the Yoders' barn. But what had struck him was how sad she seemed, her shoulders slumping as if she carried a burden almost too hard to bear. Once the service was over, she disappeared, and he hadn't given her much thought after that.

As the months passed, though, her complexion had cleared up, and her weight had gone down. She wasn't thin by any means, but she looked healthier. She also rarely said much, even to the Stolls, the family she lived with. At least, he'd never seen her talk much to them. She did her job and when she was finished with her tasks, she spent the rest of her time making top-notch baskets. They'd never been in close proximity before, and he'd been busy learning the job from Loren and his son Levi, who both owned and ran the inn along with Loren's mother, Delilah.

Her left brow raised. Knowing she had to be wondering why he was standing in front of her, he started to explain. "Uh, hi—"

"Ezra!" Charity's voice carried from the front of the barn. "Where are you?"

Oh *nee*. He looked over his shoulder, then back at Katharine, who still remained silent. He'd never met such a quiet woman in his life, and after spending a few hours with Charity, he was starting to appreciate that quality. "Can you hide me?" he pleaded in a loud whisper.

"What?" Now both of her eyebrows were arched.

He heard Charity's footsteps nearing, and without asking he dove under the table, then pulled a few of the hay bales nearby in front of him. Still crouching, he held his breath.

"Ezra—oh." Charity's surprised pause lasted less than a second. "What are you doing here, Katharine?" she asked, her tone borderline snotty, as if Katharine didn't have the right to be in the same barn as her.

"This is *mei* workstation," Katharine replied, sounding unruffled.

"Aren't you a maid, though?"

"I am. But I also make baskets and sell them at the inn. You might have seen some of them—"

"*Ya*, whatever, but where's Ezra? He told me he had to do something here before we went on our date this afternoon."

Ezra gasped, losing a bit of his balance. That little twerp. How dare she lie about him, or rather, them? Wait, there was no *them*. He settled himself, then realized his backside was against Katharine's legs. He should move, but if he did, he might draw Charity's attention, and that was the last thing he wanted. He just hoped Katharine wouldn't kick him out from under the table, even though she had every right to.

Instead she remained still. "I haven't seen him."

"Are you sure? Because I saw him *geh* into the barn and I *didn't* see him come out."

He imagined Charity's thin arms crossed over her boyish frame. He'd suspected she was young, but now he wondered if she was even old enough to date, much less find a husband. She certainly was sounding childish.

"I don't know what else to tell you. He's not here."

Her voice had a surprisingly pleasant lilt to it. When Charity didn't respond, Ezra was relieved. Hopefully she would move on, and he could stand up and give Katharine the apology he owed her.

He wasn't that lucky. "You make baskets, huh," Charity said.

"*Ya*." He heard Katharine sliding pieces of willow around on the tabletop above him.

"That sounds boring."

"It's not." A pause. "I can show you how to make one if you want."

No no no. He did not want Charity lingering any more than necessary. His legs were cramping as it was. He was the tallest in his family, and although he was turning twenty-one in two months, he'd grown two more inches over the fall, and that had put him at six foot four. And a half, but no one was counting. He was practically folded up in a ball under the table and balancing on his toes while being keenly aware that a part of him that shouldn't be pressed against Katharine's legs still was. He shifted his line of sight and his eyes widened. All Charity had to do was look down at her feet and she would be able to see him through the gap in the hay bales he'd hastily arranged in front of him. *Great. Just great.*

"Nah," Charity said, taking a step back from the table. "I need to *geh* find Ezra."

"You must like him a lot."

"Oh, I do. He's so tall. He's cute, you know."

Katharine didn't respond.

Ezra frowned. What—she didn't think he was cute? He wasn't prideful, but he wasn't oblivious either. Charity wasn't the only single woman in Birch Creek who had pursued him or been complimentary of his looks. Now that he thought about it, Katharine was the only one who hadn't.

"Are you *positive* you don't want to learn how to make a basket?" she said to Charity. "I just started a square one that's big enough for lots of storage. It should only take me, oh, an hour or two to teach you. I'm sure *wherever* Ezra is, he won't mind waiting for you."

He nearly groaned out loud. Had Katharine lost her mind? There was no way he could stay under this table for an hour, much less two. When Charity didn't answer right away, he started to panic. Was the girl actually considering Katharine's offer?

"I don't like doing crafts," she sneered, as if she were referring to snakes and cockroaches instead of an industry that was bread and butter for a lot of Amish. "*Mamm* says the only Amish who make crafts are the ones who aren't *gut* at doing anything else." She turned and left.

Wow. Not only was Charity wrong, she was also a brat.

After several of the longest minutes of his life, he felt Katharine nudge him with her foot. "You're safe now. She's gone."

He shoved away the bales and scrambled from under the table and rose. Intense tingling shot through his right leg. Rats, his foot had gone to sleep. He hopped on the other one and faced her. She was organizing the willow pieces as if he weren't there. "*Danki*," he said, touching the table with his fingertips to help keep his balance. "I haven't been able to shake her all morning."

Katharine looked up at him, and this time he noticed her eyes were a pretty shade of bluish green. Those pretty eyes were also slightly narrowing. "Maybe you should have been honest with her, instead of dating her."

That clipped his ego a bit, but she wasn't wrong. "I can clear that up. I never said I was going to ask her on a date. Or that we were going on a date together. She's basically a child."

"She's eighteen."

"Really?" He frowned. "She doesn't act like it."

"And hiding under a table is so mature."

She had him there. Gingerly, he set his foot down, glad that the unbearable tingling had almost stopped. Now that Charity was gone, he was embarrassed. "I'll admit, this isn't *mei* best moment, but I did tell her I was busy and she still insisted on following me. And then she lied to you about us going out. Not to mention the crack she made about doing crafts."

Katharine went back to organizing the willow strips.

He sighed. "Right. This isn't *yer* problem, it's mine. *Danki* anyway for *yer* help." He headed for the front of the barn.

"Do you want me to talk to her?"

Stunned, Ezra whirled around. That was a great idea and would get him off the hook. But while he was tempted, he couldn't take her up on her offer. "*Nee*. I have to fix this myself. I'll make sure she listens to me this time." Then he paused. "You weren't really going to teach her how to make a basket, were you? Not while I was waiting—"

"Hiding," she corrected.

"*Hiding* under the table, where she could have caught me at any time."

A tiny smile played at the corner of her lips as she picked up some more willow strips and set them on the table.

Huh. That was unexpected. All the other times he'd seen Katharine, she had been serious and aloof. Playful wasn't something he associated with her. He couldn't help but grin, then left to find Charity. He wasn't sure what he was going to say, but he was sure that he was never hiding from a woman again. If his brothers found out about this, he'd never hear the end of it.

Katharine couldn't help but smile as Ezra hurried out of the barn. She'd had a hard time keeping her amusement hidden as he explained the situation with Charity. She shook her head and gathered the willow strips, set them aside, and reached for the large square chip board that would be the bottom of the basket. She knew Charity wouldn't have agreed to learn how to basket weave. That girl had one thing on her mind—snagging a husband. Obviously Ezra was her latest target. She didn't know who she should feel sorrier for—Charity, because he wasn't interested in her, or Ezra, because she was relentless.

Using a pencil and ruler, she started marking off evenly spaced holes on the chipboard. She agreed with Charity on one thing—Ezra was cute. She'd noticed that the moment Levi introduced him to her on his first day of work. She already knew who he was. Everyone knew the Bontrager family, who had eleven male children and one female, Phoebe, who was the oldest. She also knew that nearly half of the men were married or engaged to be married, and the rest were in their late teens and younger. Not that she'd had any interaction with the family, or anyone else other than the Stolls. Selah, Levi's wife, had tried to befriend her. But when Katharine arrived at Birch Creek, she vowed to keep her distance, and she had kept that promise. Delilah was the only person she ever had more than four-word conversations with.

She paused, her heart growing heavy as it usually did when she thought about her predicament. Most of the time she kept busy, either working at the inn or making her baskets. Delilah had insisted on selling some of them at the inn, and they were also used in the rooms and in the Stolls' home. And like her business in Hulett, the baskets were almost always sold out the minute they were on display. She had agreed to sell some of them in Schrock's Grocery, and with the extra work she was able to keep to herself almost all the time.

But it was a lonely life. After living in Birch Creek for a year, she wondered if this was the way her life would permanently be.

She spent the next two hours working on the baskets, then went to the house to help Delilah prepare supper. She stopped at the bathroom to wash up, and in spite of herself, looked at her reflection in the mirror. Her face was still chubby, despite the fact that she had lost almost forty pounds over the past year. At least her complexion had almost cleared up, thanks to a homemade cream Margaret Yoder made for her two months ago. The concoction had been a miracle for her acne, and now she had only a few bumps on her forehead and chin. The dresses she brought with her from Hulett were too big, and she needed to make some new ones. Maybe after she finished weaving the new basket. Finding time to sew, or to do much of anything else, was difficult. But she had to keep busy. The rare times she wasn't, memories of Simeon intruded, along with homesickness. She missed her parents, and her friendship with Elsie.

Shoving the past out of her mind, she left the bathroom and went into the kitchen. Delilah wasn't there, but Katharine didn't hesitate to start on supper, something she had done many times in the past when Delilah was caught up with inn business. Loren and Levi were the official innkeepers and Delilah the official cook, but that didn't keep her from dipping her toes—and nose—into the day-to-day workings of Stoll's Inn.

She looked at the menu pinned to the small corkboard on the kitchen wall. Delilah was so detailed and organized that she made menus for the inn and her family a month in advance, and she did all the shopping for the ingredients at one time. Ham pot pie was today's scheduled dish, along with maple-glazed carrots, rolls, and fruit cocktail. Katharine had gathered the broth, potatoes, celery, onion, and ham and started chopping the vegetables when Delilah appeared.

"*Danki*, Katharine," she said, bustling toward the stove, her face flushed. "You won't believe what just happened. We had a late check-out today while you were working on your baskets. When I went in the room to get the bedclothes, there were marks all over the wall. In *permanent marker.* I can't believe that family let their toddler color on our pristine walls, and then didn't bother to say anything before they left!"

"Why didn't you tell me?" Katharine turned to her, stunned. "I would have cleaned up the room."

"I don't mind cleaning a room once in a while. But this one—*ach*! The marker wouldn't come off. It needs repainting." She blew out a breath and glanced around the kitchen. "Can you finish up supper? I need to talk to Loren and Ezra."

"Of course."

Delilah nodded, then paused and looked Katharine up and down with surprise. "Land sakes, I think you've lost five pounds since breakfast this morning."

That made Katharine smile, but she didn't reply. While she was friendly with Delilah, they weren't as close as she wished they could be. She couldn't afford to let anyone else get caught up in her mess of a life. Elsie keeping her secret was bad enough.

"You'll need a new wardrobe soon at the rate you're losing weight. How about we start on a new dress for you next week?" Delilah gave an emphatic nod, decision made.

"*Danki*," she said without protest. She knew the woman well enough not to argue with her. And it would be nice to have a new dress that was actually smaller for a change.

Delilah headed out of the kitchen only to stop in the doorway and turn around. "Oh, before I forget," she said, pulling a letter from her apron pocket. "This came for you today. I'll set it on the table."

She nodded, already knowing the letter was from Elsie, the only person who knew her real location. Ever since Katharine left Hulett, she and Elsie had kept in touch through letters, Katharine mailing hers to the post office box Elsie had rented. As far as anyone else knew, she was still in Montana.

After Delilah rushed out of the kitchen, Katharine continued to cook. As she spent the next forty-five minutes preparing the casserole and making the carrot dish, she thought about her parents again. They had been confused, of course, when she called them shortly after she arrived in Ohio, pretending to be in Montana and deciding to extend her stay. A week later, she called them again, saying that "Frannie" had caught pneumonia and needed her help.

A week after that, she called and told her mother and father that the wedding was off. "I met someone," she said, barely able to say the words.

"What do you mean?" her mother had asked.

"I . . . I've fallen in love with someone else. His name is Michael Miller." She bit her lip, dismayed at how easily she was able to lie to her mother and father. She drew in a deep breath, this time telling them the truth. "I'm not marrying Simeon."

Daed had gotten on the line at that point, more confused than angry. He asked her to come home and talk things over, but Katharine refused.

"What about Simeon?" he asked. "Does he know about this?"

"Not yet," she whispered. "I will let him know, though."

"I don't understand," *Mamm* had said, her voice sounding farther away.

Katharine could imagine both her parents huddled in their small phone shanty, trying to make sense of why their daughter, who had always been obedient and had never given them a moment's trouble, was now backing out of her betrothal to a man they loved like a son. "This is for the best."

"Please," *Mamm* said, her voice thick. "You can bring this young man with you if you want. Just come home. All we want is for you to be happy. We miss you, *lieb*."

"I miss you too." Then she hung up the phone, and it was the second hardest thing she'd ever had to do. She was taking advantage of the fact that her father couldn't travel far due to the accident and her mother would never leave his side. All she could do was pray they would eventually forgive her deception.

Katharine blinked, her thoughts coming back to the present. She and her parents had spoken sporadically over the past year, but the conversations were strained and short. She never did call Simeon, and he never called her. If he had gone looking for her in Montana, he hadn't told her parents or Elsie. It was as if their relationship had never existed. At times that saddened her, but lately not as often. It also validated her decision to leave him.

Once the casserole was baking and the carrots simmering on the stove, she sat down at the table and opened Elsie's letter.

Dear Katharine,

I was so happy to get your last letter and to find out that you're still okay in Ohio. I miss you and wish you could come back home. I also wish I could say that Simeon is leaving your parents alone, but he's still weaseling his way into their lives. I probably shouldn't tell you this, but he's been eating supper at their house almost every night during the week after he gets off work. I'm convinced he's up to something, but Galen says I'm imagining things, and that Simeon and your parents are comforting each other over their "loss." I want to tell him the truth, but I know he wouldn't understand.

Katharine stopped reading, her heart squeezing in her chest. She didn't like that Elsie couldn't be honest with Galen. But her friend had insisted it wasn't a problem and that she would always keep her secret. That was necessary now since Simeon was still spending time with her parents. The last time she talked to them was almost a month ago, and the conversation had been strained. As usual they asked her to come home with "Michael," her imaginary boyfriend. And as usual, she put them off. They didn't mention Simeon during that call, or the three that preceded it, and that had given her a spark of hope that she could return to Hulett soon.

She should have known better. Whenever she dared to have hope, it was eventually dashed.

> I wish you could see Jason now. He's gotten so big, and he's walking everywhere! And he's going to have a sibling soon. I'm due in two months. I thought about telling you in my last letter that I was expecting, but I held off. Galen is so excited to be a father again, and he's hoping for a little girl this time. I am too, but another boy would also be wonderful.
>
> I miss you, Katharine. I know I said this already, but I truly mean it. Even though you've been gone for a year, I feel we've become closer friends through our letters to each other. But I hope you're also making friends in Birch Creek. Maybe even finding a future husband. Don't let your experience with Simeon keep you from loving someone else. If the right man comes along, don't let him get away.
>
> Love,
> Elsie

Katharine folded the letter, clinging to it for a moment before putting it in the pocket of her apron. Although her homesickness had eased the more time she spent in Birch Creek, anytime she heard from home, her yearning for Hulett returned. Now she wondered if she'd ever be able to go back to Wyoming. *Not until I know Simeon has moved on and is out of my life for good.*

Then there was Elsie, who was encouraging her to move on. And she had—from Simeon at least. She held no love for him, or respect. Only shame for the things he said and did to her, and how she had allowed him to treat her. She would never allow that to happen again, because she would never let another man capture her heart. Her dream of marriage and a family was gone, and she accepted it.

Delilah entered the kitchen, a wide grin on her rotund face. "Set an extra plate, Katharine," she said, her blue eyes twinkling behind her glasses. "Ezra is joining us for supper tonight."

Chapter 2

Ezra?" Katharine said, surprised. She had lived with the Stolls for a year, and this was the first time one of the handymen they had hired—and there had been several—joined them for a meal. Lester, who had been here when Katharine arrived, was as standoffish and aloof as she was. But he had also been kind, in a gruff way. After he suddenly left, a succession of English handymen had been employed, the one who had been there the longest being Ralph, who stayed three months. Most of them left because they found better-paying jobs. Stoll's Inn was successful, but only three years old. No one was rolling in money, and the Stolls couldn't afford to pay what the English men had wanted.

"*Ya*. Ezra." Delilah grabbed the pitcher of iced tea and started to fill the glasses on the table. "That young man is an answer to prayer. As soon as he saw the mess in Room 3, he offered to stay late and repaint the wall. Fortunately we saved all the paint from when we renovated the inn, and he said he would have it finished by suppertime." She set the pitcher on the table and put her fists on her plump hips. "But the next time I see Bob at the hardware store, I'm giving him a piece of *mei* mind. He said that everything could be cleaned off this kind of paint. Apparently, everything but permanent marker. I still can't believe that couple let their child draw on *our* walls!"

Loren entered the kitchen in the middle of Delilah's rant and glanced at his mother. His normally calm expression mirrored her upset. "*Gut* thing we don't have inconsiderate guests that often," he muttered, taking a seat at the table. "Ezra is washing up. He said he'd be here in a few minutes."

Katharine placed another plate on the table, then added a fork, knife, and spoon. She and the Stolls didn't always eat alone. Occasionally Levi and Selah joined them for a meal, but they usually stayed at their own house on the other side of the inn. Levi's sister, Nina, and her husband, Ira, and their son, Nathan, also came over sometimes, but usually it was just Katharine, Delilah, and Loren who took their meals together.

The timer went off for the casserole, and Delilah pulled it out of the stove, filling the kitchen with the mouth-watering scent of smoky ham and seasoned vegetables. Katharine had set a breadbasket filled with rolls on the table when Ezra walked in. Most of the time she averted her gaze around everyone but the Stolls, but after his escapade with Charity she couldn't help but look at him. He gave her a sheepish smile before sitting down next to Loren. Again she was struck by how handsome he was, his good looks almost the polar opposite of Simeon's . . .

A sudden attack of nerves hit her. Did Ezra like ham casserole? Would he like *her* ham casserole? Why did she even care if he did? Simeon had never liked her cooking and had always complained about something during the meal. Too much salt, too little salt, too much gravy, too little gravy. It had gotten to the point where she was a jumpy wreck when he came over to her house once a week for supper. Her mother had insisted she make the meals for him. "You'll be cooking for him the rest of *yer* life after you marry," she said. "Now is the time to practice."

"Katharine?"

She turned to see Delilah seated at the opposite end of the table from Loren. Everyone was ready for prayer, and she was still standing behind her chair. "Sorry," she mumbled, then quickly sat down.

Loren bowed his head. "Let's pray."

As they all silently prayed, Katharine tried to settle her jitters. She'd never had a problem cooking for Loren and Delilah, and she shouldn't be worried about what Ezra thought. He wasn't Simeon. Then again, she wasn't the best judge of character.

"Do you want a roll, Katharine?"

She opened her eyes to see Ezra holding up the plate of bread in front of her. She hadn't realized the prayer was over. The rolls smelled heavenly, and more than anything she wanted one. Bread with butter was one of her weaknesses. "*Nee*," she said, barely looking at him.

He nodded, then took three rolls from the basket and put them on his plate.

Delilah handed her the serving spoon for the casserole, and she took a small amount and placed it next to the carrots on her dish. Ezra, on the other hand, had given himself a huge serving of the casserole and twice the number of carrots. She didn't begrudge him the large helpings, only the fact that he could eat so much and stay thin, while she could gain weight just looking at food. Even though she wasn't stress eating anymore, she was determined to cut down on her calories. She still had more weight to lose.

"Katharine made this basket." Delilah grinned as she set two rolls on her plate. The woman didn't skimp on her meals either, and while she carried extra weight, she carried it well. She also enjoyed her food, instead of resenting it like Katharine did. Hopefully someday she would be comfortable not only with herself but also with eating. "Don't you think it's lovely, Ezra?"

He stopped chewing, his mouth full with a huge bite of the roll. He nodded, then swallowed. "Lovely indeed."

Her cheeks warmed at the compliment. There was something different about the people in Birch Creek. In her district in Hulett, there was an unspoken rule about compliments, even though occasionally they were doled out, especially when someone needed encouragement. Here the people gave them more frequently, and not to pump up someone's pride either. While Simeon had said he loved her and wanted to marry her soon after they started dating, he'd never complimented her on anything, although she couldn't hold that against him considering the community rule. But she also couldn't ignore that Ezra praising her basket felt good. Very good.

"She made supper tonight too," Delilah said. "Using *mei grossmutter*'s recipe, of course."

"Of course," Loren mumbled, then turned to Ezra. "Did you have any trouble covering up the marks?"

"*Nee*. Only took one coat and they disappeared." He lifted a generous spoonful of casserole.

Delilah clucked her tongue. "Unbelievable. If I had done something like that as a *maedel*, *mei* parents would have had *mei* hide."

"Mine too." Loren looked at his mother. "More than once."

She lifted her chin. "Spare the rod, spoil the child."

"I definitely wasn't spoiled," Loren said. At Delilah's sour expression he added, "I'm just teasing, *Mamm*. You did an excellent job raising me and helping to raise Levi and Nina."

Her expression grew soft, and she looked down at her plate, a pleased smile on her face. Then she glanced at Katharine. "Perhaps sometime soon you can invite *yer* parents to visit us," she said. "I'd like to meet them, and I'm sure they're curious about Birch Creek."

She could feel the color drain from her face. Delilah had never mentioned her parents before. Why was she bringing them up now? Any other time she asked questions about home, Katharine had been able to stall or change the subject. She'd told the Stolls she was from Montana, and that was all she had revealed, not wanting to lie any more than she had to. "They, uh, don't like to travel much," she finally said. At least that was the truth.

"Surely they'd travel to see their daughter." Delilah dipped a piece of her roll into the last bit of casserole on her plate. "I'm surprised they haven't visited you yet."

Now what do I say? When she saw Ezra's puzzled expression, panic set in. She had no choice but to lie now. Not just to Loren and Delilah, who had been nothing but kind and open-hearted with her. She would also have to lie to Ezra. Her hands clenched in her lap.

"Don't pester her," Loren said, his voice firm. He pulled his napkin out of the neck of his shirt and wiped his mouth. "*Gut* supper, Katharine. Better than *Mamm* makes."

"Excuse me?"

While Delilah protested, Katharine caught Ezra's smirk out of the corner of her eye. She lifted her gaze and their eyes met. His mouth lifted into a grin as he gestured with his head toward Delilah.

Katharine's fists unfolded. Saved by Loren, praise God.

"Loren, your *vatter* adored *mei* ham casserole," Delilah fussed.

"I remember. Pretty sure he would adore Katharine's too." He winked and pushed back from the table. "If you'll excuse me," he said, standing up, "I'll be back in a little while to do the chores."

"Off to see Rhoda?" Delilah said, her expression switching from offended to curious.

His brows flattened. "Maybe. Or maybe not. That's for me to know, *ya*?"

"Humph."

Loren looked at Ezra. "*Danki* for staying late and taking care of the room. See you in the morning." Then he faced Delilah. "*Gute nacht*, *Mamm*."

"But—"

He hurried out of the room.

Delilah sighed. "He might be close to fifty, but he acts like a teenager sometimes."

If she wasn't so tense, Katharine would giggle at Delilah's frustration. The woman did *not* like being kept in the dark, especially when it came to her family and their plans. Before Delilah started questioning her again, Katharine stood and picked up her plate. "I'll take care of the kitchen."

"You'll do *nee* such thing. You cooked and I will clean." A mischievous twinkle appeared in her eyes. "Why don't you *geh* outside and enjoy the evening air?"

"I'd rather wash the dishes—"

"Take some dessert with you." Delilah popped up from her chair and scurried to the counter, then picked up a small plate of blondies, leftovers from the snacks she'd made early this morning for the inn's guests. Turning, she handed it to Katharine. "You and Ezra can eat these on the patio."

She looked at the thick, tan squares filled with chocolate and more butter than she wanted to think about. Her mouth watered, and she was sure her stomach would growl any minute. She'd eaten only a few bites tonight, and the scrumptious treats were almost more than she could resist. When she first arrived in Birch Creek, she was still eating everything in sight, including Delilah's blondies, so she knew how delectable they were. And how could she decline the dessert, and eating outside with Ezra, without hurting Delilah's feelings?

"*Geh* on," Delilah said, walking over to Ezra and snatching his plate from in front of him, even though he was still finishing up the last of the carrots. As his eyes widened, she added, "Soon it will be too cold to *geh* outside after supper, so take advantage of the nice nights while you can."

Katharine lost the battle before it began, and she wasn't so sure that Delilah wouldn't pull Ezra's chair out from under him. He likely had the same thought because he sprang up from his seat. "Um, okay," he said, sounding a little hesitant, although he was eyeing the blondies with interest. "Those sure do look *gut*."

"They are." Delilah waved her hands at them until they walked out the back door. "Now shoo so I can finish cleaning in here."

Katharine spun around. "But—"

Delilah shut the door.

For the next few minutes, Katharine gripped the edge of the plate, trying not to breathe in the scent of the blondies. Neither one of them spoke or moved, their feet planted on the concrete patio. *Awkward*. No, not just awkward. *Painfully* awkward.

Finally Ezra moved closer to her. "Mind if I have one?" The motion sensor light above the back door illuminated his face.

"Oh, sure. Sorry." She held out the plate to him. He took a blondie, then sat down on one of the chairs as if nothing out of the ordinary had happened. He bit into the dessert, leaned back, and looked at the stars. "She's right," he said after he finished eating the bite.

"About the blondies?"

"*Ya*. And about the evening air." He chuckled. "It is a nice night."

She glanced up at the dark sky, the twinkling stars filling the black backdrop. Her instincts told her to stay in place. Better yet, she needed to come up with an excuse to go back inside. But Delilah would just send her out again, making the situation even more peculiar than it already was. She slowly sat down in the chair farthest from him and balanced the plate on her lap.

"Aren't you having any?" he asked, turning to her.

"*Nee*."

Ezra frowned. "You don't like blondies?"

"I do, but . . ." Did she really have to explain why? Obviously, she shouldn't be eating dessert. Was he trying to tempt her on purpose? Simeon sometimes did when her parents weren't around and he knew she had started a new diet. He seemed to enjoy watching her struggle to fight temptation—a fight she almost always lost. Was Ezra doing that too?

He shrugged and polished off the rest of the blondie. "You're missing out," he said over the mouthful.

Yes, she was missing out. But she wasn't about to let him make a fool out of her. She put the plate on the plastic table in front of them and shoved it toward him. Without skipping a beat, he grabbed another square.

They sat there together, more silence stretching out between them, which gave her time to realize she was judging Ezra without knowing him. So far he was nothing like Simeon, and it was nice to enjoy a starry night with someone and not have to walk on eggshells or have her feelings trampled on. The coil of tension around her shoulders eased.

"By the way," he said after a few more silent minutes. "I spoke with Charity right after I left the barn. She finally got the message."

None of my business . . . none of my business . . . "What did you tell her?" she blurted, unable to keep her curiosity from overriding her vow to be detached.

He continued staring at the sky, his hands behind his head. "I told her the truth. That I wasn't interested in her, and that she needed to be with someone who was." He turned his head and looked at her. "Something I should have done in the first place. No one likes being deceived or made a fool of."

She knew that better than anyone.

"Are you going to eat that other blondie?" He leaned forward in the chair.

"*Nee*. You can have it."

He picked it up off the plate and settled back in his chair.

She watched him as he took bites of the dessert and stared up at the stars. His nose was slightly larger than average, but it fit his face, balancing out his large, heavy-lidded eyes and square jaw. His light brown, slightly wavy bangs covered his forehead.

"Did you make these?" he asked, then crammed the last bite into his mouth.

She had avoided making desserts from the moment she stepped foot in Birch Creek. The apple pies she'd helped her mom make before she left Hulett had been the last ones. "*Nee*. Delilah did."

"She's a *gut* cook. So are you. Loren was right, the ham pot pie was delicious."

She dipped her head, unsure how to react to so many nice words in one day. But she should at least say something. "*Mei mamm* taught me," she said.

"Back in West Kootenai, right?" He got up from the chair, then grabbed it and set it down in front of her.

Startled, she jerked back. "What are you doing?"

"I like talking face-to-face." He sat back down and asked, "What's it like in Montana?"

His question had her scrambling, not to mention that now that he was facing her, she couldn't exactly *not* look at him without coming across stranger than people probably thought she already was. Weather. That was a safe subject. She'd never been to Montana, but she figured the climate was the same as Wyoming's. "Freezing cold in the winters," she mumbled. "Hot in the summers. Fall and spring are short, but pleasant." That was vague enough.

His legs stretched out in front of him until his shoes were almost touching hers. He had the longest legs she'd ever seen. The only man she knew taller than him was Noah Schlabach, and Ezra wasn't that much shorter than he was. "I've never been out of Ohio."

She pulled her feet underneath her chair. Better yet, she should get up, tell him goodbye, and go inside. Surely they'd been out here long enough to satisfy Delilah. Instead, she stayed put. It had been so long since she'd had a normal conversation with someone other than the Stoll family, and she couldn't bottle up her question. "Do you want to travel?"

He crossed his ankle over his knee. "Nah. I like Birch Creek. I haven't always lived here, though. *Mei familye* moved here from Fredericktown when Phoebe got engaged to Jalon. I've only gone back once, for *mei* oldest *bruder*'s wedding. He got married last year."

She didn't reveal that she already knew everything he was telling her. Remaining on the outside of the community allowed her to pay attention to things and conversations busy people might miss. Like how the former bishop, Emmanuel Troyer, had left the community he founded nine years ago in disgrace, and how Loren had become friends with his wife Rhoda. Their relationship was platonic since no one knew what had happened to Emmanuel, but Katharine had to wonder if there wasn't something romantic between them.

"Do you have any siblings?"

Ezra's question made her flinch. He seemed determined to learn about her. "I'm an only child." No harm in telling him that.

"I can't imagine not having a passel of siblings. Brothers around all the time, never having more than a few moments to myself."

She'd always longed for a brother or a sister. Being an only child had been lonely at times, even though she and her parents were close. *Were* close. The thought brought on a pang of homesickness.

"Don't get me wrong," he continued. "I think *mei familye* is great. I just need a break from them sometimes."

"Is that why you took the job here?"

"*Ya*. For the most part. I also wanted to do something other than farming. I guess I'm trying to figure out what I want to be when I grow up."

Katharine held back a smile. The idea of Ezra growing any taller than he already was brought an amusing image to her mind.

He put his foot back on the ground, then stood. "I better head home. Tomorrow's an early day. Then again, aren't they all early days?"

She nodded, not trusting herself to say anything else. She rose, picked up the plate, and turned to go inside.

"*Gute nacht*, Katharine."

Glancing at him, she saw his easy smile. More often than not he had a smile on his face, almost as if nothing could ruffle him. Except Charity. She whispered, "*Gute nacht*," then opened the back door and walked into the kitchen.

She half expected to see Delilah there, pretending she wasn't eavesdropping on them. To her surprise, the woman wasn't. The kitchen was as spotless as usual when Delilah cleaned. Katharine washed and dried the empty blondie dish, then put it away and headed upstairs.

When she entered her room, she shut the door and sat down on the edge of her bed. After their initial awkwardness, talking with Ezra had been nice. For the first time since she had arrived in Birch Creek, a question she kept deeply buried rose to the surface. *Will I always be alone?*

She took Elsie's letter out of her pocket, ready to place it in her nightstand with her other letters. Instead she read the last paragraph again. *Don't let your experience with Simeon keep you from loving someone else.*

She folded the letter. Sighed. And for a fleeting moment thought about a different future than the one she had resigned herself to. A future where she was happy. Where she was genuinely loved.

Then she came to her senses. It was easy for Elsie to give her that advice. Galen was a good man, in spite of his blind spot for Simeon. And Elsie had what Katharine didn't—beauty. Before her first pregnancy she had been thin, and her complexion unblemished. Pretty girls never had trouble finding men to love them. Look at the married young women in Birch Creek. While beauty was always subjective, none of them were very fat or had scars from out-of-control acne. A few of the older women, like Abigail Bontrager and Delilah's granddaughter, Nina, carried a few extra pounds, but not as many as she did. Even before Katharine had gained so much weight, she'd never been thin. She had thought Simeon saw past her surface to her heart. She had trusted her feelings. She had trusted him.

She had been so wrong, about everything.

Katharine crammed the letter in the drawer and slammed it

shut. She'd rather be alone for the rest of her life than be controlled or pitied by another man. Elsie had gotten her happily ever after, but that didn't happen for everyone. Katharine didn't dare expect it to happen for her.

Chapter 3

Rhoda Troyer picked up her tea mug and smiled at the man sitting across the table from her. Loren Stoll. He'd been her friend and rock over the past several months since she'd decided to hire a private detective to find out what happened to Emmanuel. The decision hadn't been easy, and she had doubted herself more than once since hiring Jordan Powell, but Loren had supported and encouraged her every moment they were together. So far the detective hadn't found any trace of Emmanuel, but he assured her he would continue searching until he found something.

"You're quiet tonight." Loren sipped the coffee she made for him when he'd arrived half an hour ago. Three nights a week, like clockwork, once he had finished supper at his house, he came over for coffee and conversation. "Anything on your mind?" he asked.

She smiled, as always treasuring the time they spent together. She thought about telling him she wasn't thinking about anything, but not only was that deceptive, she had vowed not to lie to anyone ever again. She had done enough of that while married to Emmanuel, and almost all of the lies had been to herself. "I'm thinking about the past. Again."

Loren started to reach for her hand, then pulled away. That wasn't the first time he had done that, and she tried not to be upset that he changed his mind every time he moved to touch her. It wasn't his fault that they couldn't be anything other than friends. That was Emmanuel's doing. Even though he wasn't here, he was still controlling her life.

A change of subject was definitely needed. "Do you want more *kaffee*?" she asked.

He shook his head. "Your *kaffee* is the best in town, but I better not. The caffeine will keep me up all night." He looked down at his mug, then back at her. "Staying warm enough at night?"

"*Ya*. I have plenty of firewood."

"Good." He gripped the mug handle. "Rhoda, I . . ."

"I know."

He held her gaze, and the unmistakable longing in his eyes reached to her heart. Then he sat back and stared at his mug again, both hands gripping the sides.

Guilt, always a close companion, churned inside her. She was being selfish and she knew it. Every time she saw him her feelings for him grew, and she knew he felt the same way, even though he hadn't said so. To voice the truth would not only be wrong, it would also make it real. Right now they could both pretend their feelings didn't exist . . . but not for much longer. "Maybe we shouldn't see each other anymore," she whispered.

His head jerked up. "*Nee*. I don't want that."

"Loren, this isn't fair to you. You should find someone who's—" Her throat caught. "Who's free."

"Rhoda. Look at me." When she raised her eyes, he took her hand without hesitation. "I don't want to find anyone else. You're the only person who understands the pain I felt after *mei frau*'s death."

His hand, warm and strong, felt right in hers. "But we have to be realistic—"

"*Nee*. We don't. What we have right now is enough. Besides, where else am I going to find a sweet, beautiful woman who not only makes a tasty cup of *kaffee* but bakes an angel food cake so *gut* it should have wings?"

She smiled at his reference to the dessert she'd served tonight—angel food cake topped with blueberries. Other than their first year of marriage, Emmanuel rarely spoke to her in a way that made her heart sing. Loren's words were like a cool breeze on a stifling hot day.

He squeezed her hand, then let it go slowly, as if reluctant to end the connection. "I'd rather have your company as a friend than to not have it at all. I mean that, Rhoda."

"Oh, Loren. I feel the same way." She also felt a lot more for this strong, gentle man who cherished her more than her husband had during a marriage that had lasted almost thirty years. Even more than thirty, counting the ones after he left. They were still married, after all. "It's just so hard—"

"Shh. Let's not say any more about it." He held up his mug. "I'll take another cup of *kaffee* after all."

Half an hour later and after the usual disappointment she felt when he went back home, she washed and dried the percolator coffeepot and filled it with fresh coffee for the morning, Emmanuel still not far from her mind. The list of his wrongs against his family and community was extensive—verbally and physically abusing his family, hoarding the community fund, trying to obtain all the natural gas rights in Birch Creek, among many other things. Birch Creek had rich deposits of natural gas, and several members of the community leased those to a gas company. Emmanuel had stolen those leases but their son Aden had returned them to everyone, while Bishop Yoder made sure the monies in the restored community fund were available to any person or family in need. Something Emmanuel had refused to do.

She shook her head. She'd never known what a greedy, callous man she'd married until after Aden was born and more and more natural gas leases were being sold. He changed, and she never saw a glimpse of the man she had fallen in love with after that.

But dwelling on the past was never good, and she had decided to retire upstairs for the night when she heard the phone ring in the barn. Her sons, Sol and Aden, had insisted she have a phone, even though she mostly forgot it existed due to the lack of calls she received. She put on her navy-blue cardigan, grabbed a flashlight, and hurried to the barn to answer the phone. "Hello?"

"Hi, Mrs. Troyer. It's Jordan."

While Jordan sounded as if he were in his early thirties, the same age as her sons, when she met him the night he took her case and saw the threads of gray in his coal-black hair, she realized he had to be in his forties or early fifties. Old enough that she trusted him with finding Emmanuel. He called her only when he had news. Hopefully this time it would be . . . She wasn't sure what she wanted to hear. "Hello, Jordan."

"We haven't spoken in a few weeks, and I wanted to update you on my progress."

Her heart stilled. "Have you found . . . ?"

"I'm sorry, I haven't. All my leads except one have dried up, and I plan to pursue it. But Mrs. Troyer, if that one doesn't pan out, there's nothing more I can do. As of right now, Emmanuel Troyer is a man who doesn't want to be found."

She nodded, her disappointment growing that she might not ever get the closure she desperately needed. "Thank you, Jordan. I appreciate everything you've done."

"I haven't done much, Mrs. Troyer. I'm sorry about that. I'll call you soon. Have a good night."

"You too." She hung up the phone and kept her light shining on the receiver, anger and resentment building to the point that she had to take several deep breaths as she listened to Penny rustling the hay in her stall. Despite decades of practice stuffing down her thoughts and feelings to the point where she was numb, fighting the bitterness edging her heart was getting harder. Why hadn't he contacted her or her sons at least once? Why had he left them all in limbo?

She dragged herself back to the house, exhausted. She slipped off her shoes, hung up her cardigan, and walked into the kitchen. Looking at the kitchen table, she thought about Loren. His gentle touch. His kind words. For that brief blissful second, she'd had hope for a happy future.

Rhoda yanked her gaze from the table and shut off the light. She had been hopeful before—when she first married Emmanuel, and then again when he'd left that he would return and repair their broken family.

Hope had failed her twice. She wasn't stupid enough to be hopeful a third time.

"Did they finally *geh* to bed?"

Sadie Troyer nodded, then gave Aden a sly smile. "You shouldn't have given them so much ice cream after supper. They were both too wound up to fall asleep right away."

He shook his head. "You were the one who added extra chocolate sauce."

She laughed. "Obviously it was a team effort." She waited for him to chuckle. When he didn't, she frowned. Their two girls, Rosanna and Salina, hadn't been that difficult to put to bed, but Aden had been so preoccupied lately that she tried to at least make him smile.

They both readied for bed, and as was their habit every night, Aden climbed in first, then held the covers open for her to snuggle under. She laid next to him, then put her head on his shoulder, closing her eyes when he put his arm around her. She could hear the comforting thump of his heartbeat. Her steady, loving husband meant everything to her, and she was concerned about him. "Aden?"

"*Ya*?"

"When are you going to tell me what's bothering you?"

A pause. "*Nix* is bothering me."

She lifted her head and propped herself on one elbow. The bedroom was too dark for her to see his face clearly, but she didn't have to. "We've been married for nine years, *lieb*. I can tell when something is wrong. You've been too quiet lately. And when the *maed* asked you to go outside with them this afternoon, they had to ask three times before you answered."

He sighed and rolled over on his back. "I'm worried about *Mamm*."

Sadie nodded. When wasn't he worried about his mother? She knew he tried not to, fully believing God's word about not being anxious for anything. But there was a fine line between worry and concern, and he was crossing that line more and more. "I noticed she's been spending a lot of time with Loren lately," she said, assuming he had the same suspicions she did.

"*Ya*, she has." He turned on his side again and faced her. "I want her to be happy. All those difficult years she had with *Daed*, and then after he left she was still insistent he was coming back, until recently. It's not right that she has to keep suffering because of his cowardice." His tone took on an uncharacteristic edge.

Sadie kissed him until they both settled back onto the mattress, this time with her cradling him in her arms. "God has a plan," she whispered, gently stroking his red hair.

"I know. You and I are living proof of that."

He was right. Over the years Sadie tried not to think about how she and Aden had been forced to marry because of Emmanuel's greed and control. He initially tried to coerce her into marrying Sol, Aden's brother, for the sole purpose of gaining control of her late parents' natural gas rights. Aden had stepped in and agreed to marry her in place of Sol. At first she had been angry, not wanting to marry either of them. Then she realized he was a good man. Nothing like his father, or how his brother used to be.

Instead of focusing on the difficult circumstances that brought them together, she marked the day she had fallen in love with him as the beginning of their relationship, more than a month after they had exchanged vows. She discovered Aden had loved her long before that, and he had proven his love then, and many, many times over the years. She longed for the day his past wouldn't affect him anymore, when the nightmares would stop and when he wouldn't carry the weight of his childhood on his shoulders. Emmanuel had abused not only him but also his brother and his mother. Those experiences weren't easy to get over, even if he had forgiven his father years ago.

Aden lifted his head. "Now you're the one who's quiet."

"I was just thinking about how much I love you."

He smiled. "What a coincidence. I was thinking how much I love you."

Sadie touched his jaw, feeling his soft beard under her palm. "What a pair of saps we are."

Aden laughed. "And for a minute I thought you were going all mushy on me."

"Never." But she laughed too. He was the romantic one in their relationship, while she was practical to a fault. "Your *mamm* will be fine. She's a strong woman, and both she and Loren know the *Ordnung*. They would never violate the rules."

"Of course they wouldn't. But I know how much she cares for Loren, and I'm positive he feels the same way." He paused. "I can't imagine not being able to be with you, Sadie. If that ever happened, I would be devastated."

Her heart skipped a beat. "Me too." She hadn't thought about Rhoda and Loren's relationship that way or realized that they cared for each other that deeply. Since Emmanuel's disappearance, Aden and Sol spent at least one evening a week with Rhoda, usually for supper. The three of them were close, and she shouldn't be surprised that Aden, always perceptive, had caught on to how Rhoda and Loren felt about each other. "There's *nix* we can do," she said. "They're adults, and they will deal with this the best way they can."

"Loren is a *gut mann*. He treats *Mamm* well. If things were different—"

"But they're not." She moved to whisper in his ear. "Don't fret about them so much."

He buried his face in her neck and they held each other. When she finally pulled away, she said, "Let's not talk about *yer mamm* and Loren anymore." She kissed him again. Long. Passionate. "Let's not talk at all."

He drew her into his arms. *Conversation ended.*

Chapter 4

"Don't look at me like that, Cevilla Schlabach Thompson."

Cevilla picked up her cup of hot tea. "Like what, Delilah?"

"Like you think *mei* idea is a bad one."

Cevilla took a sip, then set the cup down. She didn't like chastising her good friend, but in this case, it was necessary. "It's a terrible idea. Remember our promise?"

"To not interfere? *Ya*, *ya*, I remember." She waved her plump fingers. "But this is an exception."

"Of course it is." She leaned back in her chair. It was Thursday afternoon, and Delilah was over for tea. Whenever she could get a break, she came over between two and four o'clock to share a cup at Cevilla's house. Cevilla's husband, Richard, was at Asa Bontrager's, helping the young accountant with tax season. Although he was a retired Los Angeles businessman who had left that life behind, become Amish, and married Cevilla, he often volunteered to help Asa during the busy periods of the year. She didn't mind. The activity kept his mind sharp and gave Cevilla some time to herself. Or in this case, some time alone with her friend.

"Delilah," she said, "we vowed not to matchmake anymore. We need to keep that promise."

Delilah sat back in her chair, her lips pursed in a slight pout. "This is an emergency."

"I thought you said it was an exception."

"That too." She sighed and leaned forward, her tea barely touched. "Katharine is such a sweet girl. She works so hard at the inn, and spends hours making her pretty baskets. She has so much to offer a man, and I can't stand that she's so lonely."

"She told you that?"

"Um, not in so many words." Delilah averted her gaze.

She was obviously fibbing, but Cevilla couldn't hold it against her. She liked Katharine too, even though most of what she knew about the girl was through Delilah. She was standoffish, and, bless her sweet heart, conventionally unattractive. If someone took the time to notice, she had lovely, uniquely colored eyes, and a pretty smile she seldom showed. Since moving to town, she'd started looking much healthier, but overall she was the type of woman many people overlooked, especially men. Despite all that, Cevilla hadn't gotten the impression Katharine was lonely. In fact, she had wondered more than once if the girl was making herself unavailable on purpose. Most of the single women who came to Birch Creek had gone to singings, frolics, and other gatherings, letting the dwindling number of single men in the community know they were interested in them. According to Delilah, Katharine hadn't attended one single event. If she had come to Birch Creek to find a husband, she was going about it the hard way.

"And then there's Ezra," Delilah continued, this time looking straight at Cevilla. "Handsome, charming, a good sense of humor, and just as diligent a worker as Katharine. The perfect catch if you ask me."

"I'm sure there are many women who think the same way."

"That doesn't matter." Delilah huffed.

"It does, if he's dating someone right now."

"He's not. I'm sure of that. He has more than enough to do working at the inn and his *familye*'s farm."

"Then he's probably too busy to date."

Delilah scoffed. "You make time for what's important."

Cevilla picked up her tea again. Now that the beverage had cooled somewhat, she could take a longer sip and also gather her thoughts. Against her better judgment, she was warming to the idea of getting those two together, despite all the obstacles. She was always up for a challenge. But Richard, not to mention Loren, would be livid if they meddled in Katharine and Ezra's love lives. And while Ezra might not be pursuing anyone in particular, she was sure plenty of young women had pursued him. Pretty girls. Confident girls. Girls who were desperate for a husband. Then a thought struck her. "You're not giving Ezra extra work to keep him at the inn, are you? Perhaps making sure he doesn't have the opportunity to date?"

"Of course not. You know there are a million things that need to be done. Shall I list them for you?"

"Please don't." But Cevilla wasn't fooled, especially when Delilah fiddled with the hem of her long sleeve instead of speaking directly. "Why are you so invested in the two of them?"

She didn't say anything for a moment, then finally spoke. "Katharine reminds me of . . . me. I wasn't the prettiest girl in the district. Not even close. I've always carried extra weight, and although

I didn't have the same skin issues, I was *nee* beauty. But when Wayne started courting me"—her eyes sparkled—"I felt like the most treasured woman on earth."

"And you think Ezra can make Katharine feel that way?"

"*Ya*, because he's just like my Wayne." A sad expression crossed her face. "I miss him so."

Cevilla patted Delilah's hand. She hadn't been married before Richard, and she didn't know what it was like to lose a spouse. But she didn't like the possibility that Delilah was projecting her past onto Katharine and Ezra. "You could be wrong about this," she said gently. "Just because they remind you of you and Wayne doesn't mean that they're meant to be together."

She nodded. "I know. I thought they might have spent more time together last night after supper. I gave them the opportunity to be alone, but it wasn't long before Katharine came back inside and Ezra went home."

"Like you said, he's busy. And we both know we can't force them together, especially if it's not God's will. Richard and Loren would have our hides."

"I know that too."

"But you still think we should interfere."

Delilah hesitated, then nodded. "There's been ample opportunity to play matchmaker since that advertisement became public." She gave Cevilla a knowing wink. "That was a brilliant idea, by the way."

"Wait," she said, leaning forward. "You think I put the ad in the paper?"

Delilah's mouth formed a small *O* shape. "You didn't? I thought for sure you had."

"And I thought you did."

"I didn't have a reason to. *Mei grosskinner* were already married. Besides, I vowed not to play matchmaker anymore."

"So did I."

Delilah shook her head, a small laugh escaping. "And here we are talking about doing exactly that. For a *gut* reason, though. Almost every *maedel* that has come here looking for a husband has stayed at the inn. Not once did I sense that I had to take hold of the reins and steer any of them in a particular direction. Except now, with Katharine and Ezra."

Oh dear. Delilah was actually making a decent case for herself. Cevilla usually listened to her gut too. She'd be a hypocrite if she told Delilah not to. But that didn't mean they needed to dive in and immediately plan the wedding. She tapped two fingers on the tabletop. "I wonder if there's a way to see if they're actually compatible."

"They seemed compatible last night," Delilah said.

Or was Delilah trying to rationalize her own desire to see the two of them together? "Have they spent any time alone otherwise? And I mean a decent amount of time, not just a few minutes after supper at your insistence."

Her face fell. "*Nee.*" After a moment, her eyes lit up. "I could send them on an errand. Or multiple errands that would take them all day. That would give them plenty of time together."

Cevilla chuckled.

"What?" Delilah said, looking offended.

"I'm just remembering that I did the same thing with Noah and Ivy. I asked them to take me to Barton, then hung out at the craft store while they got to know each other better." She also remembered her own certainty about her nephew and Ivy being a perfect match for each other. Now they were married, had a successful antique business, and were the parents of a lively little girl. Her instincts had been right about the two of them. She had also been right about Seth and Martha and Lucy and Shane. What if Delilah's instincts were also right? In her experience, some couples just needed a little push in the right direction. "All right," she said with a definitive nod. "I'm on board."

"With sending them shopping?"

"For starters." She grinned at Delilah. "Let operation Katharine and Ezra commence."

"Excellent." Then her smile faded, and she frowned. "But, Cevilla, if you didn't put the ad in the paper—"

"And you didn't either," Cevilla supplied, "then who did?"

Delilah shrugged. "I have *nee* idea."

Chapter 5

On Friday afternoon, two days after Ezra stayed for supper, Katharine walked into the kitchen to get a glass of water before spending some time working on the square basket she started earlier that week. She was halfway finished, although usually the basket would be closer to completion by now. It wasn't that she didn't have time to work on it. She'd had plenty lately, since there had been no new guests booked until tonight and she had finished cleaning and getting everything ready for their rooms yesterday, including Room 3. Ezra's paint job on the scribbled wall was perfect. She couldn't tell he had painted over anything.

That wasn't the first time he intruded on her thoughts, so much so that when she did work on her basket, she couldn't focus. She'd seen him only twice since their talk on the patio. The first time was when he was replacing a light bulb in one of the rustic wall sconces in the upstairs hallway. He'd nodded to her but maintained focus on his task. The second was when they passed by each other on her way to the barn. She kept her gaze down like she usually did, and he didn't say anything to her. Unable to help herself, she glanced over her shoulder, feeling a little disappointed he hadn't said hello, and saw him briskly walking toward the house. Then again, he was in a hurry, and she hadn't said anything either. *Everything is back to normal.*

Except she wasn't. Not only was she confused, she was also annoyed with herself. Try as she might, she couldn't stop thinking about the short time they'd spent together. Only now was she realizing how desperate she'd been for some normal conversation. Ezra, with his easygoing manner, had given her that with his small talk. He also hadn't pressed her for any more information than she was willing to give, which she appreciated. Although she had gone to bed bitter after reading Elsie's letter, at least there was one man who on the surface wasn't like her ex-fiancé.

She had finished filling the glass with water from the tap when Delilah entered the kitchen carrying a large pad of paper. "Oh, I'm glad I caught you." She sat down at the table and patted the chair next to her. "I want to discuss tomorrow's plans."

Katharine took a sip of the water, and the minute she sat down Delilah pushed the pad in front of her. She glanced down at the handwritten column on the page. "What's this?"

"Your list for tomorrow." She ripped the top page off and handed it to Katharine.

As she read through all the errands, her brow furrowed. Had the woman lost her mind?

Delilah tapped the side of the pencil eraser on the pad. "I know it's a long list, but those tasks need to be done ASAP."

All Katharine could do was nod. As her boss, Delilah had the right to ask her to do anything related to the inn, within reason. "I'll call and arrange a taxi for tomorrow morning."

"Not necessary. Gary will pick you and Ezra up tomorrow at eight o'clock sharp. I do appreciate a man who is punctual."

"Ezra?" she said, confused.

"Ezra is punctual too, but I was referring to Gary."

"Gary," she mumbled, still processing Delilah's words. Wait, Ezra was going with her? *Oh* nee . . .

Delilah flipped the pencil around and held it above the pad. "Do you think we should serve oatmeal bars next week, or banana nut muffins?"

Right now she didn't care what they served for breakfast. This was the second time in a week Delilah had sprung a surprise that included Ezra. She looked at the list again. The first few stops were in Barton—Walmart, the fabric and hardware stores, then Schlabach's Antiques. After that they were free to have lunch—naturally Delilah had scheduled it on the list—and then they were to pick peaches at Smith's orchard, drop a bag off at Rhoda Troyer's, and then go to Cevilla's before coming home. Even with Ezra's help, it would take the whole day to do everything Delilah wanted.

"I think muffins will suit." Delilah scribbled on the notepad.

Katharine lifted her gaze. "What do you need us to do at Cevilla's?"

"I'm not sure." Delilah studied her notes as if the word muffins was of great interest. "She wanted you to stop by her house, but she didn't tell me why."

Katharine started to rub her temple, then jerked her hand away. She didn't need Delilah to see her stressing about this assignment. "Is Gary okay with spending the entire day shuttling us around?"

Delilah set the pencil on the table and looked at her. "He's fine with it, Katharine. I explained all of the errands to him, and he was happy to help out."

"Does Ezra know?"

"*Ya*," she answered, her tone suddenly laced with impatience. "I told him earlier today. It's not like you to question me, Katharine. Do you have a problem with *mei* requests?"

Katharine quickly shook her head. Delilah was a kind woman, but when the inn was involved, she was a taskmaster. This was the first time she'd given Katharine so many tasks, though. "Can I ask one more question?"

Delilah huffed. "*Geh* ahead."

"Tomorrow's Saturday. Don't I need to be here to help out with the guests?"

"Oh." A small frown appeared on her face, deepening the wrinkles at the corners of her mouth.

"Maybe it's better if I run the errands on Monday—"

"*Nee*!" Delilah cleared her throat. "That's not necessary. Selah can take care of any maid duties that arise. So that frees you up for tomorrow." She sat back in her chair, flashing Katharine a satisfied smile.

But Delilah's solution only caused Katharine more uncertainty. Selah was the inn's hostess, and also the special events coordinator. Often she was at home or in the office working on an upcoming event or developing marketing ideas to advertise the inn. When she was first hired at the inn she'd been a maid, and Katharine knew she wouldn't mind filling in for a day. None of that explained why Delilah insisted on sending her and Ezra out on their busiest day, however.

"Katharine?" Delilah peered at her over silver-rimmed glasses. "Is there something wrong?"

"I'm concerned I won't get everything done." Yes, that was true, but it wasn't the only reason she was apprehensive. Knowing she had to spend an entire day with Ezra had her stomach in a tizzy, and not in a good way.

"I agree, if you had to make the trip on your own. That's why I'm sending Ezra with you. Four hands are better than two, I always say."

Katharine had never heard her say that.

Delilah picked up her pencil again, her grin still triumphant. "And take as much time as you want for lunch. The Mexican restaurant in the center of town has delicious food. You should eat there."

"Okay," she mumbled, not bothering to mention that she didn't like Mexican food.

"I need to finish up this menu," Delilah said. "Do you have any requests?"

That I don't have to go tomorrow? "Anything you decide on is fine." She got up from the table and picked up her almost-full glass. "I'll be out in the barn if you need me."

Delilah nodded, her smile fading. "Are you sure you don't want me to make anything special?"

She poured some water on the potted plant in the windowsill above the sink. "I'm sure."

"Hmm."

Katharine turned around, but Delilah was already working on her list. *I must be hearing things.*

After quickly washing and drying the glass, she went outside. The sun peeked through billowing clouds in the sky, but Katharine barely noticed the warmth as she folded her arms over her chest and started to fret about tomorrow. Staying aloof with Ezra for hours would be difficult, if not impossible. Engaging in small talk all day sounded tortuous too. Before Simeon, she preferred to get to know someone on more than a superficial level, and she had to give that up when she moved to Birch Creek.

She entered the barn, then stopped by the stalls of Bob and Brad, the Stolls' two new horses, and patted their noses. "I'm being ridiculous," she said to Bob—or was it Brad? "It's just a shopping trip."

The horse bobbed his head, as if agreeing with her.

"And it's only for a day. I can do anything for a day."

The other horse whinnied his approval.

"*Ya*. I can do this." She smiled at the two animals before heading back to her workspace. When Delilah found out Katharine liked to make baskets, she had Loren set up a table and folding chair for her to use. Over several months Katharine had made three large baskets to hold her supplies, and next to those was a bucket she used to hold the water she dipped her pieces in. It needed filling, and she needed to select the strands of wicker she wanted to add to the basket. Instead she put her elbow on the table and rested her chin in her hand, the self-confidence she'd uttered to Bob and Brad disappearing. *What am I going to do?*

"Hi."

She jumped at the sound of Ezra's voice. How had she missed hearing him enter the barn? Then again, when she was engrossed in her thoughts the world around her disappeared, something that had happened when she started dating Simeon. To cope with his verbal abuse she disappeared into herself until there was nothing but silence in her head replacing his voice. Blissful silence—

"Looks like the basket is coming along nicely."

She frowned. "What?"

"The basket. Right. There." He pointed to the half-finished container on her table.

"Oh. *Ya*. This basket." Wow, she sounded dumb. Her face

flushed, and she quickly grabbed a handful of dried wicker from the container next to the bucket.

"Maybe you could teach me how to make one of those sometime."

She stilled, halfway to a seated position. "Are you serious?"

"Sure." Ezra stuck his hands in his pockets and grinned. "I like learning new things. I've sure learned a lot in the short time I've been here. Besides, you never know. Weaving could come in handy someday."

She sat up, the edges of the wicker digging into her hand. "You want to learn weaving," she said, still gaping at him.

"Why are you surprised?" He smirked. "Is basket making only for *maed*?"

Simeon had thought so. Once she showed him a large basket she'd made, her best one yet, and she offered to teach him how to weave.

He scoffed. "I don't do women's work." Then he inspected her craftsmanship. "The edges are uneven."

"A little." But only another basket weaver—or a picky, critical person—would notice.

"If you can't make a basket right, you should stop making them."

That was the last time she had shown him any of her baskets.

"Uh, you don't have to teach me if you don't want."

She blinked and Ezra came into view, or rather his torso did. She lifted her gaze to his face, searching for a response and not wanting to be rude. "I—I can teach you. Some day." She quickly reached for the water bucket, ready to make her escape.

"Want me to fetch you some water?" he asked. "I've seen you dip those willow strips to loosen them up."

Alarmed, she released the bucket's handle. "You've been watching me?"

"Just once last week when I hitched Bob to the buggy. I'm surprised you didn't hear me get him out of his stall." He pulled his hands out of his pockets and took a step back. "I wasn't spying on you or anything."

She didn't know if she could believe him . . . until she met his eyes. There was no guile or harshness in them. Only candor, and that bothered her more than the idea of him observing her unnoticed.

His smile returned, although it wasn't as bright as before. "I don't mind getting you some water."

"I don't want water," she said, her tone sharp. "I want to know why you're being nice to me."

Well that was an unexpected question. And a weird one. Ezra had been repairing the dripping faucet outside the barn—the inn and its property and buildings seemed to have a fair share of plumbing problems—when he saw Katharine walk into the barn. She had been spending extra time there this week, he'd noticed. He also didn't understand why he'd noticed, or why she had been on his mind since the other night. After he left the Stolls', he had thought about how calm he was around Katharine, probably because she had a peaceful presence he wasn't used to being around. He'd grown up in a loud, crowded family, and lately he'd been chased by several overeager females ready to settle down and who never seemed to stop talking. But Katharine was different. She was quiet. Serene. Even her voice had a soothing quality to it.

Right now her expression was anything but soothing, and her

forehead had been wrinkled up since the moment he'd startled her with his arrival. "Why wouldn't I be nice to you?" he asked, genuinely puzzled.

Her cheeks turned red again. "Never mind." She reached for a willow strip only to knock over the bucket. Good thing he hadn't filled it with water. He quickly picked up the bucket and set it upright on the ground.

When he lifted his head, their eyes met. He stilled, fascinated by her eyes again, and this time he was close enough to see them in detail. Vibrant, bluish green, and he could make out the ring of gold around each pupil. Wow. He vaguely made note of some imperfections in her skin, but they didn't detract from her perfectly shaped eyebrows and completely smooth forehead.

He'd never been one to take stock in looks, having met plenty of women who were pretty on the outside and not so nice on the inside, and vice versa. His future sister-in-law, Margaret, happened to be both pretty and a great girl. Like all of his sisters-in-law, actually.

Then there was Gloria, a young woman who had arrived in Birch Creek soon after the bachelor advertisement hit the paper. She wasn't the prettiest of the girls that had flocked to his community, but she was nice . . . or so he had thought. They had secretly dated for almost a month, and he thought he might be serious about her, until he discovered she was also dating another guy back in her hometown. "I like to keep *mei* options open," she'd said, like dating two men at the same time was no big deal. But to Ezra it was a huge deal, and after that punch in the heart he quickly ended the relationship. Fortunately she went back home soon after, but the experience was part of the reason he had kept the other women interested in him at arm's length.

But Katharine was different. He wasn't sure how, and he couldn't explain why he couldn't stop staring at her. Yet something kept him there, half standing, half bending, looking into a pair of eyes that kept him mesmerized.

She jerked her head and stood. "I need to get back to the inn," she said, almost knocking the chair over. "I forgot I, uh, have to do something."

Funny, that was the same excuse he'd used on Charity the other day, which was why he doubted her words. What he didn't doubt was that she wanted to get away from him. Had he been offensive in some way? Did he smell bad? Maybe he should check his armpits, but then she would think he was weird, on top of thinking he was . . . well, whatever she thought he was.

"Excuse me," she muttered, finally managing to get the chair back under the table.

They were in a tight space and he tried to give her enough room to pass, but she still had to squeeze by him. Her hip pressed against his thigh.

"Sorry," she said, her voice breaking.

Ezra frowned, able to hear the distress in her tone. "It's okay . . ." he said as she fled the barn.

Confused, he played through their conversation. *I asked her to teach me to weave . . . I offered to get her water . . . She asked me why I was nice to her . . .* Wait. That was a strange question. And when he questioned her back, she deflected. Was she upset because he was being *nice*? That didn't make any sense.

This wasn't good, especially since they were spending tomorrow together, per Delilah's orders. He'd been surprised that she wanted him to run errands with Katharine, but he was also looking forward to the opportunity to get away from the inn for a day. He didn't go to Barton often, and he was sure that Delilah wouldn't mind if he picked up a few things for himself while they were out. He enjoyed fruit picking, and seeing Cevilla was always a hoot. Tomorrow could be fun, but not if Katharine was upset with him. *For being nice. Good grief.*

The idea of being at odds with her didn't sit well with him, so he decided to seek her out. He checked the inn, and when he didn't find her there, he figured she went home to the Stolls' house.

But he stopped short in front of the door. He had a lot of work to finish today, including repairing the mailbox, and he was spending time chasing Katharine. *What am I doing?*

He spun around and went to the large shed that held tools, both garden and regular ones, along with the bag of concrete he'd ordered earlier in the week from Schrock's Grocery and Tool. He didn't have time for games, or whatever this was between him and Katharine right now. He'd talk to her in the morning, and they would either settle things or it would be a long, silent trip. Either way, he vowed to enjoy himself. He wasn't going to let some slight he had no idea he'd made keep him from having a fun and productive day off.

Chapter 6

"I'm sorry I don't have better news, Mr. Smith."

From his seat on the exam table, Lester stared at Dr. Chen. Was it possible to be both surprised and resigned at the same time? "I kinda figured it was bad," he mumbled, staring at the opposite wall of the examination room. A poster with the words, "Doctors need patience. Patients need doctors," caught his attention. Right now he'd do anything not to be a patient.

Dr. Chen adjusted her black, square-framed glasses and looked over his chart. "Late-stage pancreatic cancer is difficult to treat," she said, not looking at him.

"Because it's terminal?"

Her eyes flicked to his, as if she was surprised he knew his prognosis. She shouldn't be. But with his thin frame covered with jeans and a T-shirt stained with paint, and an oversized black-and-red plaid flannel shirt he'd picked up at a thrift store a year ago, he probably looked homeless. Add to that his full mustache and a beard that reached to his collar . . . Yep, he was a sight all right. These were his work clothes, having taken a job six months ago with a commercial painting company. Truth was, though, his regular clothes weren't much better.

"There are treatments you can undergo, Mr. Smith," she said. "Radiation, chemo—"

"Stop right there." He held up his hand, also covered with flecks of white and gray paint. He had had to take off the afternoon to go to this appointment, and he hadn't bothered to shower or change. "I'm not letting anyone put that poison in me."

"But it will prolong your life."

"I don't have much of a life to prolong."

She closed his chart and took off her glasses. "Mr. Smith, while I respect your decision, I encourage you to read the literature we have available about our treatments. We're the best cancer center in West Virginia, and we will do everything we can to help you. None of us can predict the future. Perhaps you'll be the first one to beat this disease."

He scoffed. "Then I'll just end up as your guinea pig. No thanks."

She pressed her lips together and pulled several thin pamphlets from the holder on the small built-in table next to an equally small sink. "I'm giving these to you anyway. Just in case you change your mind."

Lester accepted them, but he wasn't going to change his mind. "Thank you."

"Stop by the desk on your way out and Alicia will make your next appointment." She held out her hand. He shook it, and then she left the room.

The silence in the exam room was so heavy he could hear his heart beating. Oddly enough, he wasn't anxious for once. Anxiety and agitation, he'd discovered, were some of the symptoms of late-stage pancreatic cancer. That along with the twenty pounds he'd seemed to lose overnight, his poor appetite, and the pain in his gut and back. Lack of sleep had made him careless at work, and it had been his boss who forced him to go to the urgent care two weeks ago. That scored him an oncology referral, followed by tests and blood work, and lots of money flying out of his pocket to pay for everything. All that trouble to find out he was dying, and there was nothing anyone could do to stop it.

He realized he hadn't asked the doc how much time he had. Then again, did it matter? Every person on earth was in some stage of death. He just happened to know that his end was coming soon.

Lester got off the table, the constant dull ache in his side and abdomen more acute than before. Odd. He thought he'd gone completely numb the moment he heard his fate. He walked to the desk to check out.

"Dr. Chen would like to see you in two weeks," Alicia said. "What time is good for you?"

"I'll get back to you on that."

Alicia looked up at him. The young woman had the plumpest cheeks he'd ever seen. They reminded him of that girl back in Birch Creek, the one who had moved in with the Stolls. What was her name? He couldn't recall. All he remembered was her being overweight, having a bad complexion, and having a sad countenance that made even his hard heart soften a bit.

"Dr. Chen encourages her patients to make their appointments right after their visit," Alicia said, pulling him out of his reverie.

He met her eyes. "Because some of them don't come back?"

She paused, then nodded. "How about the twenty-fifth of this month?"

"Whatever."

"Great, I'll put you down for one thirty."

He nodded. "Sure." He reached in his pocket for his wallet.

"There's no co-pay this time," Alicia said, folding her hands on her desk and smiling.

He frowned. "Why?"

"Per Dr. Chen." She continued to look at him.

"I can pay my bill." He yanked out his wallet and almost threw the cash at her, stopping himself because it wasn't her fault the doctor thought he was too poor to pay. "Here," he said.

"But—"

He turned around and walked out of the office to his third-hand car that was almost as beat up as he was. He opened the driver's side door and sat behind the wheel. He never bothered to lock the doors because no one in their right mind would break in or steal anything from such a piece of junk. He stared at the cracked leather steering wheel in front of him. Pancreatic cancer. That wasn't the way he'd expected to go.

Lester leaned back in his seat, the sun shining through the windshield and heating up the car. He barely noticed and closed his eyes. He'd heard that a person's life flashed in front of them before they kicked the bucket, and while he wasn't sick enough to be at death's door just yet, his past dashed through his mind. That was nothing new. As usual, regrets and shame filled him, mostly from the distant past, although one regret was more recent. He thought about the Amish kid he'd left in front of the hospital last year, his head concussed and bloodied, while his girlfriend had gone into the ER to get help. Owen and Margaret. He couldn't forget their names. He should have stayed and made sure they were both okay. But his two ever-present companions, fear and self-preservation, had kicked in and he took off, first to West Virginia and then to Kentucky, where he lived in a pay-by-the-day motel and painted buildings for a living. A far cry from who he used to be and what he used to do.

Time to mail those letters.

He drove back to the motel, walked inside the dark room, and flipped on the light. Half-empty water and soda bottles littered the table, and since he allowed the maid to come in only once a month, the bed hadn't been made in weeks. He made sure to tidy up before she came in, but there was still plenty of cleaning to do. When he glanced at the clock on the nightstand, he realized he hadn't had lunch. Or breakfast. Did he eat supper last night? He couldn't remember.

He walked over to the nightstand, opened the drawer, and looked at the three envelopes he'd placed there when he first moved in. He'd written them over a year ago and had carried them with him through his moves, still undecided whether he should send them. He wasn't undecided now. He picked up the envelopes, locked his room, and went to the front desk at the end of the row of motel rooms.

"Hey, Lester." Pauline, the day clerk, greeted him with a gap-toothed smile. "Haven't seen you around lately." She tilted her head, peering at him. "You don't look so good."

"Having an off day." He set the envelopes on her desk. "Do you have any stamps? I need to mail these."

"I can take care of that for you." She picked them up. "Birch Creek, Ohio, huh?"

"Yes." His jaw jerked.

She thumbed through the envelopes. "All Troyers too. Ain't that an Amish name? Jeb and I used to live near Amish country in Northeast Ohio."

"Are you gonna mail them or not?"

"Sorry." She reached under the counter and brought out a roll of stamps. "Jeb's always saying I'm too nosy for my own good."

As he watched her put a stamp on each envelope, a different pain developed in his gut. He should have done this the moment he wrote the letters. But he must have a shred of conscience left because he had held off, not able to go through with the lie. Now it didn't matter. That lie would eventually become the truth.

"I'll put them with the rest of the outgoing mail, right here." She set the letters on a small stack in a wire basket on the counter. "Anything else I can do for ya?"

He shook his head. "Thanks, I'm good." He turned around and started to leave.

"Jeb's cooking ribs on the grill tonight," she said. "You're welcome to join us if you want." Pauline and her husband not only ran the motel, they lived in the room next to the office.

Her kindness made him smile. "Maybe another time."

"You know you're always welcome."

He nodded, then left, heading back to his room. This wasn't the first time she'd invited him to join them for supper. They were friendly like that, especially to people who stayed for a while at the motel. Lester figured she must be on a mission to get him to say yes, and he had to admire her tenacity.

If she knew the truth about him, she would never invite him again.

Chapter 7

Stupid . . . stupid . . .

The word played over and over in Katharine's mind as she waited for Gary to arrive. She should be enjoying the sunrise. The comfortable hickory rocking chairs on the wraparound porch in front of Stoll's Inn provided a serene view of the rising sun. But all she could think about was yesterday's conversation with Ezra.

She jumped up from the chair and started to pace. A year of keeping her distance from everyone had been difficult, and all that effort was starting to unwind. *Why are you being nice to me?* Of all the questions she could have asked him, that one popped out. She shouldn't be asking him questions anyway. Fortunately she'd been able to redirect his attention—this time.

When she reached the end of the porch, she halted, then rubbed her palm across the white banister. Anytime Simeon was extra nice or did something kind for her, he wanted something in return. She kept telling herself Ezra wasn't like that . . . but how could she be sure? When they had made eye contact, it took her a few seconds to realize he was staring. Every scar, every imperfection, every bit of her double chin was inches from his scrutinizing gaze.

On top of that, she'd had to squeeze by him. Not a problem for a thin girl. But there wasn't enough room for her bulky body to move past without brushing against him. How mortifying.

Katharine closed her eyes. She was making this into a bigger deal than it was. If Ezra did have a problem with her face or body, so what? They were coworkers doing a job. And once today was over things would be back to normal. They hadn't interacted much before, and that would continue. As lonely as she was, she preferred that to constantly worrying about what he thought of her.

She sat back down on the hickory rocker. The sun was halfway past the horizon, and Gary would arrive shortly. Her stomach grumbled, and she placed her hand over it to muffle the sound. She should be helping Delilah in the kitchen with breakfast, but she'd skipped eating and didn't want the temptation. When she put on her dress this morning, she noticed it was even looser around the waist than it had been lately. The last thing she wanted to do was ruin her progress.

Besides, last night after giving her money for today's purchases, plus insisting on providing extra for lunch, Delilah had told her not to do her usual morning chores. "Just focus on the errands," she said, her smile cryptic.

In the half light of dawn, she saw a tall figure walk down the road, then turn into the inn's driveway. Ezra always walked back and forth to work even though the Bontrager farm was more than two miles away. The only exceptions were days when it was storming, and even then, he waited until the rain stopped or he caught a ride from Levi or Loren, or even Jackson, if he was around.

Katharine waited until he was almost to the front porch before she stood. "Hi," she said, moving to stand at the edge of the top step. She didn't want to be friendly to him, but she refused to be outright rude either.

"Morning." He remained at the bottom of the steps, his hands in his pockets, his gaze on his shoes, clearly keeping his distance.

Gut. But it felt anything but good. Now things were more awkward between them than they had been at Delilah's. She gripped her fingers together, waiting for him to say something.

He didn't.

Her empty stomach filled with familiar shame. Now that he had gotten a close look at her, he was repulsed. Just like Simeon had been. She couldn't go to Barton, or even spend another minute on the porch, now that she knew what Ezra thought of her. She turned to go inside and tell Delilah she was too sick to run errands. That wasn't far from the truth.

"Looks like it's going to be a nice day, *ya*?"

Katharine paused, then faced him. He was looking at her, absent his usual smile. But there was no revulsion in his eyes. Only uncertainty. He pressed the toe of his boot on the edge of the bottom step.

"Uh, *ya*. It does."

Another stretch of silence. Ezra glanced over his shoulder at the driveway. Then he faced her again. "I'm sorry about yesterday."

She frowned. *He* was sorry? "Why?"

"You were upset. I figured I had something to do with it."

Katharine descended the steps, stopping before the last one. Now they were almost eye to eye, and she could clearly see his distress. "I'm the one who needs to apologize," she said. "I shouldn't have run off."

"Why did you?" When she didn't answer right away, he added,

"If I said or did something, please tell me. Whatever it is, I won't do it again."

She blinked, wondering if she heard him right. Simeon would never admit he was wrong, even when he was. "You didn't do anything," she said. "I'm . . . I'm not used to people being nice to me." That wasn't exactly true. Elsie was a godsend, and the Stolls were too. Her parents were supportive and loving. But they were also being influenced by Simeon.

His eyebrows shot up. "You're not?"

"By men other than *mei vatter*, *nee*." That was as close to the truth as she dared admit.

He rubbed his chin, not answering her. The sun was directly behind him, his body blocking the bright glow. He seemed in deep thought, and she couldn't help but take advantage of the moment to focus on the cleft in his chin. Not too deep or big. Exactly right and it suited his handsome face.

When Gary pulled into the driveway, Ezra turned and headed for the car.

Katharine grabbed her purse off the porch. She followed him, wondering what he was thinking about. *Never mind*. They had cleared the air concerning yesterday, and that's what mattered.

By the time they reached Ivy and Noah's antique store right before noon, Ezra was starving. The trips to the discount, fabric, and hardware stores had been easy, since Delilah needed only two or three items from each, and he'd been able to buy the few things he needed for himself without a problem. Gary, who had always been good-natured every time he taxied Ezra and his family around, didn't mind hanging out in his car most of the morning. But since Bob, the owner of the hardware store, was a good friend of his, he had gone inside. When Katharine told him they had to go to Schlabach's Antiques, only a block away, he nodded and went back to talking to Bob.

But Ezra's mind wasn't on his stomach, and it hadn't been on his errands. He kept thinking about what Katharine revealed right before Gary picked them up. They hadn't talked much in the car, mostly because he was silently fitting the pieces together. She'd been hurt, and now her aloofness made sense. He also suspected that giving him a tiny peek into her past had been difficult. He sympathized. Gloria's betrayal had wounded him—mostly his pride. But it was obvious Katharine's pain ran much deeper.

"Ezra? Are you coming inside?"

He blinked, snapping back to the present in front of Schlabach's large picture window. "*Ya*," he said, hurrying to the front door. He held it open for Katharine. "Sorry. I guess I was woolgathering a bit."

She gave him an odd look before they both went inside.

"Hi, Katharine." Ivy Schlabach smiled as she walked over to them. "Nice to see you, Ezra. What brings you both by?"

Ezra searched Ivy's face for the familiar sly look people often gave when they saw a single male and female together outside of church. But Ivy's expression was guileless and friendly.

"Delilah sent us on some errands today," Katharine said, stepping toward her. "She said you have some picture frames held back for her."

Ivy nodded. "That I do." She walked over to Noah, who was standing behind the counter. Raising her voice slightly as she looked up at him, she said, "Could you get Delilah Stoll's frames from the office? Katharine and Ezra are here to pick them up." Noah had severe hearing loss due to Ménière's disease and although he wore hearing aids, he also read lips.

"Sure." He caught Ezra's gaze and nodded hello. Ezra returned his nod and Noah headed for his office in the back of the store.

"I haven't seen you in here before," Ivy said to Katharine. "Is this your first time visiting us?"

"*Ya*." She glanced around the store. "You have a lot of lovely things."

"Let me show you around." Ivy glanced at Ezra. "Just make yourself at home."

Ezra wasn't much interested in antiques, so he went back to the office to chat with Noah. He knocked loudly on the door before poking his head into the office. "Hey," he said, when Noah turned around.

"Come on in." Noah gestured to the frames sitting on a desk covered with papers. "Ignore the mess. I'm purging some old records I had from my days as an auctioneer." Wistfulness entered his eyes. "Every time I think I'm over the past, I see something that makes me wish I was still in the game." He glanced at the papers. "But Ivy is right. It's time to get rid of all this stuff."

"What is it?"

"Mostly notes about items I've auctioned off. I liked to do a lot of research when I held an auction. That way items were priced right." He held up one of the frames, a small rectangular one that had gunmetal faceted stones attached on each side and a fancy wrought iron bow at the top. The glass insert was missing, and the backing was faded linen, not cardboard or paper. "This is an odd choice for Delilah," he said. "I didn't take her for an art deco kind of woman."

"Is that what that is?"

"The style, *ya*. Not exactly plain. Or Amish." He set the frame down on top of two larger, less decorative wooden ones. "I was surprised when she came in here yesterday and purchased these."

Ezra frowned. "Wait, Delilah was here yesterday?"

"Yep. Right after we opened. I expected her to take the frames with her, but she said she didn't have room for them in the taxi. A little strange, but you know Delilah. She has her own way of doing things."

"That she does." He looked at the frames again. They wouldn't take up much room in a car unless the taxi had been stuffed to the gills with other things. Still, she could have held them on her lap during the ride home.

Noah picked up the frames. "The paper and bubble wrap are up front behind the counter. Won't take long for me to package these up for you."

"*Danki*." He followed Noah to the front. Something was off here. If Delilah was in Barton yesterday, why did she send him and Katharine here today? The items on her list weren't exactly emergency supplies. Maybe she'd forgotten to get them yesterday. But at all these different shops? And how could she forget to buy fabric when the fabric store was on the other side of Schlabach Antiques?

When she talked to him yesterday about her list, she'd insisted he and Katharine go together, even when he offered to run the errands himself and save her the trouble. So insistent that he couldn't tell her no, in spite of all the work he had to do at the inn. "You both have to *geh*," she said, her tone brooking no argument. "*Together*."

Ezra reached the counter and stopped. When he first started working at Stoll's, Levi had made an offhanded comment about how his grandmother liked to poke her nose in other people's affairs—especially single people. "But it worked out in mine and Selah's favor," he'd said. Until now, Ezra hadn't given any thought to Levi's words. Were he and Katharine Delilah's new targets? Katharine wouldn't like that at all, and he wasn't too happy about it either.

Now he was convinced Delilah was behind the bride advertisement. For some reason, the woman was determined to match up the whole town.

As Noah wrapped up the frames, Ezra saw Katharine a few feet away, peering inside a curio case filled with small, decorative objects. She touched the glass in front of a jar with a silver metal lid on top. The lid was covered with tiny decorative flowers painted in muted pinks, lavenders, and tiny specks of green for the leaves.

Then he turned his gaze from the jar to Katharine's soft expression and stilled. The perpetual lines of tension around her eyes and mouth had disappeared. A tiny, yet sweet smile played on her lips.

Pretty.

The word popped into his head. He jerked back his thoughts, finding it surprisingly difficult to do. He was a sucker for a great smile. That was the first thing he'd noticed about Gloria. *And look how that ended up.*

Ezra scratched at his ear. Delilah was messing with his head. That had to be the reason he'd paid attention to Katharine's smile and then thought about his doomed relationship with Gloria. If Delilah's intent was to make him and Katharine a couple, she was going to be disappointed. He didn't want any part of a matchmaking scheme. He'd already let Gloria manipulate him. He wasn't going to let another woman—or anyone else—do that again.

Katharine stared at the jar in front of her. Such a beautiful piece, and very fancy. Too fancy for an Amish home. But she had always been drawn to pretty, ornate things that were endlessly available in the English world. This sparkling jar with the lovely lid was appealing to the eye, but not very practical. But that didn't stop her from imagining for a minute how it would look on her dresser in the room she rented from the Stolls.

Reluctantly, she pulled away from the curio and turned around, almost jumping out of her skin. How long had Ezra been behind her? He had the stealth of a cat, even while wearing clunky boots. Or she'd been so enamored with the jar that she shut out the rest of the world again.

"Sorry," he muttered. "Didn't mean to sneak up on you."

"It's fine."

His expression grew tense. "Noah's wrapped up the frames. We need to get going." Without waiting for an answer, he headed for the door.

She gave the jar one last, longing look, then followed him. Ivy was behind the counter next to her husband. Katharine thought they made a visually interesting pair due to their height difference. Ivy was short and petite while Noah was probably more than a foot taller. They were a nice couple to be around because of their obvious respect for each other. As Noah handed her each frame, Ivy put them in a large, handled paper bag. They even worked together as a team. Just like her parents did, and Elsie and Galen.

She tugged at her loose cardigan. She had to stop thinking about home . . . and about what she would never have.

"I'll be outside," Ezra called out, then left the shop.

Ivy put the last frame in the bag. "Is he all right?" she asked.

Katharine nodded, but she wasn't sure. He'd been acting a little peculiar since Gary showed up that morning, and they hadn't said much to each other since they left. At first she was confused, expecting Ezra to at least try to talk to her. Then she was grateful. The less she had to interact with him the better.

"Not everyone is as enamored with antiques as we are," Noah said with a grin. "He's not the first guy—or gal—to lose interest quickly."

She nodded again, but wondered if boredom was the real reason he was in such a hurry to leave. Either that or hunger. It was lunchtime.

"I noticed you were looking at the powder jar in the curio cabinet," Ivy said. "That's one of *mei* favorites."

Noah nodded. "That was a *gut* find. I went antiquing with Judah in Akron a few weeks ago and found that in one of the shops. Got it for a nice price too."

Katharine knew who Ivy's youngest brother was, but she'd never interacted with him. He was in his late teens, and she was surprised that he was interested in antiques.

"At least one of my family members likes old things." Ivy handed Katharine the bag. "He's always been interested in history."

"Maybe someday he'll come work for us," Noah said.

"Oh, you won't have to twist his arm. Anything to get out of farm work." She faced Katharine again. "I can open the cabinet for you if you want to get a closer look at the jar."

While she was tempted, she shook her head. Not only was it too extravagant, it was too expensive. "This was all we needed to get. *Danki*."

"Don't be a stranger," Noah said. "We get new inventory all the time. Just as many people like to sell us their antiques as they do buy them, so we always have something different."

"I'll keep that in mind." Although normally she would have just left, she couldn't help but smile at Ivy and Noah. They were both so friendly and nice, and she knew that wasn't just for show or to sell their antiques.

When she stepped outside, she saw Ezra pacing in front of the hardware store. There was definitely something wrong. Ignoring her instincts, she went to him. "Are you okay?"

He stopped pacing and faced her. Opened his mouth to say something, then closed it.

Alarmed, she asked, "Ezra, what's wrong?"

"Did you know?"

"Know what?"

He paused again, then blew out a breath. "That Delilah is trying to set us up?"

Her chest tightened. "What do you mean, set us up?"

"Just what I said." He ran his hand through his hair, having left his straw hat in the car. "We're her latest matchmaking project."

Katharine shook her head. "That can't be true." Could it? She'd never told Delilah her reason for coming to Birch Creek, but she thought she had made it clear by not engaging in any of the activities the other single women did that she wasn't there because of the bride advertisement. Hadn't she? "Why do you think she's doing that?"

"Doing these errands together, for starters. Did you know she was in Barton yesterday morning?"

"*Nee*," she said. Delilah often disappeared for hours at a time when she wasn't needed at the inn. Katharine never asked her where she went, but she figured it out the times she came home with groceries from Schrock's or with items she could buy only in Barton. She couldn't remember if she'd noticed Delilah had been gone yesterday morning or not.

"So you didn't have any idea?" Ezra asked.

"Not a clue." She wasn't happy about Delilah's meddling, if that's what she was actually doing. But it wasn't the end of the world. When she got home tonight she would explain to Delilah that she wasn't in the market for a husband, or even a date, with Ezra or anyone else.

"That's something, at least." He shook his head. "Of all the underhanded things to do, forcing us together," he muttered, then looked at her, anger and frustration in his eyes. "Just because you're looking for a husband doesn't mean I'm looking for a wife."

At his words, she jerked back and her heartbeat tripled. He thought she was seeking a husband. That was the ruse she'd used to move to Birch Creek, and she had forgotten about that. No one had questioned her when she arrived at the inn a year ago. There were so many single women that had revolved in and out of the community that she hadn't had to explain why she was there. Of course he would assume that about her. She hadn't given him any reason not to.

That was bad enough, but worse, she'd seen those same emotions in Simeon's eyes many times before he said or did something cruel. She tried not to confuse the two men, but she failed. Was he going to take his anger out on her?

Katharine's instincts kicked in and as she made to move away from Ezra, her foot hit the curb and she stumbled into the street.

Honk!

"Katharine!" With both arms, Ezra grabbed her around the waist and yanked her close.

A car skidded to a stop halfway into the space behind Gary's vehicle.

Ezra's arms tightened around her. "Are you okay?" he asked. "That car almost hit you!"

Every vein in her body filled with ice. "*Ya*," she said, then she started to shake. If Ezra hadn't gotten her out of the way, the car would have struck her.

"I'm so sorry." A slender woman with short, gray hair ran toward her. "I didn't see you there. I thought the space was empty."

"It's *mei* fault," she said. "I wasn't paying attention."

"She's all right," Ezra said. "No harm done."

The woman let out a relieved sigh. "I'm so glad." She gave them a weak smile, then hurried back to her car.

Only then did Katharine realize she was still in Ezra's arms.

Chapter 8

Logically, Ezra knew Katharine was safe. But that didn't stop his pulse and emotions from thinking otherwise. The incident was a blur now—fear suddenly leaping into her eyes, her falling back into the street at the same moment the English woman pulled her car into the spot. He didn't think, just reacted, and yanked her against him to keep her from getting run over. Thankfully, she wasn't hurt and she had stopped shaking. There was no reason to keep holding her. *I can let her go now.*

But for some reason he didn't. Maybe it was because he'd never been this close to a woman before, not even Gloria. They had held hands, and he had given her a chaste kiss on the cheek, his arms staying at his sides. That was the day before she told him about the other man.

Or maybe he hadn't moved because of the way she was looking at him, as if he was her hero and enemy at the same time, even though he was neither.

Or it could be that she was soft in all the right places, and simply holding her felt so good.

"You kids okay?"

At the sound of Gary's worried voice, they both jerked apart. "Uh, yeah." *Understatement of the year.*

"I'm fine," Katharine said, holding the bag with the frames in front of her, as cool as a crisp March day. By some miracle she hadn't dropped it. "I lost my balance, that's all."

He glanced at her. That wasn't all, not by a long shot. Not for him, anyway.

"Whew. I heard tires squealing and got worried." Gary turned to Ezra. "I saw you get her out of the street when that car was coming. Good thing nothing bad happened."

"Yeah," he managed to say. "Good thing."

Gary looked at Katharine's bag. "Do you want me to put that in the car while you get lunch?"

She nodded, handing him the bag. "Are you joining us?"

"Nah. I've got plans with a friend of mine nearby. Don and I retired from the post office around the same time and we've stayed in touch. He and his wife invited me over for lunch. But thanks for the invite." He adjusted his Cleveland Indians baseball hat. "I'll pick you two up here in a couple of hours. Does that work?"

Ezra nodded, barely comprehending what Gary just said. He watched as the man got in his car and drove away. That left him and Katharine. Alone. For at least the next two hours. He almost smiled.

"Does Mexican sound okay to you?" she asked.

He faced her. "Uh, sure." If she could shake off what happened so easily, he certainly could. "I love Mexican food. There's a great place just a few blocks from here."

"That's what Delilah said." Katharine's eyes widened, as if she let the words slip.

"Oh *really*?" If he hadn't been sure before—and he'd been

99 percent sure already—he was positive this whole errand trip was one big setup.

"Uh, maybe she did?" She wasn't looking at him now. Then suddenly she rushed off in the direction of the restaurant.

"Wait up!" He hurried after her, then fell in step with her. As they walked to the restaurant, he tried to figure out how to approach the topic of Delilah fixing them up without her running off again, but he decided to keep that question to himself. Better to focus on feeding his hungry belly than wonder about her habit of taking off without warning. Not to mention his confusing reaction to holding her, something he hadn't completely shaken off yet. Some chips and salsa would be a good distraction.

They walked in silence to the restaurant. The few times he'd been here the place was packed, and he was surprised to find it wasn't busy on a Saturday afternoon. Then he remembered this was around the time of year when Barton High School held their graduation ceremony. Good thing he and Katharine were here for lunch today, because they probably wouldn't have found a table around dinnertime.

"Right this way," the middle-aged hostess said with a thick accent. As soon as they sat down in a booth at the other side of the restaurant, she handed them menus and asked for their drink orders. After she took them down and went to the kitchen, a waiter arrived with a basket of tortilla chips, two small shallow bowls, and a container of salsa. He placed them all on the table and hurried away.

They said a silent prayer, and then Ezra poured half of the salsa in one dish. When he went to pour hers, she held up her hand.

"No thank you." She put her hand back in her lap.

"You sure? The salsa here is delicious. *Gut* and spicy."

"I'm sure."

He set down the small bottle next to his bowl, then dipped a chip in the salsa and took a bite. Just as good as he remembered. He opened his menu and searched for his favorite dish—stuffed poblano peppers, beans, and rice. When he found it, he shut the menu, then noticed Katharine hadn't opened hers. "You're not getting anything?"

She shook her head.

The waitress appeared with their drinks—Coke for Ezra, water for her. He rarely drank soft drinks, but a cold glass of Coke paired perfectly with the cheesy peppers.

"Ready to order?" the waitress asked.

Katharine said, "Nothing for me."

The waitress lifted one thin black eyebrow, then turned to Ezra. "And you, sir?"

"Lunch special #6." He handed her the menu, then she picked up Katharine's and walked away.

Ezra frowned. "Are you sure you don't want anything? If you don't like spicy stuff, they have chicken strips."

"I'm fine."

"You don't like Mexican food," he said. A statement, not a question.

After a pause, she admitted, "I don't."

"Then why did you suggest coming here? We could have gone somewhere else."

She glanced at her lap, her blond hair peeking out from under her white *kapp*. "Because you said you love it."

It didn't set right with him that she wasn't eating because he wanted Mexican food. "I would have been fine eating at a place we both liked." He glanced at the chips. A second ago he'd been ready to inhale half the basket. Now he felt guilty eating even one.

She pushed the basket closer to him. "*Geh* ahead."

"Aren't you hungry, though?"

"*Nee*. I had a big breakfast." She stared out the window into the restaurant's parking lot.

"I'll cancel my order," he said, starting to lift his hand to signal for the waitress. "We'll find a place we both like. Barton has three other restaurants."

"*Nee*." She was looking at him now with dismay. "They're already preparing your food." After a pause, she reached for a chip. "If it makes you feel better, I'll have some of these."

It did make him feel a little better, but not much. "Is there anything on a Mexican menu that you could have? There are so many choices."

She nibbled on a corner of a chip. "Guacamole is all right. I like avocados."

"Then order some guacamole."

Katharine shook her head. "It has a lot of calories."

"So?"

Her cheeks blushed slightly, but she didn't answer.

The waitress brought his dish and set it in front of him. "The plate is very hot," she said.

He glanced at Katharine, then said to the waitress, "Could I have a small side of guacamole?"

"Of course. I'll bring it right out."

An angry spark flashed in Katharine's eyes. "I told you I didn't want any guacamole."

"Who said it was for you?" He picked up his fork and dug into the peppers as if he and Katharine were having an ordinary lunch. What started out as an easy morning had devolved into the exact opposite. No need to make things worse. He focused on his pepper. Scrumptious, as usual.

"I'm sorry," she said.

He glanced up. She was staring at the basket of chips. "It's okay."

"*Nee*, it isn't. I shouldn't have snapped at you."

A busboy set the guacamole next to him. Mexican restaurants sure were speedy. "Thanks," he said, then looked at Katharine again. "If you change your mind, I'll share. But don't wait too long." He dug a chip deep into the dip. "This deliciousness will be gone before you know it."

She stared at the guacamole while he ate his lunch, and he gave her a few covert glances as he finished his meal. Finally she grabbed a second chip. "One bite should be okay," she said, reaching for the dip.

He grinned and moved it closer to her.

When she ate the guac-topped chip, she closed her eyes. That gorgeous smile appeared again. He wondered if she knew she was smiling. She seemed to be in her own little world.

He waited until she opened her eyes, then said, "You know avocados are good for you, *ya*?"

"They are?"

"According to Owen they are. He told me that a few years ago. Obviously we can't grow them here, but *mei bruder* knows everything about almost all plants and vegetables, among other things. The farming stuff is helpful, but otherwise he's a walking encyclopedia of useless information."

She smiled a little.

That spurred him on. "If I remember right, they have a lot of vitamins, and they're *gut* for your heart. But don't quote me on that." As she continued to eat a few more chips and guacamole, he asked, "If you don't like Mexican, what kind of food do you like?"

"Just about everything else." She glanced down at herself. "Obviously."

Ah. So she was worried about her weight. He should have realized that sooner. His mother started fretting about hers after she turned fifty. *Daed* always made her feel better, reminding her that she did have twelve kids and whether she was heavy or thin, he wouldn't love her any less. Until then Ezra hadn't realized that weight could be such an issue for women. "You've lost weight since you got here," he pointed out, trying to follow his father's example.

Her eyes widened. "You noticed?"

"*Ya*. You also look a lot happier since you first arrived in Birch Creek."

Now her eyebrows were almost touching her hairline. "You noticed that too?"

Ezra speared the last bit of poblano with his fork. "You're not invisible, Katharine."

"I try to be," she whispered.

He held the pepper halfway to his mouth. That surprised him. "Why?" he asked, then finished his bite.

"It's . . . complicated." She didn't say anything else. A minute later she moved the guacamole in front of her and started eating with enthusiasm.

He grinned, pleased she was finally eating more than three chips. He wasn't as educated as Owen, but even he knew it wasn't good to skip meals. They still had peach picking to do, and she needed energy for that.

"You were right," Katharine said after she polished off the guac and picked up her napkin. She dabbed at the corner of her mouth. "That was delicious."

She smiled again, and for some reason, he felt the same pleasant, confusing feeling he'd had when he had pulled her out of the street and held her tight. Her entire face changed when she smiled, and this time he saw tiny dimples in both cheeks that he hadn't noticed before. *Would it be so crazy for us to go out?*

The waitress appeared with the check. "No rush," she said, spearing a pen through the black bun at the nape of her neck. "We won't be busy until later today."

So he'd been right about the graduation. He reached for the check.

Katharine snatched the slip of paper before he could grab it. "This is on Delilah, remember?"

"Now we know why."

She set the bill on the table, staring at it for a moment. Then she looked at him. "Is it that bad?"

"What?"

She folded her upper lip over her lower one, lowering her gaze again. "The idea of us . . . going on a date?"

He hesitated, searching for the right way to answer. Despite his earlier thought that going out with Katharine wasn't as nutty an idea as he initially thought, he wasn't in the right head or heart space to date anyone.

"Never mind—"

"I'm not interested in dating anyone. I, uh, got burned by *mei* last relationship."

"Oh." She met his gaze again. "I'm sorry."

He could tell she was genuinely sympathetic. "It ended up being for the best. Gloria wasn't the right *maedel* for me. Someday I'll find her, but right now I'm not looking. I guess I need to tell Delilah that, before she tries to fix me up with anyone else."

"I was thinking the same thing. About talking to Delilah."

"Then it's settled."

She nodded. "It's settled." She took out her wallet, pulled out enough money to cover the meal and tip, then placed it on the table.

"Ready to *geh* to the orchard?" he asked, sliding out of the booth seat.

"*Ya*." She grinned.

Whoa. He might not want to *date* Katharine . . . but he could stare at her smile all day.

Chapter 9

Midafternoon on Saturday, Rhoda went to the mailbox to collect her mail after spending the morning cleaning her house from top to bottom. Saturday morning cleaning was always a ritual, but this time was different. From the moment Emmanuel had left, everything of his remained untouched. Now she had a pile of bags full of items to donate to charity, many of them reminders of Emmanuel—his clothes and hats, his stationery and desk supplies, his favorite coffee mug. More than once she hesitated as she gathered his items, knowing that the chances of finding out what happened to him were slim to none, despite Jordan's dogged detective work. But she was more certain than ever that if her husband was still alive, he wasn't coming back. While she couldn't move on with Loren, she could stop hanging on to the past.

A light spring breeze fluttered the lavender kerchief she'd worn all day, a sweet pastel color Emmanuel wouldn't have approved of. He wouldn't have approved of the kerchief either, always expecting her to dress in austere colors, and he never allowed her to wear anything but her *kapp* at home until they went to bed. Rhoda had never been rebellious. She was a dutiful wife, possibly to a fault. Had Emmanuel taken advantage of that trait? She was almost positive he had.

She pulled down the squeaky mailbox lid, making a mental note to oil the hinge on Monday. A single letter lay in the box. Taking it out and looking at the address, she frowned. The letter was addressed to her, but the uneven handwriting was in all caps. There wasn't a return address either. Probably junk mail. Those people were getting sneakier, and sometimes the wording on the envelopes looked like actual handwriting. She'd never seen one with all caps, but that didn't mean the companies weren't using it.

She closed the mailbox and headed for the barn, stopping by the large garbage can on the side of the house to throw away the letter. She lifted the lid, then stopped. What if it wasn't junk mail? Her curiosity getting the best of her, she opened the flap and read the contents.

> Dear Mrs. Troyer,
>
> I'm sorry to inform you of this through a letter, but your husband, Emmanuel Troyer, is dead.

She almost dropped the letter. *Emmanuel . . . gone?* She leaned against the side of the house, her chest squeezing, as if she were being suffocated by a ton of bricks.

> Instructions were found among his belongings about contacting his family. His last directives also included not disclosing the location of his burial, his cause of death, or my personal contact information, including my name.
>
> I am sorry for your loss.

Rhoda couldn't move. She read the letter again and again, but the words refused to sink in.

A buggy approached and as it neared, she recognized Aden and Sol pulling into the driveway. As soon as Aden brought the horse to a stop, they jumped out of the buggy and ran toward her, both holding letters in their hands.

"*Mamm?*" Aden stopped in front of her as Sol hung back. "Did you get a letter . . ." He glanced at the paper in her hand and paled.

"I just read it." She looked at her sons, taking in their contrasting expressions. Soft-hearted Aden concerned and confused. Sol, now impassive and closed off, had always been tougher, and at one time hard and abusive. But he had gentled over the years thanks to God, his wife Irene, and his determination not to be like his father.

"Are you all right?" Aden put his arm around her shoulders. Sol crossed his arms over his chest.

"I-I don't know." She stared at the letter. When did her hands start trembling?

"Let's *geh* inside." Aden started to guide her to the house.

"I'll check on the horse," Sol said. "*Mamm*'s too."

Aden frowned. "They'll be fine for a little while."

Sol ignored him and headed for the barn.

Rhoda put her hand on Aden's forearm. "Let him be, Aden."

He nodded, then they walked into the house.. Once they were seated at the kitchen table, he handed her his letter. "This is what mine says."

She read it over and saw that it was identical to hers except for the salutation and the substitution of *father* for *husband*. "Is Sol's the same too?"

"*Ya*. As soon as I read the letter, I went over to his place. He was still working and hadn't checked the mail yet, but his letter was there too." He set her letter next to his on the table. "Do you think this is true? Or is someone playing a sick joke on us?"

Rhoda paused. "I don't know what to think."

"This doesn't make any sense. If it is true, why wouldn't he want us to know where he was when he—" He swallowed. "When he died?"

Rhoda gripped his hand. "I don't know that either. I never understood why your *vatter* did certain things."

Aden nodded, and for a moment neither of them said anything. "What are we going to do?" he finally asked.

Sol entered the kitchen. "Penny's fed and I gave Horace some hay too."

There was a time when Sol wouldn't have done anything for Aden, including something as simple as feeding his horse. She was grateful that her sons had been able to form a brotherly bond after what Emmanuel had done to them growing up. She gestured for him to sit in the chair next to Aden.

He shook his head. "I prefer to stand."

Dread formed inside, then she tempered it with practicality. He'd just found out, in possibly the most shocking manner possible, that his father had died. She had to let him handle the news his own way. *Please, Lord. Don't let him fall back to the cold, heartless youth he was in the past.*

Aden picked up Rhoda's envelope and examined it, then looked at his envelope. He turned it over, then pointed to the stamp. " I didn't think to look at this before, but according to the postmark, these were mailed from West Virginia," he said, looking at Sol and then at Rhoda.

Sol's jaw twitched.

"Does that mean he died there?" Rhoda swallowed the knot in her throat. Despite herself, her eyes started to burn. *Oh, Emmanuel . . .*

"It's highly possible, if the letters aren't fakes," Aden said. "You need to call Jordan and tell him about this."

"I'll call him tonight."

Aden nodded. "Make sure to tell him about the postmark."

"Why?" Sol said, his tone hard.

Rhoda looked at Sol, alarmed at the iciness in his green eyes. "Maybe he can find out what happened to your *vatter*."

"We already know. He's dead. *Nix* has changed as far as I'm concerned." He turned and opened the door. "I'll be outside."

She flinched as the door slammed shut. "He's taking this hard," she said.

"That's not what it looks like to me." Aden grabbed his letter and shoved it back into the envelope. "It looks like he doesn't care at all."

"He does, Aden. He cares too much, and he's been deeply hurt."

"So have I, *Mamm*. He wasn't *Daed*'s only victim."

Her heart squeezed. She was handling this badly, but she didn't know the right words to say. "I know, and I'm sorry," she whispered.

He sighed and took her hand. "*Nee*, I'm the one who should apologize. I shouldn't lash out at you. And I shouldn't be mad at Sol either. The person I'm mad at is *Daed*."

Nodding, she let go of Aden's hand. "*Geh* check on *yer bruder*. He needs you right now."

"What about you?"

"I'll be okay." So far she'd managed to fight back the tears, and she lifted her chin as she looked at him. Seeing the doubt in his eyes, she added, "I promise. Talk to Sol, then *geh* back to work and your *familye*."

"All right." He got up and shoved the letter into his pants pocket. "I'll check on you after work."

She shook her head. "I'd rather be alone, if you don't mind."

His brow furrowed, and she knew he did mind. But like the dutiful son he was, he put his hand lightly on her shoulder, then left.

Rhoda stared at the letter, her thoughts blocked and her heart numb. There were so many things she had to do. Call Jordan for one. Now that Aden had planted the idea in her mind that the letters might be fake, she had to mention that to the PI too. Although she couldn't imagine someone being so cruel as to send such a letter. Possibly to one of them, but not all three. No, the most logical conclusion was that Emmanuel was gone.

She also had to talk to Bishop Yoder. He would know how to handle the situation. Plan some kind of service or remembrance since they couldn't have a funeral and burial. And through all this, she had to help Aden, and especially Sol, get through yet another painful time thanks to their father. Her fists clenched. He'd failed them, and her, so many times. She shouldn't be surprised that he would again.

She got up from the table and walked over to the kitchen window, seeing Aden's buggy turning onto the street. Hopefully, he and Sol were talking things over. She closed her eyes, saying a prayer for her sons and herself.

When she opened them, she couldn't hold back the tears, surprising herself with how fast they flowed. She'd spent years hoping for Emmanuel's return, then the past year getting over him. Shouldn't she be relieved that he was gone? She could fully move on with her life now, and God willing, Loren would be a part of that. But those thoughts were far in the back of her mind. All she could think about was how tragic his life had been. He hadn't seen his sons reconcile. Never met his grandchildren. Never saw how the community he had founded was thriving in his absence . . . and maybe that was the point. Emmanuel could never admit he was wrong, not even a little mistake. Perhaps that was what had kept him away all these years. He couldn't stand seeing anyone have success or happiness.

And yet, in spite of all the pain he'd caused, her heart broke. His pride had gotten in the way of everything. If only he'd been able to face what he had done. If he'd sincerely asked for forgiveness, he would have gotten it. From God, from her, from the community, and hopefully, eventually, from their sons.

Rhoda wiped her eyes and sat down at the table. Somehow, she had to collect herself. Katharine and Ezra were arriving later today to drop off a bag of peaches. Delilah had mentioned that yesterday when she stopped by unexpectedly. Although she didn't come right out and say she was trying to get Katharine and Ezra together, Rhoda suspected as much. Yesterday that amused her. Today she didn't want to deal with anyone. But she had given her word to Delilah, and she would see it through.

The two young people wouldn't be here for a few more hours, and hopefully that would give her enough time to gather her composure and pretend her whole world hadn't been turned upside down again. *Lord knows I've had enough practice.*

"I told you to stop playing with *yer* food!"

Irene flinched at the anger in Sol's voice. She looked at Isaac, their youngest son, who had shrunk back in the chair at his father's rebuke. His russet-colored hair, the identical shade of his father's, was sticking out all over his head. She gripped her fork, biting her tongue. If she didn't, she would lash out at Sol, and that was the last thing her husband needed right now.

When Aden showed up alone earlier today, she was surprised to see him. Saturdays were busy at Schrock's Grocery, and he rarely came over without Sadie and the kids in tow. Aden didn't stop by the house either. He went directly to Sol's carpentry shop at the back of the property. A few minutes later Sol hurried inside.

"*Daed*'s dead."

Irene's jaw dropped. "What? When?"

He held up a letter. "Got this in the mail. Says he's dead." His tone was flat, his eyes empty. "We're going to *Mamm*'s."

Emmanuel was gone? She had so many questions, but those would have to wait. His mother and brother were of primary importance. "Of course." She waited for him to kiss her cheek as he always did before he left, but he rushed out the door.

She didn't blame him for being in a hurry and she was still trying to process the news herself. She couldn't believe Emmanuel had died. For years she and Sol had avoided the topic of his father, with good reason. Sol was a different man than he'd been when Emmanuel was in his life. Kind, loving, considerate. He still had a temper, but he'd learned to control it for the most part. It was as if Emmanuel didn't exist anymore. Irene could hardly believe that now it was true.

Before Sol returned, she went through the motions of making turkey and Swiss sandwiches for a late lunch. Her distraction showed—there was more Swiss than turkey between the bread, and she'd forgotten to spread the inside with mayo and mustard as she always did. Sol didn't complain, but he didn't eat much either, and he'd barely looked at her or their children since coming back from his mother's. That wasn't the Sol she'd fallen in love with, but it was the younger version of him that she knew growing up.

She turned to the *kinner*. "Solomon, you and Isaac are excused. *Geh* outside and play for a little while. I'll be right out."

Normally, like all five- and four-year-olds, the children would be excited to have extra playtime while she and Sol finished lunch, something they had every day as a family. If he wasn't too busy, he would sometimes play with them in the backyard for a little bit before going back to work. Sol had a wonderful relationship with his kids, one that he worked on. Being a good father didn't come easily since he hadn't had a proper role model growing up. But this time their children knew something was wrong. Without a sound they scurried out of the kitchen and out the door.

Irene rose from her chair and walked over to the back kitchen door. Through the window she saw Isaac trot to the sandbox while Solomon started kicking a ball around the backyard. They were safely occupied for a few minutes. She turned and went to Sol, placing her hand on his shoulder. "I'm sorry about the sandwiches."

"They're fine." He stared at his iced tea glass, still almost full of sweetened tea.

"They're not, since you didn't eat much."

"I'm not hungry." He jerked off her hand, then pushed back from the table. "I'll be in the shop," he muttered as he stood.

Irene stepped in front of him, blocking his way. "Talk to me, Sol. Don't shut me out."

He halted but still didn't look at her. "I'm sorry I yelled at Isaac."

She tentatively took a step closer to him. "He shouldn't have been pulling apart his sandwich. He's old enough to know better."

Sol nodded, still not meeting her gaze.

She put her arms around his waist. "Let me help you through this," she whispered, her cheek pressing against his heart. "Please."

He stepped out of her embrace. "I have to finish that hope chest tonight. There are a lot of orders to fill, and I can't get behind." He turned and walked out of the kitchen.

Irene stared at the table filled with remnants of the measly lunch. Her heart ached for her husband, a man with a horrible past who had been healed by God's love and mercy, and whom she loved deeply . . . and was deeply loved by in return. She didn't doubt that for a moment. But the news of Emmanuel's death had rocked him to his core, leaving her at a loss. She and Sadie were close, but her sister-in-law would be comforting Aden right now.

All she could do was pray, and that's exactly what she did as she cleaned up the kitchen, then went outside to play with their children. *Comfort my husband, Lord. He needs you right now.*

Chapter 10

Katharine couldn't remember the last time she'd been this happy. Once she was free to eat the delicious guacamole, she realized she was so hungry she had to fight the urge to inhale the entire bowl. The last time she'd gone to a Mexican restaurant she was with Simeon, and he had ordered for her, like he always did. One taco only, nothing else, while he always got the largest special they had. When she wanted guacamole on the side, he told her it had too many calories. "I just want you to be healthy, Katharine," he'd said as he shoved a huge bite of cheese-covered enchiladas in his mouth. After he finished, he followed up with fried ice cream that he ate in front of her, not offering her a single bite.

Then there was Ezra. He actually *wanted* her to eat. He'd also noticed her, and she didn't think anyone in Birch Creek had outside of the Stolls. That had been her goal anyway. To be invisible. But she wasn't, of course. Not to Ezra anyway.

During the rest of the meal he had asked questions about her life back home, benign ones she could answer. She told him she was an only child, that her father was in construction—although she refused to tell him about his accident—and that her grandmother had taught her how to weave baskets. As she talked, he listened with rapt attention, as if he were genuinely interested in her life and what she had to say, and that continued in the car ride to Smith Orchard.

She found out a few things about him too. He was also twenty-two, liked to camp and fish, and considered his brothers his best friends. By the time they arrived at the orchard, she was actually having fun. Unexpected fun, and that was due to Ezra.

Once they got their buckets, he took charge. "We Bontragers always divide and conquer," he'd said as they walked down the small hill to the rows of full peach trees. "Doesn't matter what we pick—blueberries, apples, plums, whatever."

"Sounds like a wise plan." She let the empty bucket dangle from her fingers. The spring sunshine warmed her back and the heady scents of fresh earth and green peach leaves mingled together. That was one thing she loved about Ohio—everything was so green here. A stark difference from the prairie grass, short trees, and reddish-brown clay back in Wyoming.

"We divide all the tasks at the farm too." Ezra tilted back his straw hat. "There are fewer hands now, with my older *bruders* being gone and having their own businesses. Owen is staying, though, even after he and Margaret get married. He loves being a farmer."

"Do you like farming?"

"*Ya*. I'll probably *geh* back to the farm full time sooner or later. I needed to do something else for a little while. A change of pace before I settle down."

Her pulse sped up slightly. So he did want to get married. She wasn't surprised, not by that bit of news. She was more stunned at her own disappointment. Like most other people, Ezra would get his happily ever after too.

They arrived at the orchard, and Ezra took off in one direction while she walked down the row in front of her. There were plenty of peaches dangling from the branches within reach, but many still had some green areas on them and weren't ripe yet. She did find a patch that were light orange and yellow, perfect for picking. She started filling her bucket.

A short time later, Ezra walked down her aisle. "Done," he said, setting his bucket next to him.

"That was fast."

"Being tall helps."

She glanced at him, then looked up at a branch in front of her. The perfect peach was there, just out of her reach.

"I'll get it." He stood close behind her, his long, lanky arm rising over her head. He grabbed at the peach and missed. Then he moved closer until her back was against his chest, and made a second attempt.

She held her breath. Unbidden, a pleasant shiver slid down her spine.

"Got it." He plucked the peach, then handed it to her over her shoulder. "Here you *geh*."

She turned around, her face warm from sunshine and happiness. "*Danki*," she said, taking the peach from him and smiling. So this was what it was like to be around a man and not be on edge or plain scared. *Absolutely wonderful*.

He cleared his throat and stepped back. "We should finish up," he said. "We still have to *geh* to Rhoda's and Cevilla's."

That brought her back to reality. But for the shortest of moments, she'd allowed herself a second of happiness.

He helped her fill her bucket and they went back to the barn to pay for the peaches. Gary, who had spent the whole time they were picking talking to the owner of the orchard, had also bought some already picked peaches. "Can't wait to bite into these," he said as they made their way to the car. "Where's the next stop?"

"Rhoda Troyer's," Ezra said. "Do you know where she lives?"

The jovial man turned serious for a moment. "Yes, I do. I've known the Troyers a long time." He opened the car door and got inside.

At her questioning look, Ezra bent closer to her, whispering in *Deitsch*. "Rhoda's husband, the former bishop, left suddenly after some sort of scandal. He hasn't been seen since. That happened a few years before *mei familye* moved here."

They got into the car and soon they were headed to Rhoda's. Katharine had assumed Rhoda had been married, because she had two sons, Sol and Aden. She had met Aden a few times at Schrock's Grocery, and she had seen Sol and his family at church but had never formally met him. She knew little else, other than Loren's visits to Rhoda. But if Loren knew she wasn't widowed, and that her husband was still off somewhere, why did he still go over to her house so often? He might be free to marry, but Rhoda wasn't.

"Hey," Ezra said. "You got quiet all of a sudden."

"I'm always quiet," she said.

"True. But today you've been practically a chatterbox."

She flinched. "Is that okay? I'm sorry if I talked too much."

"Of course it's okay," he said, his brow furrowing slightly. "And you didn't talk too much."

She held in a sigh of relief. The last thing she wanted to do was upset him.

"Katharine," he said, "you don't have to—"

"We're here," Gary said, turning into Rhoda's driveway.

"Already?" Ezra leaned forward in his seat. "That was quick."

"I know a shortcut." He put the car in park. "How long will you be here?"

"Long enough to drop off the peaches," Ezra said.

"I'll wait in the car then."

Katharine held the bag they were giving to Rhoda and got out of the car. She expected Ezra to come with her, but he stayed with Gary. When she looked over her shoulder, she could see the two of them talking. She smiled a little. She had noticed Ezra was friendly with everyone, from the cashier at Walmart to Mr. Smith, the old man who owned the peach orchard.

Her smile faded as she walked up the driveway. She needed to remember Ezra's affable personality was directed at everyone, including her. His kindness to her wasn't anything special, just something she wasn't used to. She would explain that to Delilah when she told her that she and Ezra weren't ever going to be a couple.

But in spite of all her vows and fears and reminders that keeping her distance from everyone was for the best, once again her heart pinched with disappointment.

She knocked on Rhoda's door. It opened immediately, and Rhoda greeted her with a smile. "Hi, Katharine. I've been expecting you. Come on in. Is Ezra with you?"

She followed Rhoda to the kitchen. "*Nee*, he's waiting in the car."

"Oh. I thought Delilah said—" She shook her head. "Never mind."

When they entered the kitchen, Katharine saw a pitcher of tea and three glasses in the center of the table, along with a plate of cookies. Ezra was right. Delilah did have matchmaking motives.

Thank goodness they had made it clear to each other that they weren't interested. But Rhoda had obviously gone to some trouble with the tea and cookies, and Katharine didn't want to disappoint her. She turned to tell her that she would get Ezra, then paused. Rhoda's friendly smile had disappeared. In the brighter light of the kitchen, Katharine noticed the woman's eyes were red-rimmed, as if she'd been crying. "Are you all right?" she asked, putting the peaches on the table.

Rhoda blinked and looked at her, smiling again. "Of course." She gestured to the tea. "I assumed both of you would be staying for a little while."

"I could *geh* get Ezra—"

"*Nee*, you don't have to do that. I'm sure you two have other things to do today." She sniffed, her smile fading. "I'll be right back." She quickly disappeared out of the kitchen.

Katharine stared at the table. Should she sit down and wait for Rhoda? Or should she ignore what Rhoda said and get Ezra anyway? Although she had said everything was fine, Katharine didn't believe her. The box of tissues next to the tea pitcher confirmed that something wasn't right.

"Here we are." Rhoda returned, carrying a thin spiral-bound book. "I've been meaning to let Delilah borrow this recipe book for a while now. It's filled with recipes from *mei familye* in Winesburg." She handed the book to Katharine. "Maybe she'll find something suitable to make for her guests."

"I'm sure she will." Katharine looked at the worn cover of the recipe book, then back at Rhoda. When she saw tears slipping down her cheeks, she set the book down.

"I'm sorry," Rhoda whispered, wiping her eyes. "I was trying not to do this with you here . . ."

Katharine grabbed a tissue from the box and handed it to Rhoda, then pulled out a chair for her. "Can I help at all?"

She sat down and blew her nose. "*Nee*. This is something I have to deal with myself." Then she glanced up at Katharine. "How has your day been with Ezra?"

Hesitating, Kathrine finally said, "*Gut*. We have one more stop at Cevilla's before going back to the inn."

Rhoda smiled, although it didn't reach her tear-filled eyes. Katharine filled a glass with tea, then handed it to her. "*Danki*," she said before taking a sip. When she set the glass down, she suddenly gripped Katharine's hand. "Don't rush into anything with Ezra, or any man. Make sure that the man you marry is *gut*, kind, and true. Don't let love blind you to his faults, and don't compromise yourself to please him. If you do, you'll lose the person you are, and you'll live to regret it."

Katharine's eyes widened. Why was Rhoda telling her this? They didn't know each other, but somehow she had guessed the truth about Katharine letting her love for Simeon blind her. Just thinking about how her life would be if she had gone through with the marriage . . . She shuddered. Then her body started to shake.

"Katharine?"

Rhoda's voice sounded far away as panic gripped her. Logically she knew she wasn't in any danger. *But for the grace of God I could have been . . .*

Chapter 11

Rhoda jumped up from the chair and went to Katharine. She hadn't intended to say all those things to her, especially since they didn't pertain to Ezra, one of the nicest young men she'd ever met. But the warning flew out of her mouth as she remembered being young and bowled over by Emmanuel's attention and love to the point she had lost herself and allowed him to take over. As she spoke, though, she saw the fear leap into Katharine's eyes. Now she was shaking, and Rhoda had to help her sit down.

"I-I'm s-sorry," Katharine finally said.

Rhoda sat down next to her, keeping her hand on her shoulder. "You don't have to apologize. Do you feel sick? Can I get you some water?"

She shook her head. "I-I'll be okay." Then she turned and met Rhoda's gaze.

And then Rhoda knew. She recognized the stark fear and confusion in the young woman's eyes . . . because time and time again she had seen them in her own. Katharine didn't need to be warned about falling for the wrong man. She already had.

When the girl stopped trembling, Rhoda moved to hold her hand. "Who is he?" she asked, unable to stop the question from escaping. A part of her thought she had no business prying into Katharine's personal life. But a larger part knew she had to help her. "Is he here? In Birch Creek?"

Katharine stared straight ahead, her eyes still wide. "*Nee*. He's back home."

Rhoda almost sank in her chair with relief. "Is that why you came here? To escape?"

Slowly she nodded, then looked at Rhoda. Fortunately her fear was starting to settle a bit. "*Nee* one else can know," she said. "I haven't even told Delilah."

"I won't tell a soul. I promise." She squeezed her hand. "I'm glad you were able to get away. Are you married to him?"

"Thank God I'm not. But I almost was."

Rhoda listened as Katharine told her about Simeon, the words tumbling out of her like a waterfall thawing after a long winter freeze. The things she told her were so similar to Emmanuel, especially in the later years of their marriage, that she started to grow fearful herself. *He's gone, remember? He died and can't hurt me anymore.*

"I'm sorry," Katharine said again once she finished. Her plump fingers balled into fists in her lap. "I shouldn't have told you all that. I don't know why I did."

"Because you had to. You can only hold things in here for so long." She put her palm over her heart. "And because somehow you knew, deep inside, that I understand."

Katharine nodded, the tears in her eyes mirroring the one's Rhoda couldn't keep at bay. "I'm scared," she said. "I'm scared he's going to find me and make me *geh* back to . . . to Montana. I'm scared of him, or anyone else, hurting me again."

Rhoda understood that fear. Only now could she admit to herself that she hadn't just kept Loren at bay because Emmanuel's whereabouts were unknown. She had been afraid of going through more pain at the hands of a man, and she had to be sure he wasn't another Emmanuel. "What about you and Ezra?" she asked.

"There's *nee* me and Ezra. Did Delilah say there was?"

"Not in so many words. But the woman has a reputation for trying to bring couples together."

"Ezra says she's matchmaking us."

"I think he's right. But what do you think?"

She relaxed her hands and drew in a deep breath. "I'm confused."

Rhoda sympathized, and was about to tell her that when she heard a knock on the back door. She turned and saw Ezra peeking in the window. Katharine wiped her eyes with a tissue as Rhoda stood and went to open the door. "Sorry, Ezra," she said, trying to impose a smile and praying she was more successful than she had been with Katharine. "We didn't mean to keep you waiting." She glanced at Katharine who was now standing, completely composed. The only clue that she had been crying or upset were her red cheeks and nose. "You know how we women are," she said, attempting to chuckle. "We get to talking and time flies."

Ezra nodded, but his eyes were darting from Rhoda to Katharine and back again. Then he smiled, but Rhoda thought it was a little forced, and the concern in his eyes was still there. "Glad to see all is well. Gary and I were wondering if there was something wrong."

"*Nix* wrong." Katharine went to him, but kept her gaze averted from his. "We better get to Cevilla's," she said. "We don't want to keep her waiting."

Ezra nodded. "Bye, Rhoda. Enjoy the peaches."

"I will."

He left first, and before Katharine could follow, Rhoda went to her. "Talk to me anytime, about anything."

She smiled, and for the first time since she had started to panic, she seemed to relax. "*Danki*, Rhoda, for understanding." Then she hurried to the car.

Rhoda closed the door and heard Gary's car leave. She had known him and his family almost as long as she and Emmanuel lived here. *Had* lived here.

Then her thoughts shifted to Katharine. As tough as it had been to hear her story, she was glad the girl had been able to tell it. She could also see why Delilah thought she and Ezra could be a couple. Ezra's concern was genuine, and she wondered if he did have some feelings for Katharine that she didn't know about. Sometimes the two people in a relationship were the last to figure it out. And if anyone was the antithesis of Simeon, Ezra was. But that didn't mean Katharine was ready, or even able to have a relationship right now.

Am I?

She sat back down at the table, her head falling into her hands. Before today she had thought if things were different, she was ready to have a romantic relationship with Loren. Now that was a reality—or could be, if the letters were real. But what kind of person was she, thinking about her and Loren mere hours after finding out her husband had died? Not only that but she also felt relief. Did that make her a terrible person? A part of her thought so.

Rhoda lifted her head and sighed. Katharine wasn't the only one who was confused.

Cevilla was suffering through the most uncomfortable supper in history. Perhaps an overstatement, but not by much. Ezra and Katharine had said little to each other all evening. Worse, Richard had caught on to Cevilla's plan the moment the young people stepped into the living room, and now he was fuming. She'd known he'd be angry about her "meddling shenanigans," as he liked to describe them, but not to the point of exploding. Fortunately, he was a master of politeness and small talk, in addition to being adept at keeping his feelings under wraps. Only Cevilla could tell he was enraged, and she was going to get an earful once they were alone. No, make that two earfuls.

"Would you like a slice of bread, Katharine?" She held up the basket holding a loaf of white bread Delilah had baked herself. The woman had made the entire meal of fried chicken, roasted brussels sprouts, au gratin potatoes, and lemon cake for dessert and brought the whole thing over right before Ezra and Katharine arrived, her timing perfect. It was just enough food, since Delilah had figured out during the early days of running the inn how to plan breakfasts and snacks so there were few leftovers. But considering the only person who was actually eating anything was Ezra, and he'd only consumed a few mouthfuls, there seemed to be enough food for ten people.

Katharine declined the bread. She'd also refused the fried chicken but did take three brussels sprouts. Cevilla didn't miss Ezra's frown or Richard's curious look. It was a shame Delilah had gone to all this work, because it seemed for naught. These two had the romantic chemistry of a pair of pickles. Sour ones at that.

"So," Cevilla said, setting the breadbasket down. Being around an angry husband and an awkward couple had stolen her appetite. "Tell me how Ivy and Noah are doing."

"*Gut*." Ezra pushed a slice of cheesy potato around on his plate. "They have a lot of different things in their shop."

"I enjoy going there," Richard said. "As an old person, I like being around old things." He looked at Cevilla, but instead of winking as he usually did when he made that lame joke, his expression was inscrutable.

Cevilla glanced at Katharine. Poor girl, she looked miserable. Something must have happened between the two of them today. While Ezra was more talkative, especially to Richard, he wasn't his usual sociable self. Boy, had she and Delilah made a huge blunder.

"We have lemon cake for dessert," she said weakly, trying to infuse some life into the meal. "It won't take but a minute to cut you both a piece."

Katharine shook her head. Ezra added, "I think we should get back to the inn. We've been gone long enough."

"But you *have* to have dessert." She was grasping at anything to keep them there, at least until she figured out what had gone wrong.

"I'll have some cake," Richard said, scooting his chair back. "Why don't you cut me a piece while I walk these two out."

Richard rarely asked for sweets, since he was a diabetic, and she knew defeat when she saw it. "I'll send some home with you," she grumbled, trying to hide her disappointment.

"No thank you," Katharine said, her voice barely above a whisper.

"None for me either," Ezra added.

"But—" At Richard's exasperated look, she clammed up.

Katharine and Ezra followed him to the living room. When they arrived earlier, they brought their packages inside. Ezra explained that they told Gary to go home since the distance back to the inn wasn't too far to walk. Cevilla had hoped that meant they were planning to stay later than the allotted time Delilah gave Gary. Obviously that wasn't the case. She wasn't surprised that the two of them were so thoughtful and didn't want Gary to wait around for them. But their sullen behavior had her flummoxed.

Cevilla tossed her cloth napkin on the table in frustration. "That man can get his own cake. And deal with the high blood sugar afterward." Slowly she got up and grabbed her cane, then started clearing the table, a process that took a lot longer to do one-handed.

When Richard returned, she sat back down and prepared herself for a lecture. The platter of leftover fried chicken was still on the table, along with four glasses of water that had barely been touched.

He sat down next to her instead of in his usual place at the opposite end of the table. She waited for him to speak. And waited . . . and waited . . .

After what seemed like an eternity, she couldn't take his silent stare anymore. "Say your piece already," she told him, averting her gaze and rubbing her slightly crooked thumb along the edge of the table.

"And what would that be?" he asked.

"The one where you scold me for interfering again."

He pressed his lips together. "That's exactly what I should say to you . . . but I can't."

Her gaze flew to him. "What?"

"Oh, don't get me wrong. I am irritated, to put it mildly. Once again you went back on your word to stay out of other people's personal business."

"I'm not the only one," she said, pouting a little.

"I'm aware Delilah is your partner in crime." He sighed and sat back in the chair. "But for once I can see where you're coming from."

If she wasn't positive she would break a hip, she would have fallen out of her seat. "You can?"

Richard rubbed the back of his neck. "I've wondered about that girl since she first showed up in Birch Creek. She's not like the other ones. Shy and quiet, to the point of being withdrawn. And I know you have a tender heart for the young people in this community too. So I understand why you and Delilah want to help her."

She smiled and took his hand. Oh, how she loved this man. Even though they reunited and fell in love in their twilight years, she felt like she had loved him forever.

"But," he said, pulling his hand from hers and raising one finger.

"Uh-oh," she muttered. She should have known she wasn't going to come out of this unscathed.

"Whatever shenanigans you two have in store, drop them now. If Katharine and Ezra are supposed to be together, God will make sure it happens."

"Like he did with us," she said softly.

"*Ya.*" He switched to *Deitsch*, having started to learn the language once he decided to join the Amish. He was a quick study, of course. "Hopefully for them it won't take decades for that to happen, God willing."

Cevilla thought about their disappointing supper tonight. "Maybe we could nudge them just a tad more?"

"Cevilla," he warned, his white eyebrows flattening.

"All right, all right." She exhaled, not surprised that her and Delilah's matchmaking was nipped in the bud . . . again. In this case, she was almost convinced they would be wasting their time. "I'll talk to Delilah tomorrow after church."

"*Danki.*" He sat back in his chair, a slight frown on his face.

"Is something else wrong?"

"*Nee*. I just hope Katharine can find happiness somehow. I don't know her well, but I have this feeling that there's a lovely woman hiding inside."

Cevilla smiled. "I'm sure there is, *lieb*. I'm sure there is."

Chapter 12

The evening sky turned dusky purple as Ezra and Katharine walked back to the inn. They had split the packages between them—she carried the frames and fabric while he carried the other bag of peaches they'd picked, the bags that held the few items from Walmart, and the hardware supplies. The distance to the Stolls' was farther than he had anticipated, but she didn't complain. In fact, she hadn't said a word, and that bothered him.

Ever since he'd seen her and Rhoda in the kitchen, he'd been uneasy, and that had increased over supper. He could tell both of them had been crying, although Katharine almost had him convinced she was okay. He was learning that she was an expert at hiding her emotions, something he'd never had to do, not to the extent she did. The enjoyable companionship they'd shared since lunch had disappeared, and supper tonight was painful to get through. On top of that, she hadn't eaten anything. Surely she must be hungry.

His plan was to follow her lead. She didn't speak, so he wouldn't either. That turned out to be harder than he thought, and halfway home he couldn't stand the silence anymore. He halted and said, "Okay, Katharine. I know something's bothering you."

She stopped. Hesitated. Then finally turned to him, her expression blank. "I'm—"

"Fine. Right. Except you're not. You haven't been since we left Rhoda's." He moved closer to her. They were standing under a streetlamp that was warming to life now that darkness had settled around them. Fields surrounded them on both sides of the road, and while he hadn't intentionally chosen this isolated spot, they didn't have to worry about anyone seeing them arguing.

Irritation flashed in her eyes. "It's been a long day, Ezra. Let's just *geh* back to the inn."

He noticed she didn't call it home, even though she had lived with the Stolls for over a year. "What did you and Rhoda talk about?"

"*Nix* of your business," she ground out.

She's right. It's not mei *business.* And he shouldn't keep badgering her. But there was something wrong and he was compelled to help. He wanted the relaxed, happy Katharine back. *I want to see her smile.* "You're upset," he said, taking another step toward her.

"Of course I'm upset. You won't leave me alone!" She threw the packages on the asphalt road in front of her.

Crash. The sound of shattered glass filled the air.

Katharine gasped and knelt on the ground. "Oh *nee* oh *nee* oh *nee*," she moaned as she grabbed the bag with the picture frames and looked inside.

He set his packages down and knelt beside her. "Are they broken?"

"*Ya*," she snapped. "They're broken." She plopped on the grassy curb and covered her face with her hands.

"It's okay," he said, moving to sit beside her. "The glass can be fixed."

She didn't move.

Why couldn't he have left well enough alone? Katharine wasn't his responsibility. *She wants to be alone? Fine, I'll leave her alone*. She could walk to the inn by herself.

But he didn't get up. He couldn't, even if he wanted to. The idea of walking away from her wasn't a possibility. He'd figure out why later, but right now he was staying by her side. *Lord, what should I do?*

He put his arm lightly around her shoulders. The gesture was automatic, and he was barely aware he'd moved.

Her head jerked up. "What are you doing?"

The streetlamp was fully lit now, and he could see her confusion and fear. *Why is she afraid of me?* "Comforting you. At least I'm trying to. Do you want me to stop?"

Katharine had forgotten how to move. Or breathe. That was nothing new to her because Simeon often elicited those same reactions from her when he was upset with her. She had no idea if he would insult her, yell at her, or as he had started doing before she left Hulett, hit her. But these feelings were different. The initial fear she'd felt when Ezra reached for her disappeared. Now all she felt was his strong arm against her. Saw how his hair curled up around his ears. Heard the slight sound of his breathing in their quiet surroundings as the fear melted away.

"Is it okay?" he asked, looking down at her.

"What?" She could barely string a thought together.

"That I'm trying to comfort you."

"I . . . I don't know." She stared at the empty street in front of them. Had Simeon ever comforted her when he was upset? She couldn't remember. Surely, she would if he had apologized and put his arm around her like Ezra was doing. No, Simeon had never done anything to soothe her. In fact, it was the exact opposite. She was the one who had to apologize, to stroke his ego, to give in to him whenever he was slighted.

Ezra didn't say anything, but he didn't remove his arm either. Like her, he was staring at the road in front of them. More than anything she wanted to lean against his shoulder, but she caught herself. That was too intimate, and her feelings were so raw and muddled she couldn't take it if he rebuked her.

Finally, he spoke. "Are you feeling better?"

"*Ya*." And it was true. But she was also embarrassed that she had broken the picture frames. She looked up at him. "I shouldn't have acted so childish."

"I shouldn't have been a jerk." He glanced down at her again, smiling.

She couldn't help but smile back. There was something wholesome and pure about Ezra Bontrager. Or maybe she thought there was because she had almost married the devil himself. Any man would be better than Simeon.

But Katharine was starting to realize Ezra wasn't just any man.

He drew away from her and jumped to his feet. Then he turned and held out his hand to help her up.

She stared at it. He might be strong, but she was sure he wasn't strong enough to pull her up from the ground. Ignoring his hand, she pushed up onto her feet, almost stumbling against him but catching herself, escaping another humiliating moment.

If he had noticed her struggling, he didn't let on. "Ready to *geh*?" he said, picking up the packages off the ground.

She nodded and grabbed her bags. As they walked, the broken pieces of glass hit against one another, making a light-pitched tinkling sound. "Delilah's going to be mad at me," she said, dreading trying to explain to her how she had broken the picture frames.

"*Nee* she won't. I'll take the blame."

"I'm the one who broke them," she said.

"Because of me." He looked at her. "I shouldn't have pushed you to answer *mei* question."

She didn't say anything for a moment, then curiosity got the best of her. "Why were you so insistent?"

"I was worried."

Katharine glanced at his handsome profile. "That's it?"

"*Ya*. That's it. Well, and knowing that you weren't being straight with me when you said you were fine. I know you better than that."

His words sank in as they turned into the Stolls' driveway and walked toward the inn. He knew her. Not fully, and definitely not about her past, but enough that he could tell when she wasn't being truthful. That fact should have frightened her, since she had tried so hard to keep herself apart from everyone. But it didn't, and she wasn't sure what to think about that.

They walked past the inn to the Stolls' house. Katharine opened the door and walked into the living room. A warm fire burned in the corner woodstove, and Delilah and Loren were sitting on opposite sides from each other. She was working on a crossword puzzle while Loren read a book, and both of them looked at her when she set the bags she was carrying on the empty sofa. Ezra walked in behind her and closed the door.

Delilah's grin dimmed as she looked at both of them, then the bags on the sofa.

"Sorry about the picture frames." Ezra stepped forward. "I accidentally dropped them on the way home."

"I didn't hear Gary's car pull in," Loren said. "I guess this book is more engrossing than I thought."

"We walked from Cevilla's."

"Why would you do that?" Delilah asked.

"Gary had been with us all day, and it was a nice night for a walk. Where do you want me to put these?" He held up the bags.

Loren rose from his chair. "I'll take them."

Ezra nodded, and gave him all the bags he was holding except one. "I bought a few things while we were out," he explained.

Katharine opened her mouth to tell Delilah and Loren the truth, but Ezra gave her a pointed look. "I'll see you in the morning at Zeke and Darla's," he said, opening the door. His brother and sister-in-law were hosting church. "*Gute nacht*." Before anyone could say anything else, he hurried out the door.

"Well, that was sudden," Delilah said, frowning. "I had *kaffee* already brewing for both of you."

Loren lifted an eyebrow at his mother, then said, "I'll *geh* put these things away."

Delilah got up and went to the sofa. She opened the paper bag with the frames. "Oh my. They're both shattered."

"I'm sorry." Katharine went to her. "The actual frames are fine, and I'll replace the glass."

"Shouldn't Ezra do that?"

She shook her head. She couldn't allow him to take the blame for her tantrum, but Delilah didn't need to know exactly how the frames were broken. "I dropped the bag," she said, folding her hands together in front of her. "Not Ezra."

After a pause, Delilah nodded. "I see. *Nee* worries. They weren't that expensive."

"They weren't?"

"The glass isn't original, and I used Cevilla's family discount. *Mei* English neighbor in Wisconsin won't mind replacing the glass. I bought them for her anyway." She smiled, her expression hopeful. "Did you have a nice time today?"

Now was the moment to tell her that her matchmaking efforts were for nothing. Then she thought about her lunch with him. The fun they had at the peach orchard. Him pulling her out of harm's way and how good it had felt to be held by him when she was upset. His comforting her and taking responsibility for something he didn't do for her sake.

What if . . .

She reined in her thoughts and said, "We did everything on your list."

"Oh." Delilah's face fell. "Um, job well done then."

"If you don't mind, I'll skip the *kaffee*. I'd like to turn in."

"Sure," she said, her disappointed expression growing. "*Gute nacht*, Katharine."

"*Gute nacht*."

She went upstairs to her bedroom and closed the door. What had she been thinking, even entertaining the idea of her and Ezra being together—and not for the first time today.

She went to her dresser and started taking out the clips that attached her *kapp* to her hair. Although she tried not to, she couldn't help but glance in the mirror and see her reflection. A new pimple had cropped up near the corner of her mouth. The double chin was still there. So were her wide shoulders and busty chest. *This is what Ezra saw all day.*

Every pleasant emotion she'd experienced during the day turned to shame. There was no way Ezra would ever find her appealing. Simeon never did, and he claimed to love her. Keeping her from getting hit by a car and comforting her when she was upset didn't mean anything beyond what they were—things any decent human being would have done.

Except for Simeon. If she didn't know it before, today proved Simeon didn't love her and that he was a horrible, devious person. She would be eternally grateful to Elsie for helping her escape him.

Today did show her that there were nice men in the world other than her father and Galen. An inexplicable wave of homesickness washed over her. She missed her parents and more than anything she wanted to call them and hear their voices. But they would ask her to come home, and undoubtedly bring up Simeon. Even if she told them the truth about him, she doubted they would believe her. She had fallen under Simeon's spell, and she wasn't surprised that they had too. If she went back home now, he would punish her, and probably her parents too. Would she ever be able to return home?

She rubbed her temples and pushed those thoughts out of her mind. She had a bigger problem to deal with—Delilah's assumptions about her and Ezra. After church tomorrow she would tell her to abandon her matchmaking plans. That would put an end to any future interactions with Ezra Bontrager once and for all. *It's for the best.* She had to continue to protect her damaged heart.

Jordan Powell slipped his cell phone into his jeans pocket and looked at the notes on his small notepad, a number two pencil behind his ear as was his habit developed from when he was a police officer, then a detective with the Los Angeles police department fifteen years ago. He'd retired at forty-five, and now at forty-nine he was thinking about retiring again, this time from private detective work. But not until he solved the Troyer case. Or at least closed it, since it seemed from Rhoda's phone call that Emmanuel had solved the case himself.

To her credit, Rhoda had sounded composed as she read him the anonymous letter. Then again, her husband had been gone a long time, so the shock probably wasn't as acute as it would be if she had discovered he died soon after his disappearance. But he'd detected the emotion in her voice. That hadn't surprised him either. In the past few months he'd been working for her, he'd come to like the soft-spoken woman. And now she could start the next chapter of her life knowing what had happened to Emmanuel. Closure was always a good thing.

Except something was nagging at him. This all seemed too convenient. He'd also detected an underlying doubt in Rhoda's voice when she told him about the letters. She hadn't said so out loud, but he suspected she thought the same thing he did—the letters could be fake.

He put the pencil on the table and got up from the chair in his room, having checked into a marginally classless motel outside of Charleston, West Virginia, the night before. He had a gut feeling that Emmanuel had ended up in this state, although he couldn't completely explain how. This entire case, with almost no clues available, had been conducted on instinct and a few short interviews. Rhoda had given him a list of some of the original Birch

Creek citizens he could speak to, and he'd also paid a visit to Holmes County and tried to talk to some of Emmanuel's family members and acquaintances who knew him when he had lived there. Everyone was polite, but they either didn't have much information or were uninformative on purpose. This was his first time investigating someone Amish, and as an outsider, he had found their community tough to crack.

But going on instinct wasn't a bad thing. His gut was usually right—and right now it was saying that Emmanuel's "death" announcements were as fabricated as a counterfeit hundred-dollar bill. He'd seen more than a few of those over the years too.

He opened a bottle of water and took a long drink. At one time that bottle would have been scotch or bourbon, but he wasn't about to break his ten-year sober streak because of a tough case. He'd asked Rhoda the typical questions—was the letter handwritten, did she recognize the handwriting, did the paper look familiar—and her answers didn't give him any leads, other than the postmark. At least that was something.

He sat down at the small table near the window. His laptop was already open, and he did a search for Dixonville, the town where the letter was mailed. Just outside of Bluefield in the southern part of the state, near the Tennessee line. At least he had more than his gut to go on. Even if Emmanuel wasn't in Dixonville, he could try to trace the letter's origin. Tough, but it could be done.

Leaning back in his chair, he adjusted the old baseball cap he wore to cover up his short, black-and-silver hair. His unremarkable outfit of blue jeans, an old rock concert T-shirt, and the dingy white hat with the Cincinnati Reds logo on it had kept him under the radar. Fingers crossed, he would finally discover what happened to Emmanuel.

In the morning, he'd pack up his stuff, check out of the motel, then head to Dixonville. If nothing came from the postmark, he would close the case. He didn't like giving up on cases, but when they turned cold, he had no choice. And if he did find out that Emmanuel had passed, Rhoda said they wanted to honor his request and not investigate further.

Until then, he would keep on searching for Emmanuel Troyer.

Chapter 13

After church on Sunday, Ezra leaned against one of the fence posts surrounding the large pasture on Zeke and Zeb's horse farm. Although Zeke and Darla were technically hosting church, the twin brothers and their wives lived on the same property in different houses, so both couples were involved with hosting. When his brothers first started the farm, Ezra had spent plenty of time helping them out. And boy, did they need it. As with most new businesses there were still some bumps to iron out, but he had no doubt the farm would succeed.

Normally after service he was eager to converse with his family and friends, and of course partake of the delicious meal that the women served. Although cooking wasn't allowed on Sunday, there were always plenty of satisfying cold dishes available. But today he wasn't hungry, or in the mood for company. The pasture was yards away from the barn where they held the service, and even farther from the house where everyone was getting ready to eat on the numerous outdoor tables his brothers had set up. Birch

Creek had grown so big and there were so many people staying for lunch, he doubted anyone would notice he was missing.

He also doubted they would notice him keeping an eye on Katharine. The minute the service ended, he looked for her on the opposite side of the barn where the women were seated. She was already leaving the bench seat and a second later she had disappeared outside. Did she always do that after a service? He didn't know. He hadn't paid attention before. *I'm paying attention now.*

Ezra had followed her, making sure to keep his distance. He'd already pushed her too much on the walk home last night, and even though he apologized, he was still at fault for upsetting her. She seemed better when he left the Stolls' last night, and he wanted to make sure she was still okay.

Finally she stopped at the pond behind the barn a few yards from the end of the pasture. His brothers had dug it six or so months ago and used it to water the horses and the crops they'd planted on the west side of the property. Her back was to him, but she didn't sit down. Her dark-green dress hung loosely on her body, but the color suited her. He hemmed and hawed about going to her, then decided to stay put and try to sort out the growing confusion in his head.

He didn't understand why he was so drawn to her, or why she brought out his protective side. Up until last night, he hadn't known he had one outside of safeguarding his family. And why was that happening now? She'd lived in Birch Creek for a year, and he'd never paid much attention to her. Then again, they hadn't been in close proximity before he started working for the Stolls. On top of that, they'd spent only one day together, and a good portion of that had been spent being awkward and strained with each other.

But the time he'd spent with her when they were both relaxed and getting to know each other had been enjoyable. He'd never gotten on with Gloria like that. Then again, Gloria rarely let him get a word in edgewise. Mostly she had talked about herself. But Katharine had asked him many questions about his life and had listened attentively. He was involved in a conversation with a woman, not listening to a monologue.

Then there was the way Katharine had felt in his arms—when he had pulled her out of the street, and when he had put his arm around her. And her smile . . . just incredible. The glimpses he'd caught of the real Katharine made him want to get to know her better. But he couldn't do that if she didn't let him.

A sparrow landed on a nearby post, then tilted its tiny head and stared at him. *I got nothing*, he mouthed.

"There you are."

He jumped at the sound of a shrill, high-pitched feminine voice as the bird flew away. *Oh* nee. He ran a hand over his face and turned around. "Hi, Charity."

"What are you doing all the way over here?" She put her hands on her thin, almost boyish hips. "Why aren't you eating with the rest of us?"

"I'm not hungry." Only partly true, but there was plenty of time to eat later. He fought the urge to glance over his shoulder. Could Katharine hear Charity's voice from this distance? Hopefully not.

She rolled her eyes. "I don't believe you," she scoffed. "You love to eat."

"How do you know that?" he said, frowning.

"*Yer mamm* told me."

Oh brother. Now his mother was involved in this. Worse yet, Charity clearly hadn't gotten the message when he had told her, as kindly as he could, that he wasn't interested in her. He touched her elbow and guided her away from the pasture so they could talk privately out of Katharine's earshot. Once they were behind one of the huge oak trees on the farm property and a little farther away from the pond, he stopped and looked her square in the eye, having to bend over to do so. "Remember our talk the other day?"

"The one where you told me you weren't ready for a relationship?"

"*Ya*. That one." At least she had been listening. "I haven't changed *mei* mind, Charity. I'm not ready to—" He couldn't finish the sentence.

"I know, I know. You're not ready to date."

That's what he had intended to say. But the words escaped him. And he suddenly realized why . . . Because they weren't true, not anymore.

She scowled. "What's with all the single guys here anyway? Why did you put an advertisement in the paper if none of you want to get married?"

"We weren't the ones who did that. And some of us have gotten married since then." Although when it came to his brothers, none of them had been looking for wives. The exact opposite, actually.

Charity looked up at him with round, flirty eyes. "I can wait," she said.

"Uh, wait for what?"

She threaded her arm through his. "For you. When you're ready to date, I'll be here. You're worth it."

"Charity, I—"

"Oh, hi, Katharine."

His stomach dropped. He hadn't heard her coming, and now she was right in front of them. She nodded at Charity but didn't give him a glance.

"Nice day, isn't it?" Charity moved closer to him and held on tighter to his arm. "Even better when you have someone to share it with."

Katharine stood stock-still, and she flashed her eyes to Ezra. For a split second he saw pain, then nothing. "I'm sure it is," she said, turning to Charity. Then she smiled. "Enjoy your time together." She walked away.

"Katharine—"

"Ignore her," Charity said, tugging him away from the tree. "She's an antisocial fatty."

He saw Katharine pause, obviously hearing Charity's insult, then she hurried away.

"Now," Charity said. "Where were we?"

Lester awakened to the sound of loud knocking on his motel room door. Groaning, he shut his eyes again. A foot or two away, the TV blared out an old western movie he'd never seen before. Not that he watched much TV anyway, and he'd only recently started tuning in. Mostly it was on for background noise. He'd had trouble sleeping last night, and since he didn't attend church anymore, he got out of bed early to spend the morning watching the tube. Before long he'd fallen asleep. The old motel desk chair was surprisingly comfortable.

"Mr. Smith?" a voice called from the other side of the door.

Opening one eye, Lester pretended he wasn't there.

"I can hear the TV through the door, Mr. Smith. Spoiler, the sheriff catches the bad guy."

He couldn't help but crack a smile. The good guys always won, didn't they?

More knocking. "Mr. Smith, I can stand out here all day if you want, or you can let me in. I need to talk to you."

Lester groaned. He didn't recognize the man's voice, and if he was someone begging for money or a hungover drunk unable to find his room, he was going to lose his temper. Maybe. He was so tired he wasn't sure he could muster up the energy for a tongue-lashing. Slowly he rose from the chair, every bone and muscle in his body protesting with pain.

Knock knock. "Mr. Smith—"

"I'm coming!" He shuffled barefoot across the old brown carpet. "Give a dying man some time, for crying out loud," he muttered. Finally he opened the door, and naturally didn't recognize the guy. "What do you want?"

The man grinned as if he'd won the lottery. "Just to talk."

Lester started to shut the door in his face, but the man stopped him. "If you're who I think you are, I've been looking for you."

Peering at him, Lester said, "What are you, some kind of detective?"

"Actually, that's exactly what I am."

Dread filled him. He'd meant the comment as a joke.

He fished in the pocket of his lightweight jacket and pulled out a business card. "Jordan Powell. Private investigator."

"Is that supposed to mean something to me?" When he saw his smile widen, Lester was a little impressed. He liked a man with a backbone. That had been something he tried to develop in his sons. In the end, he had failed them in every way possible.

"Do you have a few minutes? I'd like to ask you some questions."

"No." Lester started to close the door again, only to be blocked a second time.

"Your wife told me you were stubborn. She was right."

"I don't have a wife."

"Rhoda Troyer is your wife. Your sons are Solomon and Aden. You left Birch Creek nine years ago."

His blood turned cold. At long last, his past had caught up with him.

Jordan walked into the dark living area of the musty old motel room. Drapes closed. Lights off. Paper napkins and old Styrofoam coffee cups all over the place. The room looked like a dungeon and the acrid smell wasn't much better. The glow from the TV illuminated a haggard man whose clothes swallowed him. Sunken cheeks and unruly hair and beard that needed either detangling or shearing off completely.

During his years in law enforcement and detective work, Jordan had prided himself on keeping his emotions in check. But occasionally there was a case or a person that busted through his carefully constructed barrier. In his pathetic state, Lester Smith, aka Emmanuel Troyer, was coming close.

In fact, he had to hide his shock when Emmanuel first opened the door. Due to the Amish not taking photographs, he had only a sketch the forensic artist he'd hired had made from Rhoda's detailed description. At this point he had Emmanuel's face memorized, and while he might be hiding under a wild beard, the sharp eyes were the same. Now he knew for sure he was alive. Soon he hoped to discover the reason he'd told his family he was dead.

Emmanuel sank down on an old desk chair directly in front of the TV. Jordan waited for him to speak. He expected Emmanuel to ask how he had found him, or why he was here. He hadn't missed the flash of fear in the old man's eyes that quickly changed to defeat as he left the door open and allowed Jordan in.

Emmanuel didn't say a word.

"Can I turn on the light?" Jordan finally asked. "It's hard to see in here."

"No." He stared at the drug commercial on TV.

"How about I open the drapes."

A pause. "Suit yourself."

Jordan pulled back the thick dusty curtains far enough for a sliver of morning light to shine through. He looked around for a place to sit and didn't find one other than the bed. Stepping over the pair of paint-stained pants on the floor, he sat on the end of a too-thin mattress. At least they were seated next to each other. "Rhoda hired me to find you," he said, attempting to break the ice.

His bushy brow lifted but he didn't look at Jordan. "I find that hard to believe."

"It's true. I've been looking for you for nearly a year."

Silence.

Jordan pushed back the brim of his baseball cap. He wasn't surprised Emmanuel was being uncooperative. The Amish he'd talked to in Birch Creek were tight-lipped about the scandal surrounding him. Whatever it was had caused Emmanuel to disappear . . . and fake his death. "She also told me about the letters she and your sons received. Letters I suspect you wrote."

The old man stared at the TV as if mesmerized by the bloodless shootout common in old westerns. Jordan opened his mouth to speak again when Emmanuel grabbed the remote and hit the Off button. "Fine. You found me." He faced him, a haughty fire in his weary eyes. "I wrote the letters too. My family—" His throat bobbed.

"They're better off believing I'm dead. That'll be true soon enough. Now leave me in peace."

Jordan nodded. Leaving was exactly what he should do. He'd found what he needed. Emmanuel was alive. Barely, from the looks of it. He'd seen enough death in his life, and plenty of people on the verge of dying, to know Emmanuel wasn't lying this time. Jordan's job was done, and he didn't have to let Rhoda know the truth.

But that didn't sit well with him. Walking out and letting the old man die alone didn't either. "Why did you lie to your family?"

Emmanuel leveled a hard look at him. "That's none of your business."

"True." He started to put his hands on the bed, glanced at the rumpled polyester bedspread, then placed them on his knees. "It's not my business. But when presented with a mystery, I can't help myself."

"You can help yourself out, that's what you can do."

Jordan almost laughed. This man reminded him of his father, a hard-nosed former police chief who rarely left his proclivity for strict discipline at the office. Growing up, Jordan had vowed not to follow in his footsteps, so of course he did exactly that. But while they had a troubled relationship, at the end of his life they had reconciled. Maybe that was why he hadn't given up on this case yet. This man was denying his family the right to real closure, and the opportunity to make peace. "You eaten anything lately?"

Emmanuel shrugged. "Can't remember."

"How about I take you to lunch? You might feel better once you get a hot meal."

He shrugged. "Haven't had much of an appetite lately."

Jordan detected a slight Amish accent, almost imperceptible, and probably was to most ears. "Any good restaurants around here? I can bring you something back if you don't want to go out."

Emmanuel turned the TV back on.

Jordan got up from the bed and headed for the door. "I'll be right back." Normally he wouldn't leave when he was in the middle of questioning, but Emmanuel wasn't going anywhere in his condition. As he left the motel, he decided to stop by the store and get him a few groceries, suspecting there was nothing in the room's mini fridge either.

As he opened the car door, he looked at the motel office three doors down from Emmanuel's. This was his last case, and there wasn't much waiting for him back in LA. He was one of those stereotypical workaholics who had sacrificed the opportunity to have a family for his work. At the time he'd had no regrets, but after his father's death, that had changed.

Jordan shut the door and headed for the office to book a room. He'd stick around for a day or two and try to get some more info from the old man. At the very least he could convince him to eat, take a shower, and get some sleep. Emmanuel Troyer needed help, and he was going to get some, whether he liked it or not.

Chapter 14

Charity's insult hit Katharine square in the chest. She found herself unable to simply brush off her humiliation. It was bad enough she'd been put down once again, but to have it happen in front of Ezra? Her cheeks felt on fire.

She'd known Ezra had followed her to the pond, but she ignored him, wanting to be alone. No, she needed to be alone. Even though she didn't want to. She'd never been so confused in her life.

Then she heard Charity talking to him, and she was stunned at the envy winding around her heart. What did she care if they were having a conversation? She couldn't quite make out what they were saying, but when she heard them walk away, she glanced over her shoulder and saw them by the beautiful oak tree near the other side of the pasture. A tree she had to pass on the way back to the Bontragers' house, something she also needed to do because if she skipped lunch today, Delilah would be on her case. She was already upset with her for skipping breakfast again.

Katharine had promised her she would eat after the church service, but she wanted to wait for most of the people to go home.

But hearing Charity's digs and insults broke her resolve. What else could she do, other than keep walking and pretend she didn't hear what Charity said? She hurried her steps, trying to outrun her shame. It didn't work, and her eyes filled with tears. Great. She was losing her composure in front of a bratty girl. Even worse, she couldn't get the image out of her mind of Charity clinging to Ezra. He'd told Katharine that he wasn't interested in her. But he sure looked like he was interested today.

She didn't head for the lunch tables near the Bontragers' house. Instead she rushed for the road to go back to the Stolls'. She'd come up with an excuse to give Delilah later. Right now she wanted to hide from everyone, especially Ezra.

She made a quick turn at the end of the driveway, then ran a few steps before slowing down, out of breath and unable to run anymore because Charity was right—she was a fatty.

"Katharine!"

Good Lord, no. Not Ezra right now. *Not ever.* Despite her breathlessness, she pushed herself to run again. She'd not only skipped breakfast but she hadn't eaten supper last night either, and it was past lunchtime. Everything started to rotate, and she slowed down. Her stomach lurched. Oh no. Was she going to throw up in front of him? *I have to sit down* . . . She crumpled onto the grass.

"Katharine!" Ezra hunkered down beside her.

She was shocked he'd reached her so fast. Why wouldn't he when she ran slower than a molasses river? Squeezing her eyes shut, she begged the world to stop spinning.

"Katharine?" He shifted closer to her. "Say something."

Somehow she managed to lift her head and scowl at him. Her

chest heaved as she fought for air, but at least the spinning was slowing down. Then her stomach growled. Loud. Long. Then a second time. Unbelievable. As if she wasn't mortified enough.

He waited, not saying anything. When the nausea went away, she cast a quick look at him and found him watching her, his expression a puzzling mix of concern and exasperation. "*Gut*," he said. "You finally have some color back in your cheeks."

And sweat on her forehead. Lovely. She was still a little breathless too.

"When was the last time you ate something?"

A buggy turned out of the Bontragers' driveway and headed toward them.

"Do you think you can get up?" Ezra said, jumping to his feet.

"Why?"

"I'll take that as a *ya*." He put an arm under her elbow.

"What are you doing?"

"Helping you stand."

She shook her head. "But—" Before she could finish, he hauled her up without a struggle. Wow, he was stronger than she thought.

"Come with me." He started to put his arm around her shoulder.

Shrinking back, she shrugged him off. "I don't need your help."

"*Nee* arguing."

She hadn't realized he was so stubborn. And even though he was giving her an order like Simeon always did, this was different. He was irritated, but there was no harshness in his tone. "Fine," she said, letting out a long breath. The quicker she complied, the faster she would get back to the Stolls'. "Where are we going?"

"To Amanda's secret garden."

"Must not be a secret if you know about it." She hadn't meant the snide remark, but she couldn't help herself.

Instead of snapping back, he chuckled, then took her hand. "All the Bontragers know about her secret garden. It's not far from here. Let's *geh*."

The dizziness had disappeared, and she could walk under her own steam. "I'm okay," she said. "You don't have to hold *mei* hand."

He looked down at her with a sure smile. "I know."

As they walked to the other side of the Bontragers' property, behind the pond and away from everyone else, she tried not to look at Ezra's hand in hers. If she was confused before, she was completely confounded now. If he and Charity were together, then why was he holding her hand? Even reminding herself that she had almost thrown up and fainted right in front of him and more than likely still appeared to need assistance didn't clear things. Surely, he wasn't holding her hand because he simply wanted to.

They walked under a tall arch made of wood. Grapevines wound around it, and lofty oak trees along with evergreen bushes were on either side. Then she saw the garden. Old red pavers were arranged in an arc in front of a square patio made of the same type of paver. Short perennials were planted throughout the dirt covering the space, and the scent of fresh mulch hovered in the air. A wood and metal bench that looked brand-new was at the far side of the patio square. The garden was obviously still in the beginning stages, yet already idyllic. If she wasn't so upended, she could enjoy the peaceful setting.

"Now we don't have to worry about anyone bothering us." He let go of her hand and gestured to the bench. "Have a seat."

"What if I want to stand?"

His good humor evaporated. "Then stand." He walked over to the bench and sat down.

She watched him stretch out his long arms across the back of the bench, then balance one ankle on the opposite knee. The bench did look inviting. So did the man sitting on it.

"Sure you don't want to sit down?"

It was almost as if he sensed the muscles in her legs were weakened from running. Probably from lack of food too. Unwilling to risk getting dizzy again, she sat down on the bench as far away from him as she could, folding her arms over her chest.

His brow furrowed, and he moved his arms and leaned forward. "Did you have breakfast this morning?"

She turned away from him. She was still perspiring, and she dabbed her forehead with the hem of her apron.

"Katharine—"

"Isn't Charity waiting for you?" she said, spinning around.

"Probably."

Well, that backfired, because not only was she hot, sweaty, hungry, and annoyed but she also was envious again. She also didn't want to sit here with him anymore. "*Danki* for your concern," she said, lifting her chin. "I'm going to leave now." Might as well live up to the antisocial description too.

"Not until you answer *mei* question." He pressed his lips together.

And because she wasn't bemused enough, her gaze focused on his mouth, which had suddenly relaxed. His very *kissable* mouth.

That did it. She was officially *ab im kopp*.

She dragged her gaze from his mouth, intending to focus on the woods behind him. Instead she met his eyes, and a jolt of electricity shot through her. The color had darkened from light, grayish blue to slate, making her heart pound in her chest again. Simeon had never looked this way. She had never felt like this with him. Like she knew she had filled Ezra's thoughts until no one and nothing else existed. *Oh my*.

This was bad. Very bad, because she was thinking about kissing Ezra Bontrager—who might or might not be with Charity. She was also supposed to shove all romantic notions out of her mind and heart forever, not wonder if his lips were as soft as they looked.

Jumping up from the bench, she walked over to a separate area of the garden where three perennial bushes were in spring bloom. She didn't have the capacity to enjoy the pretty flowers, not when she was fighting for control of her insane thoughts.

"Hey."

His gentle voice overcame her urge to ignore him, and she turned around. But she refused to look at him, keeping her gaze on the ground. She couldn't risk seeing the kindness she knew would be in his eyes. That would be her undoing.

"Come sit next to me," he said.

Surprised, she lifted her head. He was smiling, patting the empty space beside him. She couldn't speak, just shook her head.

He rose from the bench, his movements as graceful as hers were ungainly. "Don't," she said, taking a step back. The leaves from a purple aster bush brushed the back of her calf.

Ezra sighed, then held out his hands. "I'm sorry about Charity," he said, honoring her request to keep distance between them. "What she said was uncalled for."

"She's right, though."

He frowned. "About what?"

"I am antisocial." She couldn't look at him. "And I'm fat."

"You're not fat—"

"Stop." She held up her hand. "I have a mirror. I know what I look like."

"And so what?" He took a few steps forward, then stopped when she backed away. "You're not fat, and even if you were, that doesn't make what Charity said right. She's the last person who should be casting aspersions on anyone."

"Aspersions?" Katharine lifted her brow.

He half smiled. "I might not be as well read as Owen, but I have a decent vocabulary."

She almost smiled back, then remembered she had to keep every single emotion under wraps with him. He was attuned to her for some reason. Simeon never noticed when she was sad, or happy, or anything else. Ezra seemed to effortlessly pick up on her moods.

"I honestly thought Charity knew I didn't like her," he continued.

"Then why was she hanging on to you like that?"

"She only did that when she saw you. Then she started blabbing and—" He scowled. "Katharine, trust me when I say I don't like Charity, and I *really* don't like her now after what she said to you, and I told her as much. I also have the feeling she's been rejected by more than one guy around here, and possibly some back in her hometown. I can see why."

"I appreciate you sticking up for me," she said. Her lower lip quivered. "But she's not the first person to insult me . . . and she won't be the last."

As hard as it was to have heard Charity's offensive—and untrue—words about Katharine, it was far more difficult for Ezra to hear her put herself down. 'I'm sorry people have hurt you," he said.

She blinked, as if surprised to hear his apology. Then she looked away. "Everyone gets hurt eventually."

That was true. Gloria had hurt him. And he'd probably hurt Charity when he yanked his arm from her and went after Katharine, although he suspected only her pride was sore. But neither of those incidences seemed to compare to the anguish in Katharine's voice. He wished he could make her feel better, but he was at a loss for words.

A warm breeze fluttered through the garden. A wayward strand of hair escaped her *kapp*, and without thinking he reached to touch it.

She jerked away, terror in her eyes.

He froze, his hand still in midair. Did she think he was going to strike her?

She spun around, keeping her back to him.

Dread and compassion throttled his heart at the same time. And despite his promise not to press her too much, he couldn't stop himself. "Katharine," he said, as carefully as he could. "Did . . . Did someone hit you?"

She didn't turn around. She didn't speak. And when he thought she wasn't going to answer him at all, he saw her head nod once, the movement almost imperceptible.

His nails dug into his palms. He wanted to ask who, and if that person lived in Birch Creek, he would—He drew in a deep breath. Katharine didn't need his anger. She needed his understanding.

He moved closer, halting a few steps behind her. "I'm not going to harm you," he said. "Believe me when I say that."

Slowly she turned around, tears running down her cheeks. "I do believe you. I'm not sure why, but I do."

He exhaled, tension leaving his tight shoulders. Slowly he raised his hand, then moved it closer to her face, his eyes locking with hers. This time she didn't flinch, and he brushed the tears off her cheek with his thumb, then dropped his hand to his side.

Her gaze drifted downward. "I'm sorry about *mei* face," she whispered.

"What's wrong with your face?"

"Acne," she said, still not looking at him. "Chubby cheeks. Take your pick."

"You have acne?" When she looked at him, he held his breath again, expecting her to make a sarcastic remark. She surprised him with a tiny chuckle.

"You're not the only one who has pimples, by the way." He pointed to a small bump on the side of his nose. "This one popped up this morning."

She squinted. "I can barely see that."

"It looked huge to me. You know what else? I used to hate *mei* height. I grew so fast two years ago I kept growing out of my pants. I felt like all arms and legs, and people wouldn't stop pointing out how tall I was, like I was peculiar. But I got used to it, and I don't think about *mei* height much anymore."

"Are you trying to make me feel better because of what Charity said?"

"*Nee*. I'm pointing out that we all have stuff about ourselves we don't like. Sometimes we can change those things, sometimes we can't. It's what's on the inside that counts, though. There's a Scripture verse about that, if I remember right."

"For the Lord does not see as man sees; for man looks at the outward appearance—"

"'—but the Lord looks at the heart.' That's the one."

Her expression relaxed. "*Danki*, Ezra. Sometimes I forget what's really important."

"Any time." His stomach rumbled. "We both need to get something to eat. And don't tell me you're not hungry. Your stomach says otherwise."

She paused. "You're right. I'll *geh* back to Delilah's and make a sandwich."

"I'm sure there's plenty left at Zeke's. We can *geh* back there and both eat."

"Together?"

"Why not?"

"But we disappeared together," she said. "People might think we . . . you know . . ."

"Like each other?"

Her face flushed. "*Ya*. We don't want to give Delilah any more ideas."

Ezra pondered that for a moment. He was about to tell her that there was little likelihood anyone saw them go to the garden. If Charity hadn't already gone back to Zeke's house, they were shielded from her by the barn. And he'd recognized the buggy pulling out of the driveway. His nephew Malachi Chupp had just bought a new buggy, and Ezra's younger brother Jesse was riding with him. Malachi was nosy and Jesse was a relentless pest, and he didn't want either of them to bother him and Katharine. Walking back to Zeke's could be seen as a coincidence, not that he and Katharine had gone off alone together. But his thoughts returned to Delilah's matchmaking intentions.

"We do like each other, don't we?" he asked.

"Uh, *ya*. I think we're friends." But she stared at his chest as she spoke.

"Just friends?" Because friendship wasn't what he'd felt when they were sitting on the bench together. He'd seen her looking at his mouth, and not in a friendly way. More like she'd wanted to kiss him. And if she hadn't jumped off the bench like the seat had caught fire, he wouldn't have minded if she did.

"Um, *ya*," she said in a small voice. "What else would we be?"

That brought him back to reality. She'd made it clear at lunch that she wasn't looking for a husband. And he'd made it clear he wasn't looking for a wife. He still felt that way . . . didn't he? "Right . . . friends." Obviously he'd made a mistake and had felt something between them that wasn't there. That he'd *hoped* was there. "But if you'd rather, we'll *geh* back to Zeke's separately. You can *geh* first, I'll follow a little later."

She remained in place.

"All right, I'll *geh* first then." Disappointed, he turned and started to leave the garden.

"Ezra?"

He stopped and faced her. "*Ya*?"

"I think it will be okay if we *geh* together. As long as you don't mind."

He grinned. She had no idea she'd just made his day. "I don't mind at all."

Chapter 15

"I'm not sure what else to do." Rhoda fidgeted with the hem of her apron, despite the relief she felt at unburdening everything to Bishop Yoder, including her confusion and guilt over Emmanuel's death. She brushed a stray piece of hay with the tip of her black shoe. The Bontragers' barn was as spotless as a barn could be for church service. Rhoda had waited for everyone else to leave before approaching Freemont, asking him if he had time to talk. He said yes, as he always did when one of his congregation needed him. He was the complete opposite of Emmanuel, and he had shepherded their district well during a time when it could have fallen apart. Now Birch Creek was thriving, and although Freemont wouldn't take any credit, he certainly deserved some.

Freemont nodded, then adjusted his glasses. "I appreciate you telling me all this, Rhoda," he said in his usual measured tone. "I know it has to be so hard on you. So this PI you hired, he's still looking for Emmanuel?"

"*Ya*. Other than the letters, we don't have any proof he's really . . ." She couldn't bring herself to say the word.

"I see."

"But if Jordan doesn't find anything either way, what do *mei sohns* and I do?"

Freemont stilled, obviously deep in thought, just as Rhoda had been all night. It took everything she had to come to church this morning. She was glad to see Aden and his family were here, but Irene had come alone with the two boys. None of the women said anything before the service started, and right after church ended, both families went home. Aden asked if she wanted him to stay or to take her home, but she had refused his requests. The bishop needed to know what was going on.

"Of course *mei* first answer is we have to trust God in this situation," Freemont said. "As we do each and every day. Still, this is a quandary. Does anyone else know about the letters other than your family?"

"*Nee*. We haven't told anyone."

"That's wise. Until there's more proof, nothing should be said. I can explain that to Sol and Aden if you'd like."

"That won't be necessary. They're not going to say anything."

"I noticed Sol wasn't in church today. He's never missed a service."

"I know." She looked at her lap again. Her fears were coming true, and Sol was withdrawing again. She could see it in Irene's strained expression when she walked into the barn with the boys.

"Are you sure you don't want me to talk to him?"

Rhoda considered the offer but shook her head. "He needs time. I'm sure he'll come around."

Freemont's smile was gentle. "I'm sure he will too. I've known him since he was a *kinn*, and God has changed his heart. I truly believe that. Our faith is strengthened when we undergo adversity."

"Hasn't he had plenty of adversity? And Aden too? Having Emmanuel for a father wasn't . . . isn't hard enough?"

"*Ya*. I'd say all three of you have had enough. But it's not up to me or anyone else to decide that. Only God can. He doesn't promise that we won't have continual trials, only that he will be right beside us as we see them through. Giving us hope, comfort, and mercy."

Rhoda nodded, but right now she didn't feel any of those things. "*Danki*," she said, rising from the bench. "I'll let you know what Jordan finds out."

He stood and faced her. "Please do. Know that I'm praying for all of you too. You and your *sohns* will be at the top of *mei* list."

All she could do was nod. As she walked out of the barn, she wondered what Jordan was doing now. Was he able to track down the postmark? She hadn't heard from him since she'd told him about the letters. That was Jordan's way. He didn't call unless he had some sort of news or a progress report. She thought she'd gotten used to waiting. Obviously she hadn't, because she was tempted to call him. *How's that for trusting you, Lord?*

She was a few feet from the barn when she saw Loren approach. Her heart leaped in her chest. He smiled at her, and more than anything she wanted to fall into his arms and tell him about Emmanuel. But she couldn't. Freemont was right. They couldn't say anything to anyone else until Jordan finished his investigation.

"Hi," he said when he reached her. He looked over her shoulder. "Everything all right?"

She turned and saw Freemont walking out of the barn. He passed both of them by, his only communication a nod at Loren. "*Ya*," she said after he was out of earshot. "I just needed to talk to Freemont for a few minutes."

Loren's eyes filled with questioning, but he didn't pry or demand answers. As if he knew that was the last thing she needed right now. He would be right.

If only things were different. The thought came unbidden, along with the guilt. As far as she knew, she was still a married woman, letters or not.

"There's still plenty of food," he said. "Would you like me to get you a plate?"

"*Nee*. I'm not feeling well. I'm going to *geh* home."

"Oh. Is there something I can do to help?"

She met his gaze, and the attraction and affection she felt for him nearly overwhelmed her. But as she had for so long, she held it at bay. "I'll be okay. Just a headache."

"I'll take you home then—"

"I'd like to walk, if you don't mind."

He nodded. "Sure. Whatever you need to do."

"*Danki*, Loren." She couldn't keep herself from touching his arm, then she turned around and left. *If only I could tell him what's going on, Lord. Hopefully soon I can.*

"I can't believe we were so wrong about Katharine and Ezra," Cevilla said from her seat under the Bontragers' shady patio. Several young children were playing in the spacious backyard while the women were cleaning up the last remnants of Sunday lunch.

Delilah nodded, tapping her fingers on the plastic chair she was sitting in next to Cevilla. Her offers of cleanup help had been rejected twice, although Cevilla knew she was itching to do something anyway, considering she was out of sorts after their failure to connect the two young people together. They'd had only one attempt, but after her conversation with Richard last night, she had told Delilah that she was extricating herself from the situation. Surprisingly, her friend had agreed.

"I was so sure they belonged together," Delilah said, her finger taps growing annoyingly louder. A few feet away Caroline Yoder and her sister-in-law Mary were detaching a tablecloth from one of the tables. "I can help you with those," Delilah said, starting to get up from the chair.

"Sit down," Cevilla said, tapping her cane against the leg of Delilah's chair. "Sunday is a day of rest, especially for us older folks."

"Humph. Who are you calling old?"

"Me." She sighed, then turned to Delilah. "Right here, right now, we are officially retired from meddling. Again. For the last time."

Rolling her eyes, Delilah said, "Fine. This time is for *gut*."

"*Ya*, and we have to keep our word, or Richard will make us sign a contract." She chuckled, then looked over at the pasture. Zeb had let the horses out earlier, and Job, the spirited colt he had trained when he and his brother were first starting the farm, was now a handsome, full-grown steed who took off to run around the corral.

Then she thought she saw something in the distance, behind the pasture. She squinted. Her eyes weren't as good as they used to be. Probably time to see the eye doctor for a checkup.

"Hey," Delilah said, poking Cevilla in the arm.

"Ow!" Cevilla rubbed the sore spot above her elbow. "Keep those pointy fingers to yourself."

"Look. Do you see what I see?"

Cevilla squinted again, then smiled. "Katharine and Ezra."

"Ezra and Katharine." Delilah giggled. "Coming out of the woods by themselves. Hmm."

Cevilla turned to Delilah, her expression stern. "Now, this might not mean anything," she said.

"Or it might mean something." Delilah's grin spread over her wide face. "It might mean we were right."

They didn't speak as they saw the two young people walking toward them. Cevilla scrutinized their body language, as she knew Delilah was also doing. They weren't walking too close, but they also weren't separate either. As they neared she could see their facial expressions and even a smile on Katharine's face.

"They look happy." Delilah sat back in the chair and nodded, obviously satisfied. "And just think, all it took was one day together for the magic to happen."

Cevilla was more reticent, but she couldn't deny that they did seem comfortable around each other, in contrast to their uneasiness last night.

When they reached the patio, Ezra said, "Did we miss lunch?"

Delilah giggled.

Cevilla banged her cane against the woman's chair again. "Almost. There are a few sandwiches left inside."

"*Danki*." Ezra paused and let Katharine walk in front of him as they went inside the kitchen.

"Oh, this is so wonderful." Delilah clapped her hands together. "I haven't been this excited since Nina's wedding. *Nee*, wait. Since Nathan was born."

"Now don't put the buggy before the horse. They're just having lunch together." But she was dying of curiosity about the two of them. Last night they had barely spoken to each other, and now they had been in the woods, or maybe in Amanda's secret garden, the worst-kept secret in Birch Creek.

The back kitchen door opened and Ezra came out, holding it for Katharine as she carried their plates.

"Aren't they cute," Delilah whispered.

"Shh." Cevilla shot her a warning look, then said to Katharine, "Did you two find enough to eat?"

"*Ya*. There was plenty, like you said." She smiled, then the two of them walked to an empty table. Katharine sat down first and Ezra beside her.

Now they were catching the attention of more than just her and Delilah. She saw Selah, Nina, and Margaret standing by the watercooler, casting furtive glances at the two of them, who seemed oblivious as they talked and ate their lunch.

"I can't believe it."

Cevilla glanced at Charity, who had just come out of the kitchen.

"Him? With her?" Then she lifted her chin. "I'm sure they're just friends, that's all."

"Or are they?" Delilah directed a pointed look at the young woman. "They're sitting a little close for friends, don't you think?"

Charity scowled and walked away. Delilah and Cevilla burst into laughter.

"Now that was a flounce if I ever saw one," Delilah said, still chuckling.

Cevilla nodded. The girl needed some maturity, along with a course in manners, but Cevilla hoped that someday she would learn to follow the Golden Rule and treat others the way she wanted to be treated.

She went back to watching Ezra and Katharine. He handed

her a napkin and she wiped the corner of her mouth with it. What a nice young man. She said a quick prayer for God's will in their lives, regardless of what she and Delilah wanted. His plans always trumped theirs.

Chapter 16

Lester didn't want to give Jordan any credit, but the man was right—he did feel better after some hot chicken soup and crackers, courtesy of the one decent restaurant in Dixonville that fortunately served plain home cooking. He'd managed to eat half the soup, and thankfully Jordan hadn't forced him to finish off the rest. The detective also brought him some groceries, including an electrolyte drink the doctor had recommended. He had no clue how Jordan would have known about that. Even though he hadn't scheduled a follow-up appointment with Dr. Chen, she had sent nutritional information to him in the mail. He'd glanced at the pamphlet before throwing it in the trash.

"How's the soup?"

Lester took one last spoonful while Jordan polished off a meatloaf sandwich. Oh, Rhoda used to make a good meatloaf sandwich, and Lester hadn't had one since he left Birch Creek. He doubted any cook could compare with her. "Soup's decent."

"Make sure you finish that drink."

"Why?"

Jordan wiped his mouth with a paper napkin. "Because you have cancer."

"You found that out too?"

"No. My dad died from lung cancer. I took care of him during his last weeks. I know the signs."

Sitting back in the chair, Lester said, "Pancreatic."

"Ouch." Sympathy entered Jordan's eyes. He had taken off his ball cap and had turned on the lamp, so now Lester could get a good look at him. His graying hair and lined forehead revealed Jordan was older than he had realized.

"I'm sorry, Emmanuel," Jordan said.

"Lester. My name's Lester." He paused, staring at his gnarled hands, the veins appearing to strain against his thinning skin. "Emmanuel's dead."

"When did he die?" Jordan asked, not skipping a beat.

"Nine years ago."

"When you left Birch Creek."

Lester nodded, memories washing over him again. That was the hardest part about dying, the irony of living with regrets. "Look, you did your good deed for the day. I'm tired and heading to bed."

"It's barely noon."

"You think I don't know what time it is?" He slumped in the chair, unable to remember the last time he kept decent hours. Long before he had seen Dr. Chen.

Jordan took a swig from a bottle of water. "You need to go back to Birch Creek."

Too weary to snap at him, he asked, "Why?"

"Because you need to make things right with your family."

Lester's eyes narrowed. "What do you know about it?"

"Not much, I admit." He got up from the edge of the bed and

opened the nutrition drink for him, then picked up the half-empty soup bowl and spoon and carried them to the small trash can on the opposite side of the room. "I've been in this business a long time, Emmanuel."

"Lester."

"Fifteen years at the LAPD, ten as a detective. I've seen a lot."

"Good for you." Lester tried to get up from the chair, but he was too tired from the assault of memories and this man's prattling.

"A lot of what I've seen is bad." He paused. "Really bad. But I've also witnessed some good, usually involving families reuniting." He put the trash in the plastic can, then sat back down. "Isn't that what's important to you Amish? Family?"

"I'm not Amish anymore. And like I said, my family is better off without me."

"How do you know that?"

"Because they were bad off with me." He'd never admitted that out loud, and he was surprised he'd done so in front of a complete stranger. Then again, this man didn't know all of his past, so admitting fault was easier than going through with his plan last year.

Whether it was guilt, curiosity, or God wearing him down, he'd shown up in Birch Creek, intending to make things right with Rhoda and the boys. He took a job at the Stolls' while he figured out how to talk to his family, and eventually the community he'd wronged. But he chickened out. His family and Birch Creek were flourishing without him. Sol and Aden were married and had families. And Rhoda . . . the sweet, loyal wife he had mistreated and taken for granted . . . She was falling for someone else. His boss, as a matter of fact. Yep, God had a sense of humor. So he left town, then wrote the letters, ready to mail them when the time was right. That time had come.

"You think they're better off without you," Jordan said, picking up the water bottle again.

I know they are. "Look," he said. "I don't know why you're poking your nose where it doesn't belong, but you need to leave me alone, and leave my fam—Leave Rhoda and Sol and Aden alone. Got it?"

"So you don't want to meet your grandchildren?"

He thought about Sol's two boys and Aden's girls. He'd dared to see each family only once, and that was when he had purchased honey from Aden and dropped off an order at Sol's shop for a set of birdhouses for the inn's backyard. His sons hadn't recognized him, fortunately. He had a full beard, dressed in English clothes, lowered his voice, and didn't make eye contact. Since both of them had businesses connected to their homes, he had seen their children. His grandchildren. Even now he could remember the spark they lit in his dead heart. One that fizzled out at the first sign of cowardice.

Jordan got up. "Think about it at least. I can drive you to Birch Creek if you need me to. And by the looks of it, you need me to."

Lester lifted his head and met the man's gaze. "I don't need nothin'."

"I'll be back in the morning to check on you."

"Don't bother."

"See you then. Don't make me knock on the door so long either. That tends to draw people's attention." Jordan opened the door and walked out.

Lester leaned his head back and closed his eyes. He hadn't been on good terms with the Lord for a long time, longer than he realized. He had prided himself in being close to God when he was bishop, so close that no one else had such a direct line to the Lord. Now look at him. He'd lost everything—all the money he had hoarded and thought was so important. His wife and sons, and now their families. His position in the community. His faith. For a brief moment last year he thought he could somehow get that back. And now there was no point. He would die alone. A fitting end to a man who had done so many evil things in his life.

What about redemption? Forgiveness? Mercy?

He opened his eyes. He had never offered those things to anyone else. Another reason, among many, why he didn't deserve them.

But what if? What if Jordan was giving him the final opportunity to see his family again? An opportunity he would throw away because he was too spineless to admit he was wrong.

Could he turn that down? Should he?

Jordan went back to his room and plopped down on the bed. As far as motels went, he'd been in worse. A lot worse. But Pauline, who ran the place with her husband, was friendly enough. And unlike Emmanuel's, his room was clean.

There wasn't much to do for the next few hours until he checked on Emmanuel again. Dixonville was so small it didn't even have a stoplight, and he'd already eaten lunch, so he stretched out on the bed, turned the TV on to a college basketball game, and closed his eyes. He wasn't as tired as Emmanuel, but he was pretty beat.

Just as he drifted off, his phone buzzed. He grabbed it off the bedside table and looked at the screen. Rhoda Troyer? She was the last person he expected to hear from. "Hi, Rhoda," he answered.

"Um, hello, Jordan."

He waited for her to say something else. Or ask a question. When she didn't, he said, "Everything okay?"

"Yes."

Although he was an expert at detecting a lie, he didn't need to be to know her answer wasn't honest. "Was there a reason you called?"

"I know I usually wait for you to call me," she said, her voice almost a whisper. "But I wondered if you have found out anything yet?"

Jordan sat up, shifting his legs off the bed. He wasn't sure how to answer her. Normally he was up-front with all his clients, even when the news wasn't what they wanted to hear. But he hesitated this time. While Emmanuel was digging in his heels about going back to Birch Creek, Jordan had seen the doubt in his eyes. That convinced him he needed to keep persuading him, for a little while at least. That meant lying to Rhoda and her family, though. He rubbed his temple.

"Mr. Powell?"

"Ah, not yet." He winced.

"Oh. Okay."

"But I'm still searching. I promise you that."

"I know you are. You've been very faithful and kind to our family. Thank you for all the work you've done."

Jordan scrubbed his hand over his face. She couldn't have known how her words piled on the guilt. "I'll be in touch soon." Finally, something true.

"Goodbye," she said.

He ended the call and tossed his phone on the bed. Great. He'd just lied to one of the nicest people he'd ever worked for, and in the end it could be for nothing. He couldn't take the words back now. All he could do was try harder to convince Emmanuel to do the right thing and go back to Birch Creek.

The moment Ezra returned home from church and walked into his house, he was greeted by Jesse and Malachi.

"You and Katharine, huh?" Jesse said, lounging on one of the two sofas in the Bontragers' large living room. "Wouldn't have called that one in a million years."

Malachi smirked. He was seated at the opposite end of the couch, his bright-blond hair pressed against his head from the black hat he wore to church. He grabbed a handful of caramel popcorn from the bowl on the coffee table, then settled back against the sofa, an annoying grin still plastered on his face.

Ezra shot them both a warning glare. "Don't you two have anything better to do?"

"Other than talk about you and your new girlfriend?" Jesse shrugged. "Nope."

He blew out a long breath as Malachi munched the popcorn and Jesse grinned like a fool. He should have expected this—from both of them. Malachi was a fixture at their house when he wasn't working for Aden or on his father and uncle's joint farm. "You're both almost sixteen," he said, putting his hat on the long rack near the front door where the rest of the Bontrager males kept their church hats. "Aren't you too old for this kind of thing?"

"What kind of thing?" Malachi asked, his light-blue eyes wide with feigned innocence. "We're just keeping up on current events."

"Being nosy is more like it." His good mood was starting to evaporate. He wasn't surprised, though. Jesse in particular seemed to relish getting under his brothers' skin, and Ezra knew he wouldn't be spared. "Just wait," he said.

Both Jesse's and Malachi's expressions turned serious. "Wait for what?"

"Your turn."

Jesse scoffed. "To have a girlfriend? Joke's on you. I ain't getting married."

"Me neither," Malachi said, but he was frowning a little. "Not for a long, long time anyway."

Jesse sat straight up. "That's not what you said before. You said you were never getting married. That girls are too much trouble. Which they are."

Malachi glanced down at his fingers, covered with sticky caramel. His cheeks reddened and he grabbed another fistful of popcorn and shoved it into his mouth.

Ezra laughed and went upstairs to change clothes. Seemed Malachi might be another Birch Creek male to fall victim to the bachelor advertisement. No, victim wasn't the right word. If it wasn't for the advertisement, Katharine wouldn't be here.

His mother came out of the bathroom at the end of the hallway. "Oh, hi, Ezra. I didn't expect you home so soon. I put some fresh soap I bought from Schrock's the other day in the bathroom. Don't worry, it's not a girly scent. Just plain."

"*Danki*." He didn't care what the soap smelled like, but one or more of his brothers must have complained. The Bontrager boys who still lived at home all shared the upstairs bedrooms, and the youngest ones were three to a room. He headed for the bedroom he shared with Owen to change out of his church clothes.

"Do you have a few minutes, Ezra?" his mother asked as they met in the middle of the hallway.

"Sure. What's up?"

"You and I haven't had much of an opportunity to talk lately," she said. "I wondered how your job is going at the Stolls'."

"*Gut*. In fact, it's going great."

She smiled. "Wonderful. I know your *daed* misses working with you on the farm. Even though you do chores when you come home, it's not the same as having you here all day. But he'll be glad to find out you're content working at the inn."

"Does he need me to come back?"

"*Nee*, not at all."

Whew. If his father needed him to work the farm, Ezra would, of course, quit his job at the inn. But he wouldn't be happy about it. He enjoyed being a handyman, and he was learning about running an inn from Levi and Loren. He wasn't interested in running one himself but being a handyman and landscaper definitely suited him. Then there was Katharine. If he went back to farming, he wouldn't see her every day, and he didn't like the idea of that at all.

"Ezra?"

He blinked and looked at his mother. "*Ya*?"

"You checked out for a minute. Is there something on your mind?"

"Katharine," Jesse said, coming up behind them. He gave Ezra a mocking grin, then moved past the two of them and went into the bathroom.

Mamm lifted a brow. "Katharine?"

He was about to tell her Jesse was wrong, then realized that maybe he did need his mother's advice. "Can we talk privately somewhere?" he whispered. Something that was difficult to do in a house full of busy—and nosy—young men.

"I know just the place."

Ezra followed his mother down the stairs, through the kitchen, and into the basement. They walked past two wringer washers, a pile of laundry baskets, and a shelving unit filled with laundry supplies. They stopped in front of a door that to his knowledge had always been locked.

Mamm stood on tiptoe and felt around on the top of the doorframe. Ezra was about to help her when she said, "There it is." She showed him the key, then unlocked the door. "Don't tell your *bruders* about this."

"I won't." He followed her into a small room. She turned on a battery-operated lamp and it filled the room with light.

"Welcome to *mei* prayer room." *Mamm* smiled and gestured to a short bench opposite a hickory rocking chair. One of his grandmother's quilts was draped over the back of the chair, and two light-purple pillows decorated the bench. "*Yer vatter* built it for me while he was building this *haus*. When we lived in Fredricktown, I'd always wished for a place to *geh* and pray alone. He remembered that and made sure I had *mei* own little room."

Ezra sat down, taking in the rest of the space. While the decor wasn't fancy by any means, there were more feminine touches here than in the rest of the house. A wooden calendar with flower designs hung on the wall, a light-blue lampshade covered with tiny birds hung over the lamp, and a colorful rag rug lay in the center of the floor. "Nice," he said as she sat in the rocking chair. "You and *Daed* did a *gut* job hiding it from us *kinner*."

"That was the point." She picked up a wicker basket from the floor next to her chair and held it out to him. "Would you like a snack? I have some bottled water here too."

He glanced at the basket and for a moment he wondered if Katharine had made the container. But the wicker reeds were faded, revealing that the basket had to be more than a few years old. Inside were mini-sized candy bars, foil-wrapped chocolate drops, and a few pieces of hard candy. Never one to turn down food, he took a peanut butter cup.

Mamm selected a chocolate drop, and they both unwrapped their candies. "Now, tell me what's going on with you and Katharine," she said, before popping the chocolate in her mouth.

He grimaced. Even the sweet peanuty flavor of the candy didn't placate his annoyance with his brother. "Jesse needs to mind his own business."

"*Ya*, he does. Unfortunately he's too hardheaded to get the message." She sighed and leaned back in the chair. "I could ground him again."

"Don't bother. One day he'll get his due for teasing all of us."

"Probably." She paused. "Is he right, though? Is there something going on between you and Katharine?"

"I don't know." He smoothed out the peanut butter cup wrapper. "I had *mei* mind set on being single for a *gut* long while. Now . . . I'm not so sure."

"That's how it works sometimes. It's how it's worked for all *mei sohns*, so far anyway."

"Was it that way with you and *Daed*?"

"*Nee*. We both knew we wanted to get married. Once we started dating, there wasn't a doubt." She paused briefly. "Do you like her?"

"*Ya*. I do. But I don't think she's interested in me."

"Ah. That's a problem then."

He shifted on the bench and leaned against one of the pillows. "I'm not sure what to do."

"I have a little advice, if you're open to it." At his nod, she added, "Be patient."

"Easier said than done."

"I'm sure it is. You jumped too quickly into a relationship with Gloria, didn't you?"

Ezra stared at her. "How did you know about Gloria?"

"A *mutter* has her ways. That, and I overheard the two of you on the front porch when she broke up with you."

"You were eavesdropping?"

"Of course not." She reached into the basket for another chocolate drop. "I didn't even know she had stopped by. I had gone into the living room to get the most recent issue of *Taste of Home*. I'd left it on the table next to *mei* chair and I wanted to try one of the lunch recipes I saw. She's not exactly a quiet *maedel*, is she?"

"*Nee*," he muttered. Unbelievable. His mother had witnessed the most humiliating moment of his life. And one of the most hurtful.

"I could tell after she left that you were upset." Her tone turned gentle. "You moped about for more than two weeks afterward, so I knew you were serious about her."

"She ended up being all wrong for me." He winced. "Are you saying I can't trust *mei* own judgment?"

"I'm not saying that at all. But if you had gotten to know Gloria better before getting serious with her, you might have found out about her other boyfriend sooner. What I am saying is that you should get to know Katharine. Be sure about your feelings for her, and how she feels about you, before you jump into anything."

Mamm was right, of course. He wasn't exactly a patient person. He'd have to pray for God to help him become one. "*Danki*, *Mamm*," he said. "I'll take your advice."

"You're welcome. I'm glad you talked to me about this, and I'm happy I was helpful."

Ezra stood. "I better change out of these clothes," he said. He started for the door, but she didn't move.

"I think I'll stay here for a little while."

"All right. Fair warning, though. Now I know where you keep your candy stash," he teased. "And your key."

She laughed. "But you won't know where I'll hide that key after today, though."

Chuckling, he left the basement and went to his room. Jesse and Malachi were nowhere to be found, thank goodness. He took off his black pants and vest and his white shirt, and hung all three of them up to wear to the service Sunday after next, then slipped into a short-sleeved yellow shirt and clean pants. Then he stretched out on his bed and put his hands behind his head. He could be patient when it came to Katharine. And if it turned out that she would never be interested in him romantically, he would have to accept that. Either way, they would be friends. That was something he was sure of.

Chapter 17

"I'm glad to see you have your appetite back."

Katharine paused, a spoonful of macaroni salad hovering over her plate. When she returned home from lunch, she went straight to her bedroom and changed out of her baggy church dress, then laid down on her bed, intending to take a nap. But she couldn't fall asleep, and for once it wasn't because she was upset or angry or sad. She was happy. Happy enough to fill her plate with food at suppertime without a second thought. "The macaroni salad is *gut*," she said, then polished off the bite. Delicious. She couldn't remember the last time she'd enjoyed a meal without second-guessing the calories or worrying that people were watching and judging her portions. *Thank you, Ezra.*

"It's the same recipe I make every month." Delilah sat down next to her. "So are the chicken turnovers, sweet pickles, and cream cheese pudding. You never ate much of those before." She peered over her silver-framed glasses, a sparkle in her eyes. "What's different about today?"

She took a bite of the turnovers. They were delicious fresh out of the oven and smothered with chicken gravy, but they were also scrumptious cold. "*Nix*."

"*Nix*, you say." Delilah picked up the platter of turnovers and put one on her plate. Loren had eaten earlier and was out taking an evening walk. She arched one eyebrow. "I've never seen you look this cheerful before."

She hadn't been, not since her arrival in Birch Creek, or through most of her relationship with Simeon.

"Could that cheeriness have something to do with Ezra?" Delilah winked, then scooped some macaroni salad onto her plate.

It had everything to do with Ezra, but Katharine wasn't going to admit that to Delilah. As it was, she didn't miss her and Cevilla whispering about the two of them as they ate lunch, or that there were a few other people who had given them questioning looks. That was hard to ignore, and initially she was uncomfortable. But Ezra didn't seem bothered at all, and soon they were discussing their favorite types of pie—his raspberry, hers lemon meringue. Before she knew it, she had eaten all her lunch. Her stomach was full, and so was her heart. Not in a romantic way, of course. But his companionship had fed her emptiness in more ways than one.

Delilah sighed. "All right. I won't be nosy. I'm just glad you're eating. I've been worried about you."

Katharine knew that already, having seen the concern in her eyes during mealtimes. "You don't have to worry," she said, meeting Delilah's gaze. "I'm fine." She hadn't been, but she was now. How long that would last, she didn't know, but she would enjoy the peace as long as she could.

"As long as you keep eating, you will be."

Katharine frowned. "I still have weight to lose, Delilah."

"Pshaw." She waved her hand. "How much have you lost so far?"

"Almost fifty."

"That's plenty."

"I have thirty more to *geh*."

Worry crept back into Delilah's expression. "I understand your desire to lose weight. But starving yourself isn't the answer."

Katharine stared at the remaining half of the chicken turnover. "It's the fastest way."

"It's a dangerous way." Delilah exhaled. "I know from experience."

Her head jerked up. "You do?"

"Believe it or not, there was a short time in *mei* life when I was thin. Too thin, actually."

"I didn't think there was such a thing." She pushed her plate away.

"Of course there is. And being thin isn't going to make you happy. Carrying extra weight isn't healthy, but neither is making yourself sick to be a certain size. Before I married *mei* Wayne, I was in love with Cornelius King. When I found out he didn't love me back, I thought it was because of *mei* weight. So I went on a restrictive diet and lost twenty-five pounds in less than a month. That would show Corny, I foolishly thought."

"Did it?"

"*Nee*. He left the Amish, married an English *maedel* and moved to Minnesota. Turns out our breakup had *nix* to do with *mei* weight. Soon after, I started dating Wayne, and those twenty-five pounds came right back on."

"Was he angry with you about that?"

"Angry?" Delilah's brow furrowed. "*Nee*. I was, though. But then I realized I was being even more foolish. Wayne loved me, and I loved him. I was letting something superficial get in the way of our happiness. I gained a little more weight when I had Loren, and then over the years the scale went up and down. But my happiness was constant, and that's what mattered."

Katharine nodded. Her mother had never said anything to her about her weight, even during the time she'd rapidly gained. Then again, she had been busy taking care of *Daed*. Maybe not too busy to notice, but too tired to talk to her adult daughter about such a sensitive topic. Katharine didn't blame her. After her father's accident, taking care of him was a full-time job, and she helped out as much as she could, until she and Simeon started dating, something her mother and father had both encouraged.

"Katharine," Delilah said, patting her hand, "you're an adult, and I'm not your mother. I've tried to respect your privacy since you moved in with us. Trust me, that isn't easy for me to do."

"I know," she said, smiling a little. "And I appreciate it."

"But I do care for you. In fact, I've come to see you as one of *mei* own. I want you to be healthy and happy as much as I do *mei* own *sohns* and *grosskinner*."

A lump appeared in Katharine's throat.

"And truth be told, I could lose a few pounds. So if you still want to lose weight, maybe we can do it together, the healthy way."

Katharine's heart melted. "I'd like that," she said, her voice thick.

"So I'll pass on the cream cheese pudding today." Delilah pushed the square pan of pudding to the opposite side of the table. "And tomorrow morning I'll make—ugh—plain oatmeal with fruit for the both of us. We can also start on some new dresses for you tomorrow evening if you'd like."

"I would like that very much." Katharine took Delilah's hand and squeezed it. "*Danki*. For everything."

"Any time, sweetie." Delilah patted their clasped hands. "Any time."

Almost two weeks after Jordan arrived in Dixonville, he was at the end of his rope with Emmanuel. "I thought my dad was stubborn," he said, placing a bowl of tomato soup and crackers he'd picked up at the diner on the table in Emmanuel's hotel room. After he explained to Pauline that he had befriended the man and was taking care of him while he was sick, she gave him an extra key. "I'm worried about him," she said. "Last time I saw him, he wasn't looking too good."

Jordan was worried about him too. He seemed to have declined in the past week, despite Jordan making sure that he had plenty of nutritious food during the day and enough water to drink. He even sat with Emmanuel while he took naps in his chair in front of the TV. Always the western channel, Jordan noticed. Maybe there was something about seeing horses, ranches, and farmland that made him think of home.

When he wasn't nagging Emmanuel to eat and drink, he was pestering him about making things right with his family. Emmanuel called it pestering, but Jordan viewed it as urgent, yet gentle persuasion. It didn't matter what either one of them called it, it wasn't working. Whatever strength Emmanuel Troyer had left in his frail body, he spent all of it digging in his heels.

By the middle of the second week, Jordan knew he had failed. "Here's your soup," he said, then plopped down on the bed.

"Not hungry." He stared at the TV in front of him.

"You have to eat."

"Humph." The remote ever at the ready, Emmanuel turned up the volume.

Jordan slumped. "I can't stay here forever," he said. "At some point I have to go back to LA."

"No one's stopping you."

Emmanuel was right. The only person keeping Jordan in Dixonville was Jordan. He stared out the window at the gravel parking lot. The only car other than his and Emmanuel's beat-up sedan was an old truck that belonged to Pauline and her husband. Later on in the day there would be more cars as a few travelers showed up for an overnight stay. But the lot was never full. The old motel was almost as depressing as Emmanuel himself.

Jordan sighed, got up from the edge of the bed, and picked up the soup and crackers and took them to Emmanuel. Last week he'd bought a TV tray from the local discount store across the street and had set it next to Emmanuel's chair. He placed the soup, crackers, and a small bottle of water on the tray, along with a plastic spoon. "Eat," he ordered.

Emmanuel turned and looked up at him. His eyes were sunken, along with his cheeks, but neither masked his defiant expression. He narrowed his gaze, then shifted it back to the TV.

Running a hand through his hair, Jordan said, "This is your last chance, Emmanuel. Let me take you back to Birch Creek. We can be packed up and on the road in an hour."

No response.

"Fine. If this is how you want to exit this world, nursing your misery in a musty old motel room, that's your choice. I'm heading back to California in the morning."

"Don't let the door hit you on the way out."

Jordan stomped out of Emmanuel's room. Two weeks of his life wasted. He'd really thought he was doing a good thing by trying to help the old man, but now he realized he'd been spinning his wheels for nothing.

He threw open the door of his motel room and sat down on the chair. Stared at the same view out of his window as he had at Emmanuel's. Then dug his phone out of his jeans pocket and called Rhoda Troyer. She answered on the third ring.

"Hello?"

"Hi, Rhoda. It's Jordan."

"Hi, Jordan." There was a brief silence on the other end of the line as he knew Rhoda waited expectantly for his update. He only called with news—bad or good. "Have you found something?"

"Yes, I did. Rhoda, I'll cut to the chase. I found Emmanuel."

She sucked in a breath. "And?"

"The letters were real. He's gone."

"Oh." He waited for the words to sink in. It took longer than he expected, but she finally said, "Thank you for letting me know. How much do I owe you?"

"Nothing," he muttered. "I wish I had better news, but I don't."

"It's all right," she said.

Funny, she was comforting him, when the roles should have been reversed.

"Please send me a bill," she added. "I will pay you for your work."

If he refused her, she would keep insisting. He could use the money too. "Okay, I'll send it along soon." He inwardly sighed. "I really am sorry, Rhoda."

"Thank you, Jordan. I appreciate everything you've done."

When they hung up, he tossed his phone on the table. He'd lied to clients in the past before, but only on rare occasions when he thought it was crucial to spare their feelings. Lying to Rhoda didn't feel right, but he had no other choice. What good would it do for her to know her husband was alive and refusing to come home? That he didn't want to make amends with his family before leaving this world? He'd promised her he would find out about Emmanuel one way or another. And at the rate he was going, within a week or two the old man would be dead anyway, and she'd never have to know about his final betrayal.

Heaviness settled over Jordan's chest, and he rubbed his forehead. Even telling himself he'd tried didn't help. But there was nothing else he could do. Emmanuel had made his decision. Jordan had no choice but to accept it.

Chapter 18

Rhoda checked her reflection in the bathroom mirror. A vain gesture, but she couldn't help herself. Loren and her sons were arriving soon, and her anxiety was growing with every passing minute. Last week during one of his evening visits, he had asked her to prepare supper for him, Sol, and Aden. Not only had she been surprised but also excited. The four of them had never shared a meal together.

Three weeks had passed since Jordan's call about Emmanuel's death. Numb, she had placed the phone in its cradle and walked back to the house. She supposed in her heart she'd known Emmanuel was gone. But when Jordan validated it, she felt a strange mix of grief and relief. When Aden came by to check on her, as he had every evening since the letters arrived, she told him about Jordan's phone call. Over the next week, she and her sons had met with Freemont, who decided a short, quiet memorial was appropriate. That occurred Sunday before last, and afterward, Loren took her home. He had come over every evening since.

She touched one of the clips securing her *kapp*. Was Loren

going to propose? She couldn't help but think he might, but she also didn't want to assume anything. The thought made her smile. Although she rarely examined her face in the mirror, tonight she noticed the sparkle in her eyes, the absence of tension around her mouth and forehead. Of course she had wrinkles, but for once those were due to age and not stress. Over the past three weeks she had mourned Emmanuel's death, but she also experienced freedom like she had never felt before, along with a little guilt that she'd gotten over him so quickly. Then again, she had mourned Emmanuel for years.

She shook her head and left the bathroom. This wasn't the time to think about him, or anything else other than her sons and Loren, along with making sure tonight's meal was as perfect as it could be. She made her sons' favorite dishes—chuck roast with potatoes and carrots for Sol and baked corn for Aden. Broccoli salad and fresh rolls rounded out the meal, and for dessert she made a recipe Naomi Beiler had given her for peanut butter torte. The roast, rolls, and corn were warming in the oven, and she gave the broccoli salad a quick stir and then put it on the table. Standing back, she checked the place settings and made sure she hadn't forgotten anything.

A knock sounded at the door, making her jump. She put her hand over her heart and let out a deep breath before walking to the back kitchen door. She opened it, and Loren stood there, a simple bouquet of wildflowers in his hand.

"Hi, Rhoda."

His smile spurred butterflies in her stomach. "Hi, Loren. Please come in."

He walked into the kitchen and turned to her. "These are for you. They're from the wildflower garden Selah planted last year."

She had no idea what the names of the yellow, purple, and

dark-red blooms were, but they were perfect. "They're lovely. I'll put them in some water."

"Mind if I put up my hat?"

Rhoda turned away from the cabinet she had just opened and looked at him. Normally he set his hat on the table. "There's a tree in the living room near the door," she said, then she faced the cabinet of glassware again. "You can hang your hat on one of the hooks."

He nodded and left the room.

She paused, staring at the bouquet in her hand. He'd never brought her flowers before. Smiling, she found a small vase and filled it with water. Then she set the flowers inside and put the vase on the counter since there was no room on the tabletop.

Oddly enough, she suddenly thought about Katharine. She had prayed for the young woman every day since she left that evening after dropping off the peaches. She saw her and Ezra together after church the day after their talk. Were they courting after all? She touched a purple petal. She had no idea if they were, but if that was God's will, she hoped Katharine could put her past to rest and find happiness with the young man. The same happiness she had found with Loren.

Loren returned from the living room. "Something smells *appeditlich*," he said.

"I hope you like roast." She folded her hands and faced him.

"I enjoy anything you cook, Rhoda." He moved closer to her, enough that she could see a bit of uncharacteristic hesitancy in him. He glanced at the vase behind her. "Do you like the flowers?"

She'd already said she did. Her smile dimmed. "Are you all right, Loren?"

He started to nod, then stopped. "I'm a little nervous about tonight."

"Because of Sol and Aden?"

"*Ya*. And something else."

The butterflies increased. She didn't have the courage to ask him what that something else was.

At that moment, Aden and Sol arrived. Her sons greeted Loren and they sat down at the table and talked about their work while Rhoda brought out the food.

"Baked corn," Aden said after the prayer. He grinned. "*Danki*, *Mamm*."

"I'm ready to dig into the roast." Sol's words were light, but his expression wasn't. He wasn't as sullen as he had been when he first heard about his father's death, yet she could tell he still wasn't himself either.

As the men ate the meal and continued to discuss their jobs, she took small bites of the broccoli salad, her heart consumed with joy. So many suppers had been eaten in silence over the years at this table, and to hear her sons and Loren in easy conversation was a treat. When they had eaten almost all of the food she prepared, she said, "I'll clear the table. Anyone ready for dessert?"

Loren put his hand on Rhoda's arm. "Just a minute. I have something to say." He turned to Aden and Sol. "I know you two have been through a lot lately. Your *mutter* has too. And I thought that I might be rushing things a little. But I can't help what I feel in *mei* heart. Rhoda and I have been growing closer, as you probably already knew. What you don't know is that I love her." He cleared his throat. "And If it's all right with you, Aden and Sol, I want to ask your mother to marry me. I promise to cherish and take care of her, and to love her as Christ loves the church."

Rhoda held her breath as Loren's hand slipped into hers. This was unconventional for sure, and he was taking a risk by asking them in front of her. But when she saw Aden's happy expression, followed by Sol's quick nod, she relaxed.

"Now with that out of the way." Loren turned in his chair and faced her. "Rhoda, will you marry me?"

She squeezed Loren's hand with tears in her eyes—this time, happy ones. She never thought she would have a second chance like this. She didn't think she deserved one. But God, in his mercy and grace, saw fit to bring this man into her life, a man she loved to her very core. "*Ya*," she said, smiling. "*Ya*, Loren," she said, happy tears filling her eyes. "I can't wait to marry you."

"And that's all you have to do." Katharine pushed the round, incomplete basket in front of Ezra. They'd started the basket last week, but both of them were so busy with work at the inn, especially Ezra, that they hadn't had time to work on it.

"I just keep weaving the pieces in and out?" He arched a dubious brow at the basket. "Seems too easy."

"That's because it is." She smiled and sat back in her chair. As she watched him work on the basket, the familiar sense of peace came over her when they were together. In the three weeks since their talk in the garden, she had learned she could completely be herself around him. She didn't have to watch her words or worry about him blowing up in a rage over some perceived slight she had no idea about.

Things weren't totally conflict-free with them though. The other day they argued over whose job it was to fill the firebox next to the fireplace in the lobby. Katharine insisted it was hers, while Ezra wouldn't budge on the notion that it was his. They agreed to alternate weeks, and now that summer was approaching, the heated discussion was moot. But it meant everything to her that she could disagree with him without paying heavy consequences.

There was only one thing she was confused about—the status of their relationship. Thankfully, Charity had finally accepted that Ezra wasn't interested in her, and she had moved on to poor Judah Yoder. But with the exception of him holding her hand in the not-so-secret garden and sitting next to her while they ate lunch, he hadn't given any indication that they were anything more than friends. Which made her feel a little foolish, because lately she had been entertaining the idea that if things were different—or rather, if his feelings for her were—they actually could date. A far cry from the way she felt a mere month ago. Because of him, she no longer thought that men weren't to be trusted, at least the men who would want to be around her.

But she had to be realistic, and she would rather be friends with Ezra than not have any relationship at all.

"There." He stopped weaving and turned the basket around, inspecting his work. "What do you think?"

She leaned forward and eyed the finished row of weaving. "Not bad."

"Not bad?" He leaned close to her. "Take a gander at that perfect handiwork."

"You mean here?" She pointed to the end of a willow strip that was poking out from the tight weave. "This example of perfection?"

He laughed and looked at her. "*Ya*. That one."

She smiled. She couldn't help it when she was around Ezra. He made her experience so many wonderful feelings—safety, humor, and respect, among other things. Things she had always craved and had never gotten from her ex. She'd stopped thinking about him so often and was comparing him less and less to Ezra. The pain and the fear he'd caused weren't as acute or threatening as before.

"You did do a great job," she said, growing serious. "You can add this to the list of all your other talents."

"Which would be?" He smirked and leaned his elbow on the table, then rested the side of his head in his hand.

"A little prideful, aren't we?" She matched his smirk, then mimicked his position so they were both looking directly at each other.

"*Nee*, not prideful. Call it curiosity."

Knowing Ezra didn't have a prideful bone in his body, she pretended to have a difficult time coming up with a list. When she thought he'd waited long enough, she said, "You're a *gut* plumber."

His smirk disappeared. "Gee, *danki*."

She glanced up at the ceiling, keeping up the ruse. "And you're, uh . . ."

"Don't hurt yourself trying to think of something nice to say." But the twinkle in his eyes told her he wasn't put out. "Now it's *mei* turn."

"For what?"

"To give you *mei* list."

She sat up, glancing down at her lap. "I don't need a list."

"I know you don't need one." He sat up too, then moved a little closer to her. They were seated across from each other, only inches separating their knees from touching. "But I want to tell you the things I admire about you."

A warm feeling covered her heart as she lifted her gaze. "*Danki*," she said softly.

He frowned. "I haven't said anything yet."

"You said all you need to." Just knowing there were some things he liked about her was enough. She turned to pick up a few more willow pieces. "You can start on the second row now—"

He covered her hand with his, then took the willow and placed it back on the table, still holding her hand. "Here's what I like about you, Katharine Miller. You have a *gut* sense of humor. Sometimes it's even a little saucy."

"Oh." She hadn't realized that. "I'm sorry."

"Don't be." He leaned forward. "I like it."

Whoa. Her heartbeat was galloping so fast, she was sure he could hear it.

"You make beautiful baskets, and you're a *gut* teacher."

She squeezed his hand, drinking in his kind words as if they were water and she was dying of thirst.

His eyes darkened. "You're also beautiful."

She froze, and every pleasant emotion turned to ash. It wasn't true. Her weight loss had hit a plateau, mostly because she wasn't obsessed with every calorie anymore. Delilah had made more progress than she had, and this morning she was talking about making more dresses for herself after they finished Katharine's last new dress. Margaret's salve was still doing wonders, but she was far from a clear complexion.

Suddenly uncomfortable under his gaze, she tried to pull her hand from his . . . but he wouldn't let her go.

Ezra scrambled for patience, something that despite his nightly prayers had been more and more difficult to find when he was around Katharine. He'd taken his mother's advice and spent his time with Katharine getting to know her. Each day they spent their breaks together, and he discovered she was a great listener. They talked about his family, farming, weaving, problems at work, even Gloria. The one thing they didn't discuss was her past. A few times he had asked her about Montana, and she gave him ambiguous answers. Of course he wanted to know more, and he hoped he would, in time.

Everything he'd just told her was true. She was a talented weaver, and he liked that he could make her laugh. Like him, she took her job seriously, and if he couldn't see her due to his workload at the inn or when he had to help out at the farm, she always understood. She wasn't selfish, like Gloria, or immature like Charity. She was coming out of her shell, and he was privileged to witness her transformation.

He also thought they were making a connection, one that felt stronger than friendship. Until he told her she was beautiful. At that moment, she suddenly returned to the withdrawn woman she'd been when she arrived in Birch Creek.

Her fingers were stiff in his grasp, and he let go of her hand. *Patience, remember?*

"I-I should *geh* back to the inn." She pushed back from the table and stood up.

He didn't want her to leave, especially when she was upset. What could he say that would convince her to stay? "Kiss me," he blurted.

She whirled around, her jaw going slack. "What?"

Where had those words come from? That was an easy question to answer. He'd been thinking about kissing her for days, and now that he'd asked her, he needed to see it through. He got up from his chair and went to her. "Kiss me," he repeated.

"Is this a joke?"

Ezra shook his head. "Absolutely not."

Her bottom lip trembled as she looked up at him. "You . . . You want me to kiss you?"

"I do."

"Here. In the barn."

His gaze dropped to her mouth, and it took everything he had not to jump ahead and kiss her first. "*Ya*," he whispered.

"Why?"

"Because I want you to."

She swallowed. "I-I've never kissed anyone before."

"Neither have I."

"You seem to know what you're doing."

"Trust me, I'm winging it."

A tiny smile appeared, and her shoulders relaxed. She met his gaze again, and he was glad to see the apprehension in her eyes disappearing.

"Do you want to kiss me?" he asked, not wanting her to feel pressured in any way. He held his breath, waiting for her to answer.

Finally, she nodded.

He took her hand, held it for a second, then lightly placed it on his waist. Then he took one step forward.

She looked at her hand but didn't move it. Then she took one step forward.

Ezra's heart thumped in his chest as he touched her chin. Without coaxing, she lifted her face to his.

He smiled.

She smiled.

Snort!

They jumped apart. Bob—or was it Brad?—let out several snorts and whinnies behind them.

"It's just the horse," he said, trying to catch his breath.

"Right. The horse." She was breathing hard too.

"Shall we try this again?" he asked. *Please say yes.*

She nodded slowly. She put her hand back on his waist, stood on her tiptoes, and kissed him.

"Katharine?" Delilah called from the front of the barn.

No!

She yanked her mouth from his. Quickly he grabbed the basket, and they both pretended to be engrossed in weaving.

"There you are." Delilah appeared, then stopped. A wry grin formed on her face. "I didn't mean to interrupt you two."

"We're just working," he said, moving his fingers over the still-damp weaving.

"Making a basket," Katharine added, not looking at Delilah.

"You might want to actually use some of those willow strips, Ezra," Delilah pointed out with a smirk.

Only then did he notice his hands were empty. When he saw the old woman's knowing expression, he realized they were caught. He glanced at Katharine. Her cheeks were the color of tart cherries, but he noticed her tiny smile too.

Chapter 19

Elsie read Katharine's latest letter on her way back from the mailbox as she waddled up the driveway. While this pregnancy was going as smooth as her first one, the baby had grown exponentially over the last week. If she wasn't having another boy, then she was definitely having a big girl.

When she finished the letter, she folded the sheet of paper and smiled. For Katharine's safety, their letters were few and far apart. Unlike her other ones, this note was bright and cheery. The way Elsie had always assumed her friend really was on the inside, something she had caught glimpses of every once in a while. Although the missive was similar to her other letters in keeping to mundane details of everyday life in Birch Creek, she had mentioned her excitement at selling her new baskets not only at the inn but also at Schrock's Grocery. One line in particular was telling:

> The mornings here are so wonderful. The lovely sunrises greet me with brand new sunshine, and I'm eager to start another new day.

As she went inside the house, Elsie wondered at the change and made a mental note to ask Katharine in her next letter if something new had happened in her life recently. Jason was taking his nap, and as she headed to her bedroom to put the letter in the box with the other ones Katharine had sent her, she paused in the hallway, then put her hand over the side of her extended stomach where the baby had kicked her. "Be patient," she said softly. "You'll be arriving in two or three weeks."

"What's in your hand?"

She turned at the sound of her husband's uncharacteristically suspicious tone. "Galen," she said, quickly tucking the letter into her apron pocket. "You're home early today."

"Answer *mei* question."

"I don't have anything." She held out both hands, trying to keep the alarm at bay. She hated lying to her husband, but she had to protect Katharine.

His brow flattened over angry eyes. "Then what's in your pocket?"

Dread filled her. "A letter," she said, showing him the folded piece of paper.

"Why didn't you tell me that before?"

"I—"

He grabbed it out of her hand and started reading. By the time he finished, he was furious. "You know where Katharine is?"

"*Ya*," she said, fighting for an even tone. "You do too. She's in Montana, the same place she's been since she left last year."

"Then why is she talking about Birch Creek? You told me she was in West Kootenai." Before she answered he stalked off to their bedroom. She followed him, only to see him pull out the box of letters from under the bed.

"You've been lying to me." He flipped the lid open and dumped the letters on the bed. "All these are from Katharine. Not one mention of Montana, or West Kootenai, or a new boyfriend." He picked up one of the envelopes. "The postmark is from Ohio."

Instinctively she put her hands on her stomach. She knew in her heart Galen would never hurt her or the baby, but he was angrier than she'd ever seen him. "How did you find those?"

"Jason crawled under the bed this morning while you were fixing breakfast. He pushed out the box and dumped it on its side. When I picked up the letters . . ." He dropped onto the bed, putting his back to her. His shoulders dipped. "I don't understand, Elsie. I don't understand."

She hurried to his side, shoving the box and letters away so she could sit next to him. "I'm sorry," she said, reaching for his hand and not surprised when he yanked it away. "I couldn't tell you the truth."

"That Katharine decided to up and leave her home out of the blue? That she ran away from Simeon and lied to him about it?" Galen turned to her, pain etched on his face. "Her parents were devastated when they learned she had moved away and found someone else. So was Simeon."

Right, that's why he fought so hard to win her back, Elsie almost scoffed, but she held it in. Now was not the time to show her contempt for Galen's best friend. But she had to tell him at least part of the truth. "He was abusing her," she said, her voice stronger now. "She had to leave. If she didn't, her life would have been in danger."

He gaped at her, confusion battling the anger in his eyes. "How do you know?"

"I confronted her and she finally told me. Right before she left for Mon—Ohio."

Galen shook his head. "I can't believe Simeon would be abusive. He loves Katharine."

"You never wondered about the bruises on her arms?"

"What bruises?" he said, frowning.

"The ones she tried to cover up with long sleeves on hot summer days. Or the cut on her lip the last time she was here?"

He stilled. "I never noticed either of those things." His jaw jerked.

"Galen, please. Listen to me. I've never been dishonest with you except for this. And I had to be, to save Katharine."

He looked at her. "I . . . I don't know what to believe. I've known Simeon since we were teenagers. He's always been honest with me. This doesn't make any sense."

Jason began crying, awake from his nap.

Galen grabbed Katharine's last letter off the bed and headed for the door.

"Where are you going?" she asked, following him out of the bedroom to the living room.

"To talk to Simeon."

"Galen, don't," she pleaded, their son's cries growing louder. "You're putting Katharine in danger!"

He paused in the doorway, as if having second thoughts. Then he turned around and left.

Elsie ran to Jason's bedroom. He was standing in his crib, and if she didn't get him soon, he would climb out. She picked him up and he immediately stopped crying, leaning his hot cheek against her shoulder. Fighting to stem her panic, she tried to figure out her next move. She didn't know Katharine's address, only the post office box to send her letters. She couldn't even call her on the phone. *What am I going to do, Lord?*

She sat down on the rocking chair and tried not to cry. Her son didn't need to be upset too. All she could do was pray that either Galen would change his mind about talking to Simeon, or Simeon had gotten over Katharine enough that he wouldn't try to find her in Ohio or tell her parents where she was. He had ingratiated himself with them so much it was clear to everyone that they considered him part of their family. Elsie seemed to be the only one who could tell he was up to no good. Why, she had no idea. Once Galen calmed down, maybe he could find out. Then again, aside from her and Jason, he was more loyal to Simeon than to anyone else.

She wasn't afraid for herself. She and her husband would work through this, and hopefully she would be able to convince him that Simeon was no good and that Katharine was safer and better off in Birch Creek than she would ever be in Hulett.

Emmanuel lifted up the small water bottle with a shaky hand and took a sip. The TV blared in front of him. Ever since Jordan left three weeks ago, he never turned it off. The noise drowned out his thoughts, his memories, and when he was having a good day, his pain.

A knock sounded at the door, and before he could say anything, Pauline came in carrying a box of food. Although she never said so, he assumed Jordan told her about his condition before heading back to LA, because three times a day without fail, Pauline checked on him, brought him groceries, and made sure he ate and drank. Unlike Jordan, though, she was as strict as a warden. Apropos, considering his motel room had become a prison cell of sorts.

"Breakfast time!" She set the box on the table and pushed open the drapes. Then she walked over to him and said, "Get up."

"I like sitting here."

"I know you do, but your food is on the table." She grabbed the remote and shut off the TV. "Or do I need to lift you out of that chair like I did the other day."

"I'm getting up." He put his hands on the arms of the chair and somehow got to a standing position. He wasn't in as much pain as he expected, and that had been true since Pauline took over his care. He wouldn't be surprised if she was spiking his water with pain relievers.

"There you go." She walked beside him in case he fell. "I wish you'd use that cane I gave you."

"Don't need a cane to walk four steps." It was more than four, but he still didn't need the cane. The bathroom wasn't more than five steps away either. He still had the strength to wash up, and Pauline had insisted Jeb help him with a shower twice a week. Of course Emmanuel refused, but Jeb was even more obstinate than his wife.

"Pancakes, bacon, coffee, and a fruit cup." She put the food in front of him, then brought out a second plate and set it on the table before sitting down. "Bless the breakfast, please."

Emmanuel rolled his eyes. "God is great, God is good, let us thank him for our food. Amen," he said quickly.

They ate in silence, Emmanuel eating at least half of the pancakes and all of the fruit cup, but balking at the bacon. He should be dead by now, or at least bedridden, but he wasn't. Lately he'd been feeling stronger, and the only thing he could chalk it up to was Pauline and Jeb's care.

"Did you have a good night?" she asked after they finished their meals. She never talked during the meal, and he figured that was her way of making sure neither of them got distracted.

"Good enough."

"How many hours did you sleep?"

He pushed away his plate. "Didn't count."

"You're spunky today, so it must have been enough." She sipped her coffee. "You've got more color in your cheeks. Maybe you should go back to the doctor again. Let her know how you're doing."

"Maybe you should mind your own business."

She laughed, her dangling green and yellow beaded earrings swaying against her jaw. "Now, Lester, you know I ain't gonna do that. Jeb and I are happy to take care of you, as long as you need us."

He got up from the table, walked to the chair and sat down, then turned on the TV.

She chuckled again and put the used paper plates and utensils back in the box. "Anything special you want for lunch?"

"Nope."

"Okay, liver and onions it is."

He blanched. "Soup would be good."

"Thought so." Pauline opened the door. The temperature outside was climbing, and the warmth entered the room. "If you're up for it I can set up a lawn chair outside the window and you can get some fresh air and sunshine."

He shrugged.

"See you at lunch." She shut the door behind her.

Emmanuel hung his head. Pauline and Jeb shouldn't be taking care of him. Jordan either. He should be able to take care of himself. He'd done so for the last nine years. Before that he'd taken care of the Birch Creek community. *And look how well that went.* Who was he fooling? He'd had no business being a bishop. He thought God had chosen him because of his excellent character, which he now realized he didn't have. What he did have was pride in spades, and he was starting to think that getting terminal cancer and dying in an old motel room was his final humbling.

Stagecoach was on TV this morning, and as a young John Wayne sauntered onto the screen, Emmanuel closed his eyes.

"Well, there are some things a man just can't run away from," Wayne's character said.

Emmanuel began to dream . . .

Chapter 20

Galen watched as Simeon read Katharine's letter. When he left Elsie and walked the mile and a half to Simeon's blacksmith shop, he couldn't get his wife's pleading words out of his mind, her accusation that his best friend had abused Katharine, or the deception she and Elsie concocted. Galen was the one to see the tears in Simeon's eyes when he found out Katharine had left him for another man. And everyone knew how devoted he was to the Millers, even after her betrayal. He couldn't wrap his mind around the idea that Simeon wasn't the man he knew him to be.

Despite all that, when he reached the shop, he hesitated before going inside. He'd never had a reason to doubt Elsie's judgment before, and perhaps he should listen to her this time too. But he'd never lied to his best friend either, and now that he knew where Katharine was, he believed Simeon deserved to know the truth.

Simeon handed the letter back to Galen, his expression as calm as it was when Galen arrived. He'd been taking a break from hammering out a pair of horseshoes, but now he walked back to the anvil. "Katharine is in Ohio?" he asked coolly, as if he was inquiring about the weather.

"*Ya*. Birch Creek." Galen looked around the forge. Months had passed since he was here last. Simeon always supplied him with new horseshoes whenever he needed them and brought them straight to his house. His work area seemed different, but he couldn't put his finger on why. Then he saw the barely scratched anvil, remembering that his old one had a crack on the side. His leather apron also appeared barely worn. When had he gotten the new supplies?

Simeon pushed up the sleeves of his shirt, exposing huge forearms covered in soot. "Did she ever go to Montana?"

"As far as I know . . . *nee*." He blew out a breath. "I'm sorry. I don't know what got into Elsie, or why she thought Katharine was in trouble."

Simeon grabbed an old rag and wiped off his hands. Behind him the oven blazed, filling the forge with oppressive heat. Then he grinned. "You've kept her with *kinn* ever since you got married. Maybe the pregnancies have affected her brain."

Galen nodded, but the explanation didn't make any sense. Other than this situation, Elsie had been fine. More than fine. She was a wonderful mother and wife, and she couldn't wait for the new baby to arrive. None of this lined up with what he knew about her.

"Don't worry about it," Simeon said, clapping Galen on the shoulder.

He reeled back, almost losing his footing. This wasn't the first time Simeon had made the friendly gesture, but he'd never hit him that hard. "What are you going to do?" he asked, resisting the urge to rub the sore spot.

"*Nix*. For now." His eyes met Galen's.

A chill ran down his spine, despite sweating from the forge's heat. For a fraction of a second, he saw something in Simeon's eyes that terrified him. Just as fast, it was gone, making him think he'd imagined it. He probably had, considering how insistent Elsie was that Simeon was a villain.

"I've got to get back to work." He walked over to the anvil, then smiled at Galen again. "We should keep this to ourselves for now, though. Katharine's parents have been through enough." He picked up the hammer and banged it down on the horseshoe. Red sparks flew everywhere.

Galen nodded, waiting to see if Simeon would say anything else.

Bang.

Bang.

Bang.

Galen left the forge, glancing back at his friend. Simeon was handling the news well, all things considered. But as he went home, he couldn't shake the dread that came over him when he left the forge. *Did I just make a huge mistake?*

Emmanuel sat straight up in his chair. How long had he been asleep? He turned around and looked at the red number display on the small alarm clock on the bedside table. His jaw dropped. Five minutes? He felt like he'd slept for hours. The last time a dream had shaken him awake, he was in his cabin in Birch Creek, after Sol ratted him out to the congregation. He'd hit his head . . . or something had hit him in the head. Even now he couldn't remember what happened or what he'd dreamed. All he knew when he woke up was that he had to leave Birch Creek forever.

He ran his hand across his forehead, feeling the slick sweat accumulating there. What was going on? He tried to remember his dream but nothing concrete came to mind. No images. Only . . . only . . .

John Wayne was still on the screen, but Emmanuel wasn't listening to him. What were the words? What had he dreamed?

Home.

Despite the sweat, he shuddered. *Home.* That was the only clear word in his mind. *Home.*

He turned off the TV, got up from his chair, and walked over to the landline telephone next to the alarm clock. Jordan's card lay right by the phone, the same place he'd left it when he returned to California. Without hesitation he picked it up and called the number.

After two rings, he heard the familiar voice. "Hello?"

"Jordan?"

A pause. "Emmanuel. Glad you're still with us."

He would have chuckled if the situation wasn't so serious. He straightened his back, cleared his throat, and said, "I know I don't have a right to ask you this . . . but can you do me a favor?"

"What's that?"

"I'm ready to go back to Birch Creek. I'm ready to go home."

Chapter 21

Katharine knocked on the front door of Rhoda Troyer's home. She was surprised that after church last Sunday, Rhoda had asked her to come over today. Normally Thursday was a busy day, but she took a break from making her baskets, and once she finished her work at the inn, she took the long walk over to Rhoda's house. She didn't dread exercise the way she used to when she lived in Hulett. Not only did losing weight make it easier to take a two- or three-mile walk but she also found she enjoyed it, even on a hot day like today. Then again, everything was enjoyable now that she and Ezra were dating.

Her heart sang as she waited for Rhoda to answer. She had relived that short, tender kiss in her mind for the past two days. Unfortunately she and Ezra hadn't spent any time alone since. They were both busy with work, to the point that they weren't even able to take their breaks together. Ezra was working on a big landscaping project with Loren and Selah in preparation for the upcoming wedding season that was always busy at the inn, and Katharine had several more baskets to make to replenish the stock at Schrock's. She was surprised they had sold so fast. Both of them were so tired in the evening that Ezra went straight home, and Katharine went straight to bed.

But the three times she saw him in passing—yes, she was counting—he had flashed her a smile that reached straight to her toes and had her smiling back.

The door opened. Speaking of smiling, Rhoda had a lovely one on her face. Apparently Katharine wasn't the only one who was happy. "Hi," she said. "Come on inside. I've made some fresh bread and peach jam from the bag you brought over a few weeks ago."

"Sounds wonderful."

Once she and Rhoda were settled at the kitchen table, each with a glass of cold tea and a thick slice of bread liberally spread with butter and jam, Rhoda said, "I've been praying for you since our last talk."

"And I've been praying for you. I'm sorry about your loss." Soon after the news of Emmanuel's death had reached the rest of the community, there were quick preparations for a memorial service. Freemont said a few words, but not much else was mentioned about the former bishop. That confused Katharine, and from the scattering of bewildered expressions throughout the congregation, she saw she wasn't the only one. But so many people in Birch Creek were unaware of everything that happened when Emmanuel was bishop, and the ones who weren't were tight-lipped about the past.

Rhoda's kind expression grew somber. "*Danki*. It's been strange, and difficult in many ways. But Emmanuel was gone for so long. A big part of me had grieved for him already."

"I understand." Not fully, but it did make sense that she would have gone through a lot of the grieving process not knowing where Emmanuel was or if he was ever coming back.

"But something wonderful has also happened too." Her cheeks turned rosy as she smiled. "Loren proposed, and I accepted."

Katharine grinned. "*Nee* wonder he's been in such a *gut* mood lately. Does Delilah know?"

"*Ya*, and so do the rest of his family. Mine also know. But we won't be marrying until the fall sometime, so we haven't told anyone else, and we won't until we make the announcement in church before the wedding. The reason I'm telling you is because I didn't want you to think I was being hypocritical with *mei* advice the last time we spoke." She picked at the bread crust on her plate. "When Emmanuel and I first married, I was deeply in love with him. But he changed over the years. I hope it's okay with you if I don't discuss the particulars."

Katharine could tell by the way Rhoda was speaking that she still carried the pain of that relationship. She also guessed that Rhoda, like her, didn't want the memory of that relationship tainting her healthy one with Loren. "I don't mind at all."

Rhoda smiled. "I knew you would understand. I don't expect everyone to, though. And when Loren and I announce our engagement, I'm sure there are going to be some people who will think I'm betraying Emmanuel's memory, even after all this time."

"By moving on with someone you love?"

"*Ya*, especially so soon after finding out Emmanuel died."

Katharine was honored that Rhoda trusted her with that information. "I won't say anything."

"*Danki*." She took a sip of her tea. "You look much happier than the last time we talked."

"I am."

"Does it have to do with a certain young man?"

She paused. Yes, Ezra played a huge role in her happiness, but he wasn't the only one. Rhoda inviting her over, trusting her with her good news, and then asking about her welfare meant a lot to her. Delilah and Loren's generosity when she first arrived in Birch Creek had given her security. Now that she was more relaxed, she and Selah were talking more, and she was finding out that Selah and Levi had their difficulties before they got together. She could see the two of them becoming good friends.

Rhoda gave her a knowing look. "Never mind. We all have our secrets we need to keep, don't we?"

Katharine nodded, but Rhoda's comment flipped the guilt switch inside her. Eventually Rhoda and Loren's engagement would be known by everyone, and the families wouldn't have to keep their secret. But Katharine couldn't tell anyone about her ex, not even Ezra.

"Katharine?"

"Oh, sorry." She took a big bite of the bread, the sweet jam filling her mouth as she pushed her thoughts aside. "This is delicious," she said after swallowing the mouthful.

After visiting with Rhoda for another hour, Katharine walked back to the Stolls'. It was nice to take some time out of the day to do something other than work, even though she enjoyed the work she did. She was thankful that after Rhoda's painful relationship with Emmanuel, she was finally finding true happiness.

Katharine was starting to believe that she could too. More than anything she wanted to share with her mother and father that she had fallen for a good, honest man who cared about her and thought she was beautiful inside and out. But that would open an entire can of worms too. How could she explain why she had lied to them about Montana and had gone to Ohio? What if Simeon still had influence over them?

What about her biggest worry—that her happiness with Ezra wouldn't last?

She still had to bide her time. Things were too new with Ezra, and from Elsie's last letter her parents were still enamored with Simeon. They hadn't talked to each other once during the last month, the longest she'd ever gone without calling them. A phone call was long overdue.

When she reached the Stolls', she stopped at the phone shanty at the end of Levi and Selah's driveway. She picked up the phone and called home.

"Hello?"

An icy chill sprinted down her spine. "S-Simeon?"

"Hello, Katharine."

Her heartbeat accelerated and she tried to catch her breath.

"Are you still there, Katharine?"

Hang up. Hang up!

"How's Montana? Your new boyfriend? Have you set a wedding date yet?"

"*Nee*, not yet." Why was she still talking to him? But she had to find out what he was doing there. "Why are you answering the phone? Where are *Mamm* and *Daed*?"

"They're here. Do you want to talk to them?"

"*Ya*, I do."

"Then I'll get your *mamm*. Goodbye, Katharine."

She didn't respond, and a few minutes passed before her mother answered the phone. "Oh, Katharine, I'm so glad you called. We haven't heard from you in so long. I wish you would give me your address so I could write to you."

"I'm sorry, I keep forgetting to send that to you." As she usually did when the topic of writing to her came up, she changed the subject, but this time for a different reason. "Why did Simeon answer the phone?"

"I started to get up and answer it, but he insisted he'd get it for me."

"What's he doing over there? It's the middle of the day, why isn't he at work?"

"You don't exactly have the right to ask questions about your ex-fiancé."

Katharine took a deep breath. "You're right, *Mamm*. I don't. I was just curious."

"If you must know, he brought over lunch and he and your *daed* just finished playing checkers. They usually play every evening when he comes for supper, but he said he had a few minutes and could play a game or two. You know how your *vatter* loves checkers."

She pinched the bridge of her nose. "*Ya*, I do. So, Simeon still visits?"

"Every day. Now, about that address—"

"Gotta *geh*, *Mamm*. Love you and give my love to *Daed*."

"But Katharine—"

She hung up the phone, then leaned her forehead against it. Her hands were still shaking as she left the phone shanty and walked back to the inn. When she was almost to the parking lot she could hear Levi's phone ringing in the distance. But her focus was on Simeon. This was the first time they'd spoken to each other since she left Hulett. He didn't sound angry, like she expected him to be. Then again, he was with her parents, and he never lost his temper with her in front of anyone, especially them.

But could it be that he had moved on? She hoped so, but why would he spend every single day with her parents? His own parents were in Pennsylvania, and he rarely spoke of them. Maybe he saw

Mamm and *Daed* as his surrogate parents. She knew of couples who had broken up and were still friendly with each other's families. But that usually happened when the breakups were mutual, not when the bride ran away—

"Hey!"

She stopped short in front of something, then realized it was Ezra. She blinked and looked around. Somehow she'd made it to the inn, but she didn't remember crossing the parking lot. "I-I'm sorry," she said, stepping away.

"*Nee* problem. I saw you coming and called out your name. I figured you'd stop when you reached me. You surprised me when you didn't." He peered at her, smudges of dirt on his handsome face. "Are you okay?"

"*Ya*. Just thinking about some new basket patterns." She shrugged and hoped her smile and her lie seemed genuine.

They must have because he grinned back. Then he motioned for her to follow him to the side of the inn. "I'm sorry we haven't been able to see each other." He held up his dirt-stained hands. "Been busy with the flower beds, as you can see."

"You don't have to apologize." He smelled like dirt, hard work, and sunshine. All so very appealing. Finally she was able to relax. "I was lost in my thoughts, I guess."

"Thinking about anything—or anyone—in particular?" he asked with a mischievous waggle of his brows. "Because I have been."

"Oh?" She moved closer to him and this time her smile was authentic. She shoved Simeon out of her thoughts. She wasn't going to let him ruin the few minutes she had with Ezra before they both went back to work. "Who would that be?"

"Delilah, obviously."

Katharine laughed. "Obviously—"

Ezra stopped her words with a kiss. Longer, sweeter, than the one she'd given him. When he pulled away, he said, "Maybe I can stop by on Sunday afternoon, and we can visit for a while without work interrupting us."

"I'd like that."

He nodded, then said, "It's a date." He took off for the front of the inn.

Warmth traveled through her as she touched her lips. A kiss *and* a date. She couldn't do anything about Simeon and her parents right now, but she would have to figure out something eventually, probably with Elsie's help. Right now all she wanted to think about was Ezra's kiss and their upcoming date. *I'm a lucky girl.*

Galen poked at his supper. He could see Elsie had gone to a lot of trouble to make the hearty meal of shepherd's pie, cooked carrots and peas, fresh rolls, and sliced tomatoes. But he could barely eat more than two bites.

"Galen?"

He lifted his head and looked at his wife. Jason sat in his high chair next to her, drinking out of his sippy cup in between shoving tiny fistfuls of carrots and peas into his mouth.

"Is there something wrong with the meal?"

Worry creased her forehead and filled her pretty eyes. She didn't need this stress. Not with the baby coming, and definitely not from him. "The food is delicious, as always."

She nodded, then turned to wipe Jason's mouth.

"I'm sorry," he said. "I shouldn't have gotten angry with you."

"*Nee*, you were right to be. I wish I could have told you about Katharine. One day maybe you'll see why I couldn't."

"I . . . I think I do."

Elsie stilled, her expression questioning.

"I gave Simeon Katharine's last letter."

She dropped the napkin on her half-finished plate.

"He needed to know the truth." As she shook her head, he lifted his hand. "That's what I believed at the time. Now I think I made things worse." He explained Simeon's calm reaction. "Then I saw something. In his eyes. I'm not sure I didn't imagine it."

"What did you see?"

"I can't define it. But if it was real, and he goes after Katharine . . ." His stomach twisted. "She won't be safe."

Elsie's hand went to her mouth. "What are we going to do?"

"I don't know." Galen pushed his plate away. "I can't confront him about it."

"*Nee*. You can't."

"Can you send her a letter? You can warn her that Simeon knows where she is now."

"*Ya*," Elsie said. "I'll do that after supper."

"Do it now. I'll take care of Jason and clean the kitchen."

"All right." She got up from the table and started to leave. Then she went back to Galen and kissed his cheek. "I love you," she said, then left.

"Da!"

He half smiled, then went to pick up his son from his high chair, feeling a little relieved. At least Katharine would be warned. In the meantime, Galen would keep an eye on Simeon the best he could, without raising his suspicions. Right now, that was all he could do.

Chapter 22

"Finally, we're alone." Ezra turned to Katharine and grinned.

She smiled back. "*Ya*. Finally."

They were sitting on the plastic chairs on the Stolls' back patio. Soon after Sunday lunch at home, Ezra had walked over here, glad to discover that no one else was around. There was no church service today, but Delilah and Loren had left to attend church in the nearby Amish community of Marigold. The inn was empty since the guests all checked out before 11:00 a.m. He leaned back in his chair, happier than a dog getting his belly scratched. He'd missed talking to Katharine, and soon they were filling each other in on their activities during the past week.

"Did you enjoy your time with Rhoda?"

"*Ya*," she said, resting her hands on her knees. "We have some things in common."

"Oh? Like what?"

Her brow shot up, and then she shrugged. "You know . . . things." She glanced away.

He nodded, aware she was being vague again. He looked out

into the yard and saw a squirrel scampering across the grass a few feet away. Then it dashed up one of the oak trees dotting the Stolls' backyard. "*Gut*. I'm glad you're making friends."

"Me too."

He glanced at her, smiling again. He couldn't help it, just like he couldn't stop looking at her. She was wearing a new dress, a plum-colored one that fit her better than the baggy dresses she'd been wearing. This one accentuated her curves in a modest and *very* attractive way. Unable to stop himself, he reached for her hand. After a second's hesitancy, she allowed him to hold it.

A long moment passed, then she said, "Ezra?"

"*Ya*?"

She turned to him. "What are we?"

"What do you mean?"

"Are we friends, or . . ."

He chuckled. "I don't hold hands with *mei* friends, Katharine. And I definitely don't kiss them." But he understood what she meant. They hadn't defined their relationship, at least not out loud. He didn't think it was necessary, but clearly she did. "We're dating," he said, angling his body toward her. "Or courting, to use the old-fashioned term." And because he wanted to make sure they were both on the same page, he added, "If that's okay with you."

She glanced down at their clasped hands resting on his knee. "I can't believe it," she said, her voice so soft and low he could barely hear her. "I never thought . . ."

"Never thought what?"

Her gaze lifted to his. "That I could be happy again."

Ezra hurt for the pain she'd gone through in the past. He squeezed her hand. When he heard her contented sigh, he faced the yard again. There were the usual unseen sounds around them—a rooster crowing, a few cows lowing, crickets and cicadas chirping and singing. He'd had a long, tiring week, and there was nothing more peaceful than sitting in silence holding Katharine's hand.

A short time later, Loren's buggy turned into the driveway. Ezra and Katharine got to their feet as Loren stopped the vehicle and Delilah got out. She waved at the two of them and headed for the house.

Loren called out, "Ezra, can you meet me in the barn?"

"Sure." He turned to Katharine as Loren drove away. "I need to get back home before supper. *Mamm* and *Daed* like all of us to be together Sunday evenings if we can. I'll see you tomorrow."

She gave him a shy smile. "See you." Then she went back inside.

Loren was in the process of unhitching the buggy when Ezra walked into the barn. "I can do that," he said, moving to help him.

"I've got it." But Loren wasn't looking at him, and he didn't say a word as he finished putting Bob—he could tell the horses apart now—back in his stall. After Loren gave both horses a little extra feed, he turned to Ezra. "I realize I'm not Katharine's father," he said, his forehead creasing. "But I care for her like she's one of *mei* own."

That was obvious. His palms started to grow damp. Loren had never been this somber with him before.

"I also know she's a grown woman and can make her own decisions. But she's had a hard lot in life. I don't know any details, and it's not *mei* business." His expression tempered slightly. "*Mei mutter* tried to set you two up when she sent you to Barton together."

"I know. She wasn't too subtle about it."

"She never is." He rubbed his beardless chin. "I know you and Katharine have grown close. I'm concerned that you both feel you have to please *Mamm* because she's your employer."

Ezra's brow shot up. He hadn't expected this. "I'll admit I wasn't happy when I first figured out she was setting us up. I don't like being manipulated."

"*Nee* one does."

"But I would never be in a relationship with someone to please anyone else."

Loren nodded. "So you two are in a relationship."

"*Ya*." Normally he wouldn't appreciate the interrogation, but Loren was his boss. Then a thought occurred to him. "I promise we don't let that interfere with our work here."

"Oh, I know. And fraternizing isn't a problem. If it was, Levi and Selah wouldn't be married." He smiled a little, but it soon disappeared. "I just want to make sure you understand. I don't want Katharine hurt again."

"I don't either." Ezra straightened his shoulders. "I would never do anything to harm her intentionally."

"*Gut* to hear." Then he fully smiled. "I didn't expect anything less from you. Sorry to pry, but considering how important she is to our *familye*, I wanted to be sure. I've kept you long enough, so head on home. We'll see you tomorrow morning. Feel free to come for breakfast if you want. You know *Mamm* always makes plenty."

"*Danki*."

Ezra left the Stolls', thinking about his afternoon with Katharine and his talk with Loren. He was glad she had other people looking out for her. He'd figured she was important to the Stolls, and now Loren had shown him how much. *She's important to me too.*

Chapter 23

"I wish you'd have let me call Rhoda," Jordan said as he drove his car across the Knox County line. "I don't think it's right to just show up without giving her any warning."

Emmanuel crossed his arms over his thin chest. "She would have told me not to come."

"You don't know that."

Jordan was right, he didn't know if she would turn him away. But he was sure he couldn't explain everything to Rhoda over the phone, especially the letter faking his death. That kind of conversation needed to be had in person.

He ran his hand over his chin, still surprised when he felt light stubble there and not his thick, matted beard. A week had passed since he called Jordan, who agreed without hesitation to take him to Birch Creek. Emmanuel probably could have taken a bus and gone by himself, but he wanted to make sure he went through with it this time. He'd tried returning home by himself before, only to turn tail and run away again. Now he had no choice. Jordan wouldn't let him off the hook.

When Jordan arrived at the motel Thursday evening, he had driven from LA. The drive to Ohio took him only three days, but as he explained to Emmanuel, he had to finish closing up his office before he could leave. He spent last night helping Emmanuel shave, then cut his hair into a somewhat decent length. Before leaving Dixonville midmorning, both men thanked Pauline and Jeb. With tears in her eyes, Pauline hugged him. "It was a pleasure, Lester. I mean that. You're a lovely man when you're not being ornery."

A lump formed in his throat at the memory.

"Have you figured out what you're going to tell her?" Jordan asked.

He paused. His first instinct was to snap at him and tell him to mind his own business. What he and Rhoda would talk about was between them. But being nosy was part of Jordan's job, and after everything the man had done to help him, Emmanuel refused to be a jerk to him anymore. "No. Not yet."

"Oh. I figured you might have something in mind after five hours in the car."

He glanced at Jordan, checking to see if his comment was meant to be snide. But Jordan stared straight ahead at the road in front of them and the sun that was rapidly sinking past the horizon. They might have been in the car for five hours, but the trip was taking longer than that. Jordan insisted on several stops to stretch their legs. He also made sure Emmanuel ate the lunch Pauline had packed.

"Five hours ain't enough," he finally said. "I have a lot of explaining to do." Not only to Rhoda and his boys but also to the man courting his wife. Loren Stoll, his former boss. He'd known when he was working for Loren that the man had an interest in Rhoda. And he could have ground that prospect to a halt by revealing who he was.

But Loren was a good man with more integrity in his pinky finger than Emmanuel had in his whole body. Didn't Rhoda deserve one, after everything he'd put her through? That, along with having a yellow streak a mile wide, were the main reasons he'd fled Birch Creek last year and wrote those letters.

Jordan looked at the GPS display on the dashboard. "We'll be there in a little more than an hour."

Fear gripped Lester. Yep, he was yellow all right. "I suppose it's too late to turn back," he mumbled, staring out at the dusky evening sky. He'd avoided looking at the landscape until now, and a wave of memories and emotion washed over him. He knew every bit of land in this county and in Birch Creek. Where all the natural gas deposits were. Where the best farmland could be found. How far it was to Schrock's Grocery and Tool from his house—exactly 1.3 miles. Then there was the shed in the woods. The one that had been destroyed after he'd lost everything, then finding out that it had been rebuilt by someone. He had no idea who took it upon themself to rebuild the shed, or when it had happened, and he had beat feet out of Ohio before he found out. Not that it mattered. Just as well that the land and building be used for something good, instead of the evil he had used it for. A shrine to his pride, arrogance, and greed. His stomach, almost always sour now, turned rancid. He rolled down the window.

"You okay, Emmanuel?"

"I'm all right. Just need a little air."

The hour flew by, and when the GPS signaled their destination, the panic increased. When he had worked for the Stolls, he hadn't gotten the courage to go see his old house. Although there was barely any daylight left, he saw that nothing had changed on the outside since he left nine years ago.

The moment Jordan pulled into the driveway, Emmanuel gripped the edges of his seat until his knuckles hurt. "I can't do this," he said, trying to keep his breathing steady.

"I'll be there with you." Jordan put his hand on Emmanuel's shoulder.

"You don't understand. You don't know what I've done."

"No, I don't. But what I've learned in my career is that nothing is unforgivable . . . if you're truly repentant." He paused. "Are you, Emmanuel?"

A fine time to ask that question. Then it hit him. For the first time since he'd run away from Birch Creek, intense shame and guilt slammed into him. He was sorry, so, so sorry, for everything he'd done to his family and community. He'd tried to outrun those harrowing emotions, tried not to take responsibility for everything he'd done. *My fault alone . . . my fault alone . . . forgive me, Jesus.*

He turned to Jordan, a sudden calm coming over him. God had led him here, and he was finally obeying. "Yes. I am repentant."

"Then you have to let your family know and ask them for forgiveness."

Emmanuel lifted an eyebrow. "You sound like an Amish man now."

Jordan grinned. "Presbyterian, if you must know. But repentance and forgiveness aren't bound by religion. We both know that."

He did. In fact he knew the Bible probably better than most people, since he'd spent so much time twisting it. He drew in a deep breath, ignoring the slight pain in his lungs. No more avoiding. Or running. His time to pay restitution for all his deeds had arrived. "All right, I'm ready."

Jordan got out of the car, then helped Emmanuel out of his seat.

Emmanuel picked up his cane and headed toward the house. He stopped right before the front porch, those old feelings of pride and denial rising up in him. *Lord, help me. I can't do this without you.*

"Emmanuel?"

A surge of energy and confidence flowed through him, and he couldn't deny the source. For more years than he could count, he'd credited himself for everything. *Not this time.* He moved away from Jordan and climbed the steps.

Rhoda hummed a hymn of thanksgiving as she finished cleaning up the kitchen. Loren had just left, and he had surprised her with another bouquet and something even more special—their first kiss. Soft, quick, and perfect. She paused at the sink, remembering the light touch of his lips on hers. Afterward, they parted, his cheeks red. "I'm out of practice."

"Me too," she said.

He grinned. "We'll have plenty of opportunity to make up for lost time after the wedding."

Swoon. She was actually swooning. And why shouldn't she? She was in love with a wonderful man and had her sons' support. Nothing could ruin this moment for her.

She had finished drying the last glass when she saw headlights shining at the end of her driveway as a car pulled in. She expected the driver to turn around. That happened sometimes—English drivers were frequently getting lost on Birch Creek's back roads. But when the car pulled farther into her driveway, she frowned. She couldn't tell in the dim light what kind of vehicle it was, and she set the glass on the counter, then wiped off her fingers with the hand towel nearby, keeping her eye on who was coming out of the car.

When she saw a tall, slim figure she realized it was Jordan. She thought he would be in Los Angeles by now. Was there a problem with the check she sent him after he confirmed Emmanuel's death? If there was, surely he would have called her instead of coming all this way.

Then a shorter, thinner figure got out of the passenger side with Jordan's help. She didn't recognize him. She hurried to the front door and opened it. "Hi, Jordan," she said. "I wasn't expecting you—" But it wasn't Jordan standing in front of her.

"Hi, Rhoda."

She knew that voice, even though it was gravelly and weak. She knew those eyes, even though they were cloudy and sunken. *No, it can't be.*

Jordan appeared next to him. "Can we come inside? It's not easy for him to stand for very long."

"Emmanuel?" She took a step back.

"It's all right, Rhoda." Emmanuel leaned on his cane. "I'm not here to hurt you, or anyone else."

She brought a shaky hand to her lips. "The letter—" She shot a horrified look at Jordan. "You said—"

"I wrote the letters. I wanted you and our *sohns* to think I was dead."

"Why?"

"Rhoda," Jordan said, his voice and expression kind. "Can we come in?"

She couldn't believe this. She couldn't *handle* this. "*Nee*. You can't come in." She shut the door and leaned against it. That broken man might have Emmanuel's eyes and voice, but he wasn't her husband. This had to be a mistake.

Two knocks. "Rhoda?"

"*Geh* away Jordan. And take him with you." Her heart slammed into her chest. She'd never been inhospitable in her life, but she couldn't let them inside. Not now . . . not ever.

Chapter 24

"I messed up, Richard." Jordan sat at the kitchen table and swirled the tea in his glass. The drink looked slightly like bourbon, and right now he would give his right hand for a bourbon . . . or six. But his drinking days were behind him, and he knew Richard wouldn't have any alcohol anyway. He'd just returned from driving Cevilla to Rhoda's.

After the shock of seeing Emmanuel, Jordan knew she didn't need to be alone. He wasn't sure what to do, other than to go over to the Thompsons. Richard was the only other person he knew in Birch Creek. On the ride here, Emmanuel hadn't said a word. Jordan kept silent too, the words *What have I done?* repeating in his head. Emmanuel was in the Thompsons' spare bedroom now, hopefully asleep.

Richard sat back in his chair. It was strange to see him with an Amish beard and gray hair covering his ears. Jordan had always known him as a clean-cut, exquisitely dressed man. Now he resembled every other Amish guy he'd met over the past several months. "I'm not sure what you were thinking, Jordan," he said, stroking his white beard. "Lying to Rhoda, then bringing Emmanuel here in his condition."

"I was thinking about me and my dad. How much I would have regretted not being able to see him before he died. Taking care of him was tough, but it was also one of the few good times I had with him. He'd changed. I'd changed."

"You think Emmanuel has changed?"

Jordan shoved the tea glass to the side. "I've spent over a month with the man. He's cranky and stubborn, and not without reason. But there's a brokenness about him, and not just physically. He's alone and lonely."

"Like your father was."

"Yeah."

Richard leaned his elbows on the table and pinched the bridge of his nose. Then he said, "Cevilla's told me a few things that happened when Emmanuel was bishop here, and fewer things about how he left. I don't know enough to advise you about what to do now."

"I should have minded my own business."

"Why didn't you? Other than him reminding you of your father, there had to be another reason you would go to all this trouble."

Jordan didn't answer right away. He was a Christian, but a lapsed one. And over the past several years his cases had been hard ones, the kind that caused him to question his weak faith. But when he met Emmanuel, something had clicked inside him. "I went back to church when I was in Dixonville," he said.

"Good. It's always good to go to church."

"I hadn't been since my divorce." Pain pierced his heart. "My wife leaving me was the impetus for me to get sober, but even doing a twelve-step program hadn't made me want to attend church again."

"And meeting Emmanuel did?"

He held up his hands. "I can't explain why. I just know that I was supposed to help him, and to start going to church again. Doing both made me feel better than I had in a long time. Then this happens." He dropped his hands on the table. "Maybe I was looking for a little redemption too, and getting Emmanuel back to his family was part of that."

Richard nodded. "Maybe. You probably won't ever know. This might surprise you, but I think you did the right thing."

"You do?"

"Absolutely. Emmanuel lied to his family in the worst way possible—letting them think he was dead. I understand why you didn't tell Rhoda the truth too. But when Emmanuel changed his mind, and you didn't hesitate to help him, that says a lot about you. You could have simply done the job, gone back to California, and stayed there. But you didn't. You're aiding a lost man and making sure Rhoda and her sons know the truth. Imagine if she found out some other way that he was alive."

"Emmanuel doesn't have much time left."

"I can see that." Richard's expression grew downcast. "I hope they can work things out before he passes."

"Me too." But he didn't have much optimism. He was also kicking himself for not handling the situation better. He shouldn't have listened to Emmanuel about going straight to Rhoda's without letting her know they were coming, but he was so glad the man had finally acquiesced to owning up to his lie that he didn't want to risk him backing out.

"There's something you probably don't know," Richard said. "Cevilla's certain Rhoda will be remarrying soon."

Jordan's head jerked up. "What?"

"*Ya*. I mean, yes." He smiled. "Sorry. Too easy to slip into *Deitsch* nowadays. She's been friendly with Loren Stoll, who owns an inn not too far from here. Terrific guy, and a widower. Do you know how the Amish feel about marriage and divorce?"

"No divorce under any circumstances. No remarriage if one spouse abandons the other." He didn't think that was fair, but who was he to question Amish rules.

"Correct. Now, if Rhoda had married Loren while Emmanuel was still alive, and they had found out that he was, both of them would be devastated. Even if it wasn't their fault. That's how seriously they take their marriage vows."

That did make Jordan feel slightly better, but he was still unsure what to do. "I can't take him back to Dixonville. I'm worried he might not make it. And I'm sure him staying at Rhoda's, or the inn, is out of the question."

"He can stay here. Cevilla might not like it, but she's spending the night with Rhoda tonight."

"I don't want to leave him alone."

"We only have one spare bedroom," Richard said. "But we do have a couch, and if you don't mind sleeping there, you're welcome to stay too."

"Done." Jordan smiled for the first time since leaving Dixonville. "I've slept in worse places."

"You can spare me the details." Richard rose from his chair. "I'll get the linens for the couch."

"I don't need anything," Jordan told him. "Don't fuss on my account."

"I'm not." He started to shuffle away. "But Cevilla will chew me out if I don't at least give you a pillow and blanket."

"I believe it." His time with Cevilla had been brief, but she took charge immediately when he and Emmanuel arrived, and the look she gave Emmanuel could have melted stone. Jordan might have done the right thing by bringing Emmanuel here, but he'd had no idea how difficult it would turn out to be. From what he knew about the Amish, they were a forgiving people who didn't hold grudges. Perhaps there were situations where they did. He just hoped this wasn't one of them.

"I know it's not Christian of me, but I could wring that *mann*'s neck."

Rhoda lifted her gaze from the cup of tea in front of her. She didn't want anything to drink, but Cevilla had insisted, saying that most things could be solved over a cup of strong peppermint tea. Rhoda didn't think her situation could be solved at all, but she did agree with Cevilla's words about Emmanuel. She wanted to wring his neck too.

Cevilla pushed the cup closer to Rhoda. "Take a sip. It will help you relax."

She didn't want to relax. She wanted to scream, cry, and curse Emmanuel, and that scared her. She had never been so angry in her life as she was at this minute. Thank God Cevilla came over. The old woman's presence was steady and calming enough that she wouldn't act on those frightening emotions. But only barely. Reluctantly she took a sip of the tea. "There's something more than peppermint in this, *ya*?"

"Chamomile and lavender." Cevilla smiled. "It will help you relax, and hopefully sleep better."

"I don't think I'll be able to sleep for a long time." Rhoda stared at the tea again. Jordan lied to her. Emmanuel was alive. And of course he had to show up right after Loren proposed.

But the betrayal wasn't all that hurt or infuriated her. She noticed his sickly appearance, and it terrified her. To her absolute fury, she was worried about him. After everything he had done, after all the pain and deception and abuse . . . Her heart broke to see him so sick and emaciated.

Cevilla rose from her chair, her movements slow as usual, and grabbed her cane. She went to the sink and turned on the tap, then started to wash the kettle.

"You don't have to do that," Rhoda said. She should get up and wash the kettle herself, but she felt like there were two boulders strapped to her ankles, keeping her from doing anything. Except think and feel. She was doing plenty of that.

"Nonsense. I can wash a kettle. I can't sit too long anyway. These old joints lock up too easily."

Now guilt climbed to the top of her pile of mixed emotions. "You don't have to stay here," Rhoda said. "I'm fine."

"You're not fine. If you were, I'd be more concerned than I already am."

"I don't want you to worry."

Cevilla turned off the water and looked over her stooped shoulder. "Too late for that."

Rhoda picked up the tea again. Cevilla had gone to the trouble of making it, and she would drink it whether she wanted to or not. She didn't say anything while Cevilla continued to wash and dry the kettle, taking twice as long as Rhoda would have. When she finished, she put it on the stove and sat back down, then took a sip of her own lukewarm tea.

After a few minutes, Rhoda said, "I have to tell Sol and Aden about Emmanuel."

"*Ya*. It will be better coming from you. By the looks of him, he's not going anywhere on his own. Richard will make sure he stays put for a while." Cevilla scowled. "*Gut* thing I'm not there right now. Bad shape or not, he'd get a large piece of *mei* mind."

"I'm sorry you're involved with this," Rhoda said.

"It's not *yer* fault. This is all Emmanuel's doing."

"And Jordan's." She still didn't understand why he told her Emmanuel was dead, or why he hadn't called her when he found out he was alive. She would have been just as shocked, but at least she would have had the truth. She started to cry.

"Oh, honey." Cevilla grabbed her hand and squeezed. "It's going to be okay."

"*Nee*. It's not. Loren proposed. I told him I would marry him."

Cevilla blew out a breath. "Oh dear."

"Now what am I supposed to do?" She took a napkin from the holder on the table and wiped her eyes. "I love Loren. I don't have any feelings for Emmanuel anymore."

"You don't have to make any decisions tonight."

"That's *gut*, because the only thing I do know is that I have to talk to Sol and Aden as soon as possible." And Loren. Oh Lord, what was she going to say to him?

"Morning will be soon enough."

Rhoda finished her tea, and then she put fresh sheets and a quilt on her bed for Cevilla. When she came back into the kitchen, Cevilla was nodding off. She looked at the clock. Past ten. Both she and Cevilla were usually in bed by this time. She touched Cevilla's shoulder. "Your bed is ready," she said.

Her eyes flew open. "I told you I can sleep on the couch."

"That's nonsense. I'll sleep in one of the *buwe*'s old rooms. *Mei* bed is comfortable." And it was new. She had purchased it almost two weeks ago to replace the bed she and Emmanuel shared. She dragged the old one out on the curb for the trash men to pick up.

"All right. I won't argue with you." She yawned, then got up from the chair more slowly than she had before.

Rhoda led her to her room and showed her where everything was. "Do you need a glass of water?"

She shook her head. "*Nee*. I'm all set."

Rhoda nodded. "I'll be upstairs. Don't hesitate to let me know if you need something."

"I won't." She tilted her head and half smiled. "The tea is taking effect now, *ya*?"

"*Ya*." She stifled a yawn, and surprisingly her body felt less tense than it had when Cevilla arrived. "You'll have to give me the recipe."

"Margaret blended it for me. I'm sure she'll make some up for you."

For the first time since Emmanuel had surprised her, she was able to smile. "*Danki* for being here for me."

"Of course." Cevilla yawned again.

"*Gute nacht*." Rhoda left the door open partway, glad she had the presence of mind to leave a small flashlight for Cevilla in case she had to get up and go to the bathroom. As she made her way upstairs, weariness overcame her. She went into Aden's room, which was the first one by the top of the stairs, and collapsed onto his bed. Her grandchildren had used this and Sol's room for sleepovers at least once or twice every other month, so the sheets were fresh and the room clean. But she didn't care about that. She also didn't care about getting undressed for bed. She pulled the folded quilt on the edge of the bed over herself, then closed her eyes.

But before she drifted off, she was still thinking about Emmanuel. How ghostly sick he looked. And despite everything, she still said a small prayer for him.

Chapter 25

The next morning, Emmanuel made his way from Cevilla's spare bedroom to the kitchen. He was parched and needed a drink. Although he had slept, he didn't feel rested. How could he be, after Rhoda slammed the door in his face? Then again, what did he expect? To be welcomed with open arms? It wouldn't—and shouldn't—be that easy.

He was the only one up, and a thin beam of light from the outside lamppost shined through the kitchen window, enough that he could make his way to the counter. The kitchen was small, with only three cabinets, and he was able to find a drinking glass without much effort. Even though he slept, he was still exhausted. Waiting for Jordan to arrive and bring him here, plus the car ride and the stress of seeing Rhoda again, had taken a lot out of him.

He questioned his decision. Everything was fine with his family thinking he was dead. Now he was upending their lives. At one time he wouldn't have cared about that. During their marriage he had exerted his authority over Rhoda until she never said a word against him, or even raised her voice. As for his sons . . . He had dealt with them even more cruelly.

Crash!

Horrified, he looked down at his feet. The glass had slipped from his hands and hit the floor, breaking into pieces. He heard Jordan's quick footsteps in the living room. "What happened? Where is the light in this place?"

"There's a gas lamp in the corner on the opposite side of the room."

"How can you see that?" Jordan padded in bare feet over to the other side of the kitchen. After a few seconds of fumbling, the lamp hissed to life. "I guess I didn't notice this last night when Richard and I were talking." He went over to him, stopping short of the broken glass. "Are you okay?"

"No. I'm not." Emmanuel glanced at his hands. They were shaking. When had that started?

"Next time you need something, let me know and I'll help you." Jordan glanced around the kitchen and spied a broom and dustpan near the back door and grabbed both.

"I need you to take me back to Dixonville."

The broom hovered over the broken glass. "I will. As soon as you talk to your family."

"You saw what happened last night." Now his legs were wobbly. Try as he might, he couldn't keep standing. Trying to avoid the glass, he shuffled to the table. He'd left his cane in the bedroom.

Jordan appeared at his side. "Let me help—"

"You've done enough!" Emmanuel shook him off and fell into the seat, his pain intense. "I want to go home."

Jordan sat next to him. "This is your home."

"Not anymore."

"That hotel room isn't either." Jordan sighed. "I'm going to put my shoes on. I don't want to step on any glass barefoot."

Emmanuel ignored him, and as soon as Jordan left the room, he put his head in his hands. He didn't have the energy to fight him right now. Besides, he was the one who asked Jordan to bring him here. All because of a dream he couldn't remember and a word he wanted to forget. *Home*. But now that he was here, he didn't know if he could face his family and the community. They would see him like this—a broken man, physically and spiritually. He'd be humiliated.

"Pride goes before destruction, and a haughty spirit before a fall."

He sighed. His pride had led to his destruction all right. A well-deserved one.

Jordan entered the kitchen again and finished sweeping up the glass. As he poured the shards into the small trash can under the sink, Richard walked in.

"Did I miss something?" he asked, looking at Emmanuel, then at Jordan.

"I dropped a glass," Jordan said quickly. "I'll pay you for it."

"Nonsense. We have plenty of glasses here, more than we need. Anyone ready for coffee?"

Jordan grinned. "Absolutely." He put the dustpan and broom back and sat down next to Emmanuel.

"You don't have to lie for me," Emmanuel groused in a low voice. "I can take responsibility for myself."

Nodding, Jordan said, "Sorry."

They sat in silence as Richard brewed the coffee. "I've got some leftover breakfast casserole I can heat up," he said as the scent of coffee started to fill the kitchen. "Courtesy of Delilah Stoll. She always makes sure Cevilla and I have enough to eat. More than enough usually."

Emmanuel shook his head. "I'm not hungry."

"You need to eat something." Jordan looked at Richard. "I'll have a piece, and Emmanuel will have a small one."

Huffing, Emmanuel crossed his arms and stared straight ahead. Jordan got up and helped Richard with breakfast, and a short time later he put a kid-sized portion of casserole in front of him, along with a glass of water and a cup of coffee. Then he and Richard got their food and coffee and sat down at the table. After silent prayer, they both started eating. Emmanuel didn't move.

"I got to thinking last night," Richard said, shoving his fork into the eggs, sausage, cheese, and green pepper mound in front of him. "You two can stay here as long as you need to. Delilah mentioned they only had one guest at the inn right now. Cevilla and I can stay there."

"We don't want to displace you," Jordan said. "Isn't there another hotel around here?"

"There's one in Barton. A nice one too. It's a drive, though. Please stay here. I insist."

"Only if you're sure." Jordan glanced at Emmanuel, who was still sitting there with his arms crossed.

"I'm sure. It will be like a little vacation for us. Plus Cevilla and Delilah will be able to gab all they want."

Jordan picked up Emmanuel's fork and held it in front of him. "Eat."

"I'm not a child."

"Then stop acting like one."

His words dug deep. He was being childish. He took the fork from Jordan. "Thank you."

He took a small bite of the casserole. *Appeditlich*. He hadn't had Amish cooking since he left Birch Creek, and oh how he missed it.

Jordan must have noticed his reaction because his strained expression relaxed as he turned to Richard again. "We'll stay."

"*I'll* stay," Emmanuel said. "You can go back to California. You've done more than your fair share helping me." He didn't like being in anyone's debt, especially one he couldn't repay.

He shook his head. "I said I would help you, and I'm sticking to that promise. You don't have to go through this alone."

"But—" He swallowed hard. "What if they won't see me?"

Jordan frowned. "Your family?"

"*Ya*." He stared at the casserole on his plate. "I wouldn't blame them if they didn't."

"Then I'll take you back to Dixonville," he said.

Emmanuel looked at him. Blast it, he was tearing up. This man might be English, and he was still mostly a stranger, but he had proven his loyalty. Loyalty Emmanuel was sure he didn't deserve. "Thank you," he said, wiping his eyes with his napkin.

Richard cleared his throat. "Anyone want more coffee?"

He'd forgotten Richard was there. Normally he'd be embarrassed and angry at someone witnessing his weakness. But something was softening in him. It started after he woke from his dream and was continuing. Painful, but not altogether unwelcome. "I'll have some," he said to Richard. Then he added, "*Danki*."

Rhoda awakened far past the time she normally did. Whatever Cevilla put in her tea had worked wonders. She didn't remember falling asleep or dreaming. The last thing she recalled was thinking about Emmanuel. He was also the first thing on her mind when she was fully alert.

She glanced at the clock. It was past nine. She rushed out of Aden's room and flew down the steps. The scent of eggs, bacon, and biscuits filled the air. Cevilla made that kind of breakfast? She didn't like the idea of the woman doing work on her behalf, and she skipped going to her room to change clothes and went straight to the kitchen, only to halt. Aden was at the stove turning over long pieces of bacon, while Sol was standing at the table, a basket of biscuits in his hand. Cevilla was sitting in Emmanuel's former seat, as if supervising the meal preparations.

"*Gute morgen*, sleepyhead." Cevilla smiled, looking fresh and spry. "I hope you don't mind, but I called the *buwe* and asked them to come over. They insisted on making breakfast for us, and I'm not one to turn down food."

Rhoda tried to return Cevilla's encouraging smile, but she couldn't. She didn't know what Cevilla said to get them to skip work this morning to be here, and that caused dread to form in her stomach. Had she mentioned Emmanuel to them?

"You two must have stayed up late last night." Aden set the last strip of bacon on a paper towel–covered plate.

"Wh-What do you mean?" she asked as Sol pulled out a chair for her.

"My, this breakfast looks scrumptious," Cevilla said, her voice louder than normal. "Aden, I always love biscuits with your honey. Could you pass me the basket?"

"After we say the prayer." Aden gave her an odd glance, then bowed his head and closed his eyes.

"Oh, right. How could I have forgotten?" She bowed her head.

When the prayer was finished and everyone opened their eyes,

Sol said, "So what's going on, *Mamm*? You normally don't ask us to come over for breakfast."

"You don't sleep in either." Concern entered Aden's eyes.

Sol looked at Cevilla. "And you never answered *mei* question when we got here. Why did you call us instead of *Mamm*?"

Cevilla met his gaze, determination in her eyes. "I'm here to support her."

Aden looked surprised. "About her marrying Loren?"

Of course they would think this was about Loren. Rhoda wrung the napkin she held in her hands under the table.

"I'm surprised you know about this, Cevilla," Aden continued. "We already told her we supported their marriage. We want her to be happy."

Sol nodded, but his expression became wary as he turned to Rhoda. "You are happy, *Mamm*. *Ya*?"

Rhoda froze. Before Emmanuel showed up, she had been happier than she could remember. Why couldn't Cevilla have waited a little longer? She needed more time to prepare to tell her sons about their father. Then again, was there any way to prepare for something like this?

"*Mamm*?" Aden asked.

She stilled, then smoothed the napkin on her lap. With a calm she didn't feel, she turned to both of her children. "Your *vatter* is alive."

Aden dropped the basket of biscuits. It tipped on its side, and several biscuits dropped to the floor. "What?"

"What?" Sol repeated, the word sounding like a growl.

Rhoda fought for composure. She didn't need to fall apart right now. She had to be tough for her sons, something she had failed to do so many times in the past. "Emmanuel showed up here last night with Jordan." She felt Cevilla's hand cover hers, and she gripped her thin, arthritic fingers for strength.

Neither man said anything, seemingly frozen in place. Finally Sol said, "I knew it was too *gut* to be true." The words came out in a hiss.

"Solomon!" Cevilla narrowed her eyes. "I understand you're upset right now—"

"You don't understand anything." Sol got up from his chair.

"Your breakfast . . ." Rhoda bit her lip, dismayed that her motherly instinct kicked in now. How could she expect him to eat after what he just found out?

"I'm not hungry." He bolted out the door.

Rhoda looked at Cevilla. "I'm sorry."

"Don't be. I shouldn't have scolded him. He's a grown man and I overstepped."

Aden still hadn't said anything. He was staring at the spilled basket but didn't make a move to pick up the biscuits. Then he stood. "I'm glad you're here for *Mamm*," he said to Cevilla. "I'm going to see about Sol." Without waiting for a reply, he left the kitchen.

"Well, that could have gone better." Cevilla's hand was still on Rhoda's. "Maybe they needed a little more warning."

Shaking her head, Rhoda said, "They would have reacted the same way. I take some comfort that they have each other, though. When they were growing up, they didn't have a relationship at all."

Cevilla removed her hand. "I'm sure they'll be back for breakfast in a few minutes. They need some time to let the news sink in."

"*Ya*." But she wasn't sure it was true.

Aden slowed his steps as he saw Sol standing near the barn, staring at the tall grass behind it. His brother's posture was rigid, his hands in his pockets. Aden knew he had to tread carefully. While he was still reeling from the news that their father was alive, Sol's reaction had been expected. He also knew his brother well enough to recognize that he was on the verge of exploding, something he hadn't done in years. Aden understood. Since the moment he read the letter about his father's so-called death, he had struggled with nightmares he hadn't had in a long time. It was as if the mention of his father transported him back to the past, and he was the scared boy that never knew when severe punishment would come. As bad as his life was back then, Sol's was worse. He hadn't believed it at the time, but age, maturity, and some hard, honest conversations with Sol had shown him that. He could only imagine what his brother was going through right now.

He stopped a few feet from him. "Sol?"

A pause. "*Ya*."

Anger laced that single word, and Aden wasn't sure what to say next. Maybe he should leave him alone to work through the news. But his instincts told him Sol needed him right now, even if his brother thought he didn't. "What are we going to do?" was the only sentence he could come up with.

Slowly, Sol turned around and Aden filled with dread. He hadn't seen that much anger and pain in his brother's eyes in over nine years. Since the last time they saw their father. "*Nix*. We do *nix*."

"We have to deal with him."

"You might. I don't."

"What if he wants to see us?"

Sol pressed his lips together. "Whatever you decide to do, I won't begrudge you. As for me, I won't have anything to do with him. You tell him that too. If he comes around me or *mei* family . . ." His chest heaved up and down. "I don't have to spell it out."

Aden's blood ran cold. "You have to forgive him, Sol."

"I did. A long time ago. But I don't have to see him." He started to walk away. "Tell *Mamm* I went home."

"You should tell her yourself."

But Sol kept on walking, as if he hadn't heard anything Aden said.

He blew out a frustrated breath as he turned around and went back inside. At least Sol was focusing on protecting his family. There was some comfort in that. Hopefully that decision included staying away from alcohol. Sol hadn't had a drink since their father left, but he wouldn't be shocked if *Daed*'s return drove him back to the bottle. All he could do was pray that it didn't.

"How's Sol?" *Mamm* asked as soon as Aden entered the kitchen.

"He went home." Aden sat down at the table. The basket of biscuits he dropped was now upright and full again, but everything else on the table was untouched. Resentment bubbled up, surprising him. His brother was abdicating responsibility again. They were a united team when it came to supporting their mother, but now he was leaving Aden to do that on his own. He ran away, just like he did when they were younger.

But as soon as he had the thought, he shoved it away. Sol was going home to his family, and Aden didn't mind being here for their mother. Sol had never been able to handle his anger the way Aden could, although his brother was much better than he used to be. Leaving now was a wise decision, not a cowardly one. Once again, their father was triggering emotions inside Aden that he hadn't felt in years.

"Aden?" *Mamm* moved her chair closer to him. "I'm sorry."

He looked at his mother. As an Amish man, he wasn't supposed to hate anything or anyone. But right now, he hated the suffering he saw in his mother's eyes. "You don't have anything to be sorry about. And don't worry about Sol. He's concerned about Irene and the *kinner*—that's why he left."

Mamm nodded. "I understand." She smoothed down a lock of his hair, something she used to do when he was a small child. "How are you taking this?"

He glanced at Cevilla, who was busy buttering a biscuit that was already laden with enough butter to clog an artery, pretending not to eavesdrop. He was okay with her hearing what he had to say. She, along with other women in Birch Creek, had been a network of support for his mother, and he couldn't thank them enough for that, even though they would brush off his gratitude if he tried. "I'm angry. Confused. Why did he lie about his own death in the letters?"

"I don't know. We didn't talk last night. I was too upset."

"You have *nee* idea why he came back then?"

"*Nee*."

"You said Jordan brought him over." Aden stroked his beard. "I thought he confirmed *Daed*'s death."

"He did."

"So he lied?"

"*Ya*." Rhoda shook her head. "I don't know why either. But it doesn't matter to me how he got here, or even why. And God forgive me . . ." She looked down at her lap, her lips trembling. "I wish he wasn't here."

Aden took her hand. "I understand."

She nodded. "Very few people will, though."

"Don't be surprised if they do." Cevilla set down the biscuit. It tipped over under the weight of excess butter. "At least those of us who were here when he was bishop. I almost said those of us who know him, but I don't think anyone other than you two and Sol knew the real him."

"I'm not sure we even knew the real him." *Mamm* finally met Aden's gaze. "He looked awful, Aden."

"He has cancer," Cevilla added.

Aden was surprised he could feel any compassion for the father who had abused him, then abandoned his family. But there it was. Sympathy for what he was going through. "Then that's why he's here," he said, more to himself than the women. "He wants to set things right."

"Or he wants something else," *Mamm* said.

"He's staying at *mei haus*," Cevilla said. "So is Jordan. I told *yer mamm* I would be by her side as long as she needs me." She scowled. "Besides, it's not a *gut* idea for me to be around Emmanuel right now. I can't promise to hold *mei* tongue."

"He could show up at any time." *Mamm* faced him. "You have to be prepared for that."

Aden was aware that Sol knew that too, which was why he had left. One reason, anyway. "I know. I'll *geh* home and tell Sadie, then I'll be back."

"*Nee*." She shook her head. "You don't have to come back here. I can handle him if he shows up."

Aden smirked. "So can Sadie." His wife was stronger than any woman he'd ever known, although his mother right now was coming in a close second.

"I know," *Mamm* said gently. "But you need to be with her. She experienced Emmanuel's manipulation too. You both need each other right now."

His mother was right. He and Sadie had been victims of his father in different ways, but God had healed them through their love for each other. "Let me know if you need anything," he said, getting up from the chair.

"Of course."

"And I'll be right here too." Cevilla grabbed her cane and thumped it on the floor for emphasis. A shadow passed over her face. "I don't think he's in any shape to harm anyone, though."

"Words are enough." Aden looked at both women, and they nodded.

Aden left and headed for Schrock's Grocery and Tool, the store he and Sadie ran. She participated less now in the running of the store than she had before their children were born, but at least once a week she liked to work a shift while her sisters, Abigail and Joanna, took turns bringing their children over to play with their cousins.

This morning one of their employees, a retired English man named Harold, had opened the store, leaving Aden free to go to his mother's. A part of him wished he would have stayed home.

Aden stopped and talked to Harold for a few minutes before going inside to speak to Sadie. The kitchen was already clean and tidy, the breakfast dishes drying in the sink. He went into the living room and saw Sadie sitting on the floor with Rosanna and Salina. She and the two girls were drawing on a sheet of butcher paper. He leaned against the doorframe, none of them noticing he was there. Tears burned in his eyes. He didn't want to interrupt, drinking in the happiness of his wife and daughters, his heart filled to bursting with love for them. But he had no choice. "Looks like fun," he said, strolling into the room like nothing was amiss. "Can I join you?"

"*Ya*!" Salina, who was two, held up a blue crayon and handed it to Aden as he sat down. Four-year-old Rosanna was on the other side and Sadie sat across from all three of them. He met her gaze, seeing the question in her eyes.

"I drew a horse, *Daed*." Rosanna pointed at several lines that sort of resembled . . . something.

"Cat!" Salina beamed as she gestured to her squiggly lines.

"Very nice. What did you draw, *Mamm*?"

She smiled shyly at him and looked at the paper. Sadie was no artist, but her two adult and two children stick figures were lined up in a row, holding hands.

"*Maed*," he said thickly. "*Geh* to the store for a few minutes. Harold has a piece of candy for each of you."

"Candy?" Sadie said. "This early in the day?"

"*Ya*," he said firmly. "*Geh* on. I'll be there soon."

Without hesitation they scrambled to their feet. Rosanna took Salina's hand and they left the living room. When he heard the door shut, Sadie got up and went to him.

"Something's wrong," she said, sitting close.

He turned and faced her, nodding. No sense in dragging the news out. "*Daed* is here."

Her face drained of color. "I . . . I don't understand. The letters—"

"I don't know why he wrote the letters." He told her what little information he had about his father's arrival, including where he was staying. "He could come over at any time. Or not come over at all."

Sadie didn't say anything for a long moment. "Do you want to see him?"

"I don't know. I don't know what to do right now."

She put her arm around him, and he gathered her in his lap. "This is worse than finding out he died. I feel so guilty about that."

"I know." She leaned against him. "I feel the same way."

There was nothing more either of them could say. All he could do was hold his wife close and lean on God.

Chapter 26

On Friday morning, Katharine was clearing the tables in the lobby after breakfast. The job was easy, since there was only one couple staying at the inn. Surprisingly for a weekend, there had been two cancellations. She was carrying the coffeepots to the small kitchen next to Loren and Levi's office when the bell above the front door rang. She turned to see Rhoda walk inside.

"Hi," she said, giving her friend a smile. Then she saw her pained expression and set the pots on the nearest table and went to her. "Rhoda? Are you okay?"

Rhoda pressed her lips together and shook her head. Then she said, "Is Loren here?"

"He's working in the office." Katharine heard despair in Rhoda's tone. "Can I do anything—"

But Rhoda hurried off behind the counter and knocked on the office door. A few seconds later Loren opened it, and as soon as he saw Rhoda, he put his arm around her and they went inside, shutting the door behind them.

Katharine stared at the door, her fingers turning cold. Something was seriously wrong.

Delilah walked into the lobby. "I thought you'd have those dishes finished by now," she said as she approached Katharine, using the tone she always did when they were at work. With the exception of the day she sent Katharine and Ezra to Barton, the woman did an excellent job separating work business from personal. "I just got a call from Richard . . ." She frowned. "What's wrong, Katharine?"

"I don't know." She turned to Delilah and told her about Rhoda going into the office with Loren.

Delilah's expression turned grim. "I'm sure whatever it is, they'll work it out." Then she adjusted her glasses. "Meanwhile, you have dishes to do. Then I need you to prepare the downstairs room for Cevilla and Richard."

"They're staying here?"

"*Ya*." She frowned. "I have *nee* idea why, only that Richard wanted me to book the room for them, and they would be here sometime this evening." Then she brightened. "Maybe he's planning a surprise for her. The last one didn't work too well, but if you don't succeed the first time, no harm in trying again."

"What happened?"

"He was going to propose, they got into a fight, and that ended the surprise. Everything worked out well in the end. It usually does."

As Delilah walked away, Katharine glanced at the office again. She was worried about Rhoda and Loren, and it just dawned on her that up until a little more than a month ago, she would have never asked Delilah about Cevilla and Richard. Her life was changing. *I'm changing.*

She walked into the kitchen, and before she started on the dishes, she said a quick prayer that everything was okay between Rhoda and Loren.

"I can't believe it."

Rhoda held in her tears as Loren fell back in his office chair. She was short and to the point about Emmanuel's return. If she'd been any other way she would have fallen to pieces. Loren looked up at her, and she almost did lose her hard-fought poise at the anguish she saw in his eyes.

"That means . . ." he said, but instead of completing the sentence he went silent.

"It means we're over." The words were harsh, but they needed to be said. Whatever plans they had for the future, they had to let them go.

He didn't move. He didn't look at her. He stared at the desk as if in a daze.

"It would be wrong to continue our relationship." The words were like a knife in her heart, but they were true. "You know that, right?" Unable to keep it together, she started to sob.

"Oh, Rhoda." He walked over to her and drew her into his arms.

"He has cancer. Pancreatic."

"I'm sorry."

She leaned against him, his heartbeat strong and fast. He'd never held her this close before, and she didn't want to think that this would be the last time. But it had to be. *This is so unfair.*

He started to rub her back, and she came to her senses and stepped away. "I'm a married woman," she said, trying to regain her equanimity.

"I know. But, Rhoda, I still love you. I'll always love you." His Adam's apple bobbed. "I have to believe that God is willing this for a reason. As much as it hurts, I have to put *mei* faith in him."

She backed away, her eyes still blurry with tears. When she reached the door, she put her hand on the knob. "I love you too." Before she lost her courage and fell into his arms, she opened the door and walked out.

When she stepped into the lobby, Katharine was wiping down the tables. She looked up and saw the worry in the young woman's eyes. Rhoda turned to go out the door, but Katharine caught up with her.

"Is everything okay with you and Loren?" she asked, her voice barely above a whisper.

How thoughtful that even though no one else was in the lobby, she was keeping Rhoda's secret. And because of that, she had to tell her the truth. "The wedding is off," she said, stunned that she could say the words out loud without crying again.

Katharine gasped. "Off?"

She nodded, then rushed out the door to her buggy and climbed in. Loren didn't come after her, and neither did Katharine. She backed out of the driveway and headed for home. She'd told the three people she loved that Emmanuel had returned. There was nothing else she could do except wait and see what her husband was up to—and how he planned to hurt her again.

On Sunday morning, Irene sat next to Sadie and her sisters, Joanna and Abigail, in church, with Rhoda on the other side. She couldn't help but continue to check on Sol, who was seated next to Aden on the opposite side of the room. She was worried about him. When he arrived home from Rhoda's yesterday morning, he wasn't himself. When she pressed him, he told her he was fine and that he had a lot of work to do. That had been his usual response to everything since his father died, and he had worked so hard lately that he was always exhausted. Only when she started to lose her temper with him did he tell her the truth—Emmanuel was alive after all.

The news shocked her almost speechless. And when she went to console Sol, he shrugged her off and went to his shop. Last night she had gone to bed alone. Her only comfort was her prayers and her determination to trust God with Sol.

All the pews in the barn were filled, and Irene prepared herself for hymn singing. Everyone rose to sing the first hymn. But two verses in, Irene heard shocked gasps from different parts of the barn. The singing faded and people started turning around. Irene looked over her shoulder and saw a gaunt, elderly Amish man with a cane being escorted to the last pew on the men's side by an English man she didn't recognize. No wonder people had stopped singing and were staring at the two of them. English rarely came to services. In fact, she could think of only two—Richard's granddaughter, Meghan, and Levi's friend Jackson. She'd also never seen the Amish man before, and old men tended to have beards. This man was clean-shaven.

Then she glanced at Sol, and she almost ran over to him. His face had turned the color of freshly fallen snow. So had Aden's. She looked back at the man, who stood with his chin lifted and staring straight to the front. Emmanuel?

"I can't believe it," Sadie whispered, gaping at Emmanuel.

Irene looked at her mother-in-law. She was almost as pale as Sol. Irene reached for her hand and gripped it.

Nee, nee.

Rhoda started to sway. She felt Irene take her hand, and she was grateful for the support, both physical and emotional. This morning as she prepared for church, she'd been afraid Emmanuel might show up. But as the service started, she relaxed. He'd always been a stickler for punctuality, so she thought she was safe. *I should have known better.*

The church was full, and almost the entire community had gathered for today's service, but only a few knew who Emmanuel was. When he left Birch Creek, over half the community went with him, and then a few more moved away for various reasons. Did he know that? *What is he going to do?*

The church had gone silent, and Rhoda didn't dare look back at Emmanuel again. She didn't even look at Sol and Aden, or Loren. It was all she could do not to sink to the floor.

Freemont cleared his throat. "I see we have visitors today. Emmanuel . . ." He coughed into his hand. "Welcome back."

"*Danke*. This is Jordan, if anyone's wondering."

His voice sounded weak, a quality she would have never associated with him.

Freemont nodded, then surveyed the congregation as if unsure what to do next. They had held a memorial for Emmanuel less than three weeks ago. Now everyone knew he was alive. After a moment he said, "The second hymn is—"

"Wait," Emmanuel said, his voice a little stronger than before. "I've got something to say."

Even from this distance, Rhoda saw Freemont's jaw tighten. "All right," he said slowly. "Would you like to come up front?"

"*Ya*. I would."

She heard the thump of his cane as he walked up the aisle between the wooden benches. Two barn swallows fluttered in the barn rafters, oblivious to the unfolding drama. When he passed her, she refused to look at him, her heart hardening with his every step. Jordan accompanied him, but Emmanuel shook him off when he got to the front of the church. He stood next to Freemont, in the exact spot he used to stand when he was bishop of Birch Creek.

Surely he wasn't going to demand to be bishop again? She didn't know if he even could, especially after what Sol revealed right before Emmanuel left—his theft of the community fund. That was in addition to how he had treated his sons, her, Sadie—

"I don't see many familiar faces," Emmanuel said, sounding in charge and in control, almost like he had years before. "The ones I do know . . . Let's just say I can tell you're not glad to see me." He lifted his chin, his gaze slowly passing over the filled pews. "I don't blame you."

"He sounds like Lester!" Delilah blurted.

He slowly turned to her. "*Ya*. I do, Delilah. Because I am Lester."

Rhoda was confused, and from the murmurs around her, other people were too.

"I'm Emmanuel Troyer. I'm also Lester Smith. Former handyman of Stoll's Inn, and before that, former bishop of Birch Creek. Now that everyone knows who I am, I'll tell you why I'm here." He met Rhoda's gaze. "I've sinned against you. Against all of you."

He looked back at the crowd. "I've committed horrible sins against *mei* wife, *mei sohns*, and the people of this town who trusted me to spiritually guide them and look out for their best interests. I didn't do either one. Instead I was abusive, proud, haughty, miserly . . . and a lot more things." He paused, leaning on his cane.

"As you can see, I'm not in the best way. God has dealt with me while I've been gone, and most of the time I haven't listened. I've been fighting God and my fear all this time.

"I came back to Birch Creek a year ago, under disguise and with a new name. God led me here back then, told me I had to make things right. But like always, I thought I knew best and I ran off. But I can't run anymore. I see that now. And I owe you all more than I can possibly repay. All I can do is ask for your forgiveness and promise to never bother any of you again."

Rhoda felt Sadie grab her other hand. She didn't know what to do. She had to forgive him and thought she had done so already. Now that he was asking in person, she needed to tell him that she had forgiven him. But what if this was another lie? Another trick to gain their sympathy now that he was sick? Did he mean anything he said? How could she be sure?

"There. I've said *mei* piece." With slow movements, he started back to his seat.

"Are you okay?" Sadie whispered as Emmanuel made his way down the aisle with Jordan.

"I . . . I don't know."

She expected him to leave, but to her surprise, he stayed through the entire service, which continued as if he'd never arrived. But Rhoda saw many people turning around and looking at him. Timothy Glick, the minister who delivered the sermon and had lived in Birch Creek when Emmanuel was bishop, stumbled throughout the message. Ironically, the lesson was on humility in difficult circumstances.

When the service was over, no one moved, as if everyone was waiting to see who would approach Emmanuel, if anyone. She finally looked at her sons. They stared back at her. She wasn't surprised at what she saw. Aden was confused and unsure, while Sol's lips were pressed so hard together they almost disappeared.

Then she saw Freemont approach Emmanuel, who was standing now. He shook his hand, then leaned forward and said something to him that Rhoda couldn't hear. That spurred everyone else to move, some people waiting to talk to Emmanuel, while those who didn't know him left the barn.

Rhoda stayed put, along with her sons and their wives. Cevilla stopped to talk to him, Richard by her side. When Rhoda saw Loren and Delilah go to Emmanuel, her heart squeezed. Delilah's expression almost mirrored Sol's, and Rhoda knew she was angry about being deceived. But she still spoke to him, and Rhoda was certain she had forgiven him. Loren too, but when he started to move away, Emmanuel took his arm and said something else to him. Rhoda clutched Sadie's and Irene's hands tighter as she looked at the two men. One she now loved, and one she had loved in the past.

Loren nodded and left. Now there was only the Troyers in the barn, along with Emmanuel and Jordan. Jordan put his hand on Emmanuel's shoulder, then he walked out of the barn.

Sol moved out of the pew. Rhoda held her breath as he approached his father . . . and passed him by.

Irene let go of Rhoda's hand and looked at her. Rhoda nodded, and Irene went down the aisle. Unlike Sol, she paused and spoke to Emmanuel, then hurried out the barn door.

Aden went to Emmanuel and spoke to him, keeping his distance. Emmanuel nodded, and Aden left the barn. Sadie followed suit, also speaking to Emmanuel before leaving.

Now she was alone with him . . . And she couldn't move.

Chapter 27

Jordan stood near the buggies surrounding the Yoders' barn, unsure what to do. When Emmanuel told him he wanted to go to church, he had balked at the idea. From his study of the Amish, he knew that public repentance was a thing in the church, and he expected Emmanuel to do that eventually. Just not on the first Sunday, and not before he had spoken with his family. But Emmanuel was beyond stubborn, and Jordan had given in. To say the reception was chilly and awkward was an understatement, and even when people stopped and forgave Emmanuel, he could see that a few were just going through the motions. He still wasn't sure of the particulars of Emmanuel's sins, and he didn't need to know. The people he had sinned against knew. So did God.

He shoved his hands in the pockets of his dress pants and saw the congregation milling around, although they were subdued. Only the children, who ran and played while the adults huddled in groups and kept their voices low, seemed unaffected. He glanced at the barn. Rhoda was still in there with Emmanuel, and hopefully she was talking to him this time.

"Interesting service, don't you think?"

He turned to see Freemont, the bishop, behind him. He was the first one to forgive Emmanuel. He also offered to talk to him later if Emmanuel chose to. Jordan hoped he would take him up on his offer. "Yeah," he said. "I, uh, didn't know what to expect when Emmanuel asked me to bring him to church this morning."

Freemont adjusted his glasses, as if hiding the emotion that had entered his eyes. "I'm glad you did. I've been praying for years for Emmanuel to come back."

"You have?"

He nodded. "Everything Emmanuel said this morning was true. I thank God that he didn't go into detail, though. Some things need to be kept between the family and God. That was a wise decision on his part, as was finally letting God into his heart."

"God does deal with us. That's for sure."

"Yes, he does. One way or another." Freemont held out his hand. "Feel free to stay for lunch. Emmanuel too." Sadness crossed his face. "He doesn't look good."

"He's not feeling that great either." Jordan shook his hand. "Thanks for the invitation, but I suspect he's exhausted by now. We're staying with Richard, and I'll need to get him back so he can rest."

"Understood. Thanks again, Jordan. You did a good thing bringing him back home."

The people around him grew quiet, and he saw Emmanuel leaving the barn. He ignored everyone and walked toward Jordan. As expected, his movements were slower and took more effort than they did before the service, and weariness had sunk deep into the lines on his face. Jordan went to him, and Emmanuel didn't protest when he helped him over to his car. When they got there, Jordan asked, "Ready to go back to Richard's?"

Emmanuel shook his head. "I'm not going back there."

Wait, was that it? He was only going to confess in front of the church? "You can't go back to Dixonville," Jordan said.

"I know. And I'm not."

Jordan frowned. "Then where are you going?"

"To my house." Rhoda appeared beside Emmanuel. "He's going home."

"You've been awfully quiet since we left the Yoders'."

Katharine looked at Ezra. They were walking back to the Stolls' together, deciding against partaking in the meal after the service. Ezra suggested they leave, and Katharine didn't hesitate to agree with him. She was trying to wrap her mind around finding out that the man she knew as Lester was Rhoda's husband. "I have a lot on *mei* mind," she murmured.

"Care to share?"

More than anything she wanted to share the burden on her heart. But she couldn't, not without betraying Rhoda or revealing her past with Simeon. It was hard to believe that the frail man who appeared in church today was healthy and strong only a year ago and fooling everyone into believing he was English. It was even more difficult to comprehend that he had been abusive to his family. She didn't know the details, and they weren't her business. But she'd seen the blend of fear and anger in the Troyers' expressions, along with the struggle to keep those feelings hidden from everyone else. Their battle was something she was familiar with.

But Ezra was waiting for an answer, and she didn't want to brush him off completely. "I was thinking about Rhoda and Loren," she said, telling him a half-truth. "Now I understand why she called off the wedding."

"So they were going to get married." Ezra stuck his hands into the pockets of his black pants, seemingly unsurprised at the news. "Emmanuel's return threw a big wrench into their plans, didn't it?"

Katharine sighed. It threw a wrench for more than just Rhoda and Loren. She'd noted the shocked reactions of everyone in the congregation. The man they thought was dead was still alive. She had to wonder how long, though. Then she shoved the morbid thought away. Lester—rather, Emmanuel—would live as long as God wanted him to.

The walk to the Stolls' didn't take long, and when they reached Loren and Delilah's, she said, "*Danki* for walking me home."

He stopped. "Home?"

She halted and turned to face him, confused.

Ezra moved closer to her. "Birch Creek is *yer* home?"

She paused, only now realizing that this was the first time she had called the Stolls' house her home. And saying it out loud felt right. She still missed her parents, and when the time was right she would tell them everything that had happened with her and Simeon, along with asking them for their forgiveness for not being truthful and for leaving them. Until that time, though, this was her home. "*Ya*," she said, stepping toward him. "I'm home."

He smiled, and she could tell he was waiting for an invitation to come inside. They hadn't eaten lunch, and normally she wouldn't mind fixing something for the both of them. But right now she wanted to be alone. There were too many emotions going through her, and she was afraid she wouldn't be able to continue keeping her secret from Ezra until she settled them. "Would you mind if I take a rain check on lunch? I've got a headache."

"Oh. Sure. We can do that."

But she didn't miss the disappointment in his eyes. Which led her to stand on her tiptoes and kiss his cheek. "I promise I'll make it up to you."

She froze. She had said the exact same thing to Simeon before she left Hulett. And while she meant to keep the promise to Ezra, a terrifying thought slammed into her. *What if Simeon finds me?*

"Katharine?"

She blinked, seeing Ezra's confused face coming into focus. "*Ya*?"

He touched her cheek. "You do look unwell. Are you sure you don't want me to stay?"

She touched his hand, then moved it away from her face. "*Nee*. I'm going straight upstairs to lie down. I'll sleep it off, don't worry."

"All right." His smile returned. "I'll see you tomorrow then."

Katharine gave him a small wave as he walked away. Then she went inside, shut the door, and leaned against it, gulping air and trying to cling to reality. She had been afraid of Simeon discovering her deception and finding her in Birch Creek when she first arrived last year, but that fear had diminished. For the first time since she briefly talked to him when he answered his parents' phone, she thought about their conversation. He didn't flatter her, or cajole her, or try to manipulate her.

Her heartbeat slowed. It didn't make any sense for him to look for her now. He thought she was happy in Montana. He was calm and seemed to accept that she had moved on. No, she didn't have to worry about him showing up in Birch Creek. He had no idea where Birch Creek was.

Now her head really was pounding, and she went into the kitchen to make a cup of chamomile tea. As she waited for the water to boil in the kettle, she kept reassuring herself she was safe here. There was one thing nagging at her, though. Why was Simeon still so attached to her family?

She fixed the tea, then set it on the table to cool. She went to the desk in the living room and pulled out a paper and pen and brought it back to the kitchen. She didn't want to get Elsie more involved than she was, but she needed information. Usually she waited for Elsie to write her back, and she had just sent her a letter two weeks ago. She was sure her friend would understand.

Dear Elsie,

I accidentally talked to Simeon recently. I called Mamm and Daed and he answered the phone. Are my parents okay? Mamm sounded fine, although she's still upset with me about leaving and not giving her my address. I'm sorry to ask you this, but could you let me know if they're all right? You might have to ask them yourself. They're exceptionally good at hiding their problems.

Katharine paused, not wanting to write the next sentence. She didn't want to leave Birch Creek, or her friends, and especially not Ezra. But she would if Simeon was harming her parents in any way.

If I need to, I'll come back to Hulett.

Your friend,
Katharine

She put the letter in the envelope and sealed it. Then she placed a stamp in the corner and hurried to the mailbox. Usually she dropped her letters off at the post office, but there was no time. She lifted the red flag on the side of the box, then rushed back to the house and sat back down at the table and sipped the now tepid tea. Hopefully the brew would heal her headache . . . and hopefully Simeon had turned a new leaf, and his devotion to her parents was sincere. *Miracles can happen, right?*

Rhoda stood in her bedroom and looked at Emmanuel, asleep in her bed. Now it was their bed . . . again. Was it only a year ago that she was able to feel like this was her home, and not his? That she was able to move away from the past and embrace a new future? *Not anymore.*

She stared at his face, his eyes closed and his thin chest rising and falling as he slept. Of all of the mixed emotions flowing through her, the one that rose to the surface was pity. She believed in miracles, and if it was God's will, he would heal Emmanuel. She would pray that he did, because it would take a miracle for the wasted man lying in front of her to regain his health.

She thought about all he had missed, all he had lost and would lose. But he'd taken a step toward God now, and she hoped he would continue. That was one reason why she insisted he come back here with her. That, and the fact that he was her husband. For better or worse.

As quietly as she could, she left the bedroom and went to the kitchen. Jordan was still there, along with Richard and Cevilla. When Cevilla saw her getting into Jordan's car, she hollered at them to wait and directed Richard to go with her to the car. The three of them rode in the back seat of Jordan's car, with Emmanuel sitting up front, everyone completely silent during the drive to the Troyers'. It felt like the longest ride of her life.

"Is he okay?" Jordan asked, as she entered the room.

Rhoda nodded. "For now. He fell asleep as soon as he laid down." She looked at the three of them. "I'll fix us something for lunch."

Jordan held out his hand. "I can run and get us something."

"Not on Sunday." Cevilla scooted away from the table. "Sit down, Rhoda. I'll make lunch."

"*I'll* make lunch." Richard's tone brooked no argument, and Rhoda imagined that was the same when he'd worked in the business world. He didn't become a billionaire overnight. A sharp contrast to Emmanuel, who had been consumed with money, especially hoarding it. Richard made more money than Emmanuel could even dream of, and he gave it all up to join the Amish and marry Cevilla. Emmanuel had clung to money and power until it was taken away from him.

Cevilla knew Rhoda's kitchen almost as well as Rhoda did, so she directed Richard to prepare sandwiches. While he followed her specifications, Jordan turned to Rhoda, a sheepish look crossing his face.

"I'm sure you want an explanation about why we showed up today," he said.

Rhoda stared straight ahead at the napkin holder in the middle of the table. "Emmanuel gave me one." At least he tried to. As he drifted off to sleep, he mumbled something about finally understanding the truth. She had no idea what he was talking about, and it didn't matter. He had done what he was supposed to do—ask those he sinned against for forgiveness. She just hoped he had gone to the Lord first, the one he had sinned against most of all.

"I understand if you're mad at me for telling you he was dead. Honestly, I thought it wouldn't be long before he actually was."

She listened as he explained how he'd stayed with Emmanuel,

about her husband's stubborn refusal to go home and make things right, and then how he'd changed his mind. "I'm sorry that this is causing you so much trouble." He rubbed the back of his neck. "But I'd do it again if I had to. Without hesitation."

"You did the right thing."

"Freemont said that too. But it means more coming from you."

She asked him the one question that had been on her mind since Emmanuel showed up on her doorstep. "Why did he want us to think he was dead?"

"I don't know. He refused to talk about it with me, other than to say you were all better off without him. Sounds like he thought he was doing you and your sons a favor."

By controlling and manipulating us? But she didn't say the thought out loud. Emmanuel was never able to release control of anything, not fully. She turned to Jordan. "You're free to go back to California," she said. "Emmanuel will stay here until . . ." She couldn't bring herself to say it. She didn't love him as a husband anymore, but she didn't want him to suffer.

Jordan nodded. "After I drop off Richard and Cevilla, I'll get his clothes and bring them over. He doesn't have much. Although I think he would have snuck in the TV if he could have."

"He had a TV?"

"At the motel. He liked to watch westerns."

That surprised her. He'd always said television was of the devil.

"From what I've been able to gather, he did try to assimilate into English life."

"Then he wouldn't have come back if you hadn't intervened." Or if he wasn't dying.

Shaking his head, Jordan said, "I wouldn't go that far. Remember, he was here last year. In disguise, but he did come back."

She had forgotten about that, and now she was thinking of Loren. She would have to talk to him again, and soon. He had to be wondering why she agreed to take Emmanuel home. She'd have to explain to her sons too. Her temples throbbed. This was all becoming too much.

"Rhoda, I believe he would have come around to do what he did today, regardless of his illness," he continued.

Jordan might think that, but she wasn't convinced.

"Turkey and Swiss ready to go." Richard put the plates in front of Rhoda and Jordan. "With mustard and tomato, just like my lovely wife ordered."

Cevilla smiled at him, and he went to fetch her plate. "I agree with Jordan, Rhoda," she said.

Rhoda glanced at her. The woman had an uncanny ability to listen to conversations even while she was talking to someone else. "You do?"

"After hearing him today, I think God would have brought him back again. Actually, he did, through Jordan."

After they prayed over the meal, Rhoda thought about Cevilla's and Jordan's words. She still had her doubts, but the whole point was moot. Emmanuel had returned. He'd asked for forgiveness. She gave it to him, along with a place to rest and be taken care of. That was her focus now.

As soon as they finished lunch, Jordan took the Thompsons home. Cevilla gave her a hug of encouragement, and said she would be back tomorrow, or anytime Rhoda needed her. Before Jordan got in the car, he said, "Let me know when he . . . when he passes. I'd like to come back for the funeral."

"I will."

Once they left, she went to the bedroom. Emmanuel hadn't

stirred, and a thread of panic wound around her heart as she looked at his chest. When she saw it rise and fall again, she let out the breath she didn't know she was holding. Then she went outside and sat on her front porch, desperate for fresh air and time alone to pray. A few minutes passed and she saw a buggy turn into her driveway. Loren.

She went to meet him as he got out of the buggy. But neither of them said anything right away, only looked at each other. "I'm sorry," Rhoda finally managed, her emotions clogging her throat. "I didn't know what he was going to do today, I promise. I didn't know he was Lester either. Please believe me."

"It's all right, Rhoda." Loren took her hand, then released it, as if he'd forgotten he didn't have the right to hold it anymore. "Of course I believe you. What I can't fathom is that he's Lester. He never gave a hint of his past, or that he'd ever been Amish." He moved closer to her. "Are you okay?"

She let out a bitter laugh. "*Nee*. I'm not. You and I . . . We were so close," she whispered, looking up at him. "So close to finally being happy."

He took her hands this time and kissed her fingertips. "We have to trust God's plan, remember? Whatever that may be. You need to concentrate on Lester, er, Emmanuel."

"Are you angry that I brought him back?"

His smile was gentle. "*Nee*. I expected you would. That's the kind of woman you are. Loving. Loyal. It's why I—" His smile disappeared and his breathing stuttered. He let go of her hands and turned to go to his buggy.

"Loren."

He turned around and she ran to him and threw her arms around his waist. She leaned her cheek against his chest. "I love you. No matter what happens."

"I love you too." He pulled away and climbed into the buggy.

She watched him drive off, her heart aching. What did the future hold for her now? She didn't know, but she had to believe what Loren said. *Help me trust your plan, Lord. Give me the strength I need to do your will.*

Chapter 28

Over the following week, Emmanuel felt his life slipping away. That didn't surprise him. He'd refused treatment for terminal cancer and had accepted that he would die soon. What he didn't expect was the tender care Rhoda gave him, or Aden's two visits. They didn't say much the first visit, except for Emmanuel apologizing again, more than once. His youngest had accepted his apology, and on his second visit, he brought over his daughters, Salina and Rosanna. They were wary, of course. They had no idea that their grandfather existed until now, being too young to understand any explanations about why he wasn't around. He wasn't a pretty sight either. Although he tried to hide his sparse hair with an Amish hat, wore two shirts and had to use suspenders to keep his pants from falling down, he couldn't hide his hollow cheeks, sallow skin, and raspy voice. Still, they warmed up to him eventually.

"*Danki* for bringing them by," he said to Aden when Rhoda took them to the kitchen for fresh-baked cookies. "They're fine *maed*."

Aden nodded. "I'm glad you got to see them."

Guilt, remorse, and regret were his constant companions, and they had never been so acute as they were right now as he looked up from the chair he used to sit in before his hubris made him lose everything. "You turned out *gut* too," he mumbled, his throat thick and tight. "Better than if I had been here."

To his credit, Aden didn't deny the statement. "I've got *mei* faith, and the love of a *gut* woman."

"Even though I tried to force her to marry Sol."

"I always loved Sadie, *Daed*. Why do you think I stepped in and married her? Thank God she ended up loving me too."

After Aden and the girls left, Emmanuel stared out the window. Despite his cruel decisions and actions, his sons had persevered. Sol still refused to see him, and he wasn't surprised when he passed him by in church that Sunday after the service and his confession and didn't offer his forgiveness. Sol was more like him than Emmanuel wanted to admit—stubborn, prideful, and had a hot temper. But he'd also changed, according to Rhoda. She believed he would come around.

Rhoda. A bluebird landed on the windowsill, and he smiled, although it faded quickly. He'd accused her of being weak, but she was stronger than he realized. Faithful too. Aden told him how she stuck to the belief that he would come back, and had only given up that belief last year, for her own sake. He had lost so much. No, not lost. Thrown it away, all because of pride and greed. *Don't forget stubbornness and fear.* The bluebird flew away.

"Did you have a nice visit?" Rhoda set a mug on the side table and he recognized the scent wafting from the drink. Margaret Yoder, the young woman he found in his shed with Owen Bontrager the night he fled Birch Creek, was now engaged to the boy and was an herbalist. She brought over packets of green tea with chamomile and peppermint. He didn't care for tea or peppermint, but he drank it anyway. She asked why he left her and Owen at the hospital that night, and he was honest and explained his reasons. She said she understood, although he was certain she was just being polite. He had to admit the tea wasn't too bad. He was less nauseous than he'd been when he first arrived in Birch Creek, although his appetite had completely disappeared now.

"*Ya*," Emmanuel finally said, moving to pick up the mug. "I can see those *maed* are the apple of your eye."

"So are Solomon and Isaac." She sat down on the couch across from him. "Sol will probably bring them by one day soon."

"You don't believe that any more than I do."

Rhoda looked down at her hands in her lap. She'd taken to wearing a kerchief around the house, although she made sure to put on her white *kapp* and black bonnet when she left the house. Today the kerchief was yellow. She'd made changes in the house too. Getting rid of his stuff mostly. And he could tell the bed was different, but neither of them pointed it out.

But it was her confidence he noticed the most. She was no longer the mousy wife he could order around at will. She had an inner strength and backbone he didn't know she possessed. He'd kept her from blossoming. He could see that now. Instead he believed he was doing the right thing by being the head of the household and keeping her and their sons on a tight leash. Not for their sakes but for his own.

Those things were far from his mind right now. He was focused on the worry lines around her face. They never eased. That was his fault too.

"I deserve everything I get, Rhoda," he said, looking out the window again. Pain shot through his heart, and his chest squeezed like a vise had closed around it. Not only was his body breaking down but his heart and emotions were too. Rhoda kept a Bible in their bedroom, and lately he read that book more than he ever had in his life. As bishop he used to pick out the verses that lined up with his beliefs and motivations. Now it was as if he were reading God's Word for the first time, and it was piercing him through.

She didn't respond right away, and he turned and looked at her. She was staring at him, compassion in her eyes. After all the abuse he'd heaped on her and their sons, that she could still find it in her not only to forgive him but to take care of him . . . "I never deserved you, Rhoda. Or Sol and Aden. I see that now."

Rhoda threw her hands up in the air. "Enough!"

His brow shot up. She'd never yelled at him before.

"Is this how it's going to be? You throwing a pity party every minute until you take your last breath? Or is this another way for you to torture us? To torture *me*." She shot up from the couch. "Everyone has forgiven you. It's past time to forgive yourself." She stormed out of the room.

He sat back in the chair, reeling from her words, letting them settle in his slowed-down mind. She was right. His self-flagellation served no purpose. It would be near impossible for him to forgive himself. But what he could do was not drag her and everyone else down.

Slowly he got up from the table and grabbed his cane. He tried to pick up the mug, but he couldn't do it without his hands shaking. Not wanting to make a mess for Rhoda, he left the mug there and went into the kitchen and saw her leaning against the sink, her head down.

"Rhoda?"

Her shoulders tensed and she turned and looked at him. "What?"

"I'm sorry. You're right. I'm being unfair. I promise, *nee* more pity parties." He moved closer to her. Tilted his head. Intense tenderness filled his heart. "You're still beautiful, you know that?"

Her cheeks reddened as she looked away.

"I never told you that enough when we were married. I never said it at all after the *buwe* were born."

"Because you didn't think so."

"Because I'm a *dummkopf*. And that's not me being self-pitying, it's the truth. Remember when we were first married? How much we enjoyed each other's company?"

Finally she faced him. "What happened? Why did you change so much?"

"I took *mei* eyes off God and put them on money, control, and power. Now that I'm back here, I can see the best thing God did was rip all that away from me. He's humbling me, Rhoda. And I've stopped fighting him."

Tears formed in her eyes. She reached out her hand and tentatively touched his cheek. "I'm sorry you're going through this."

He closed his eyes, her touch soothing his soul. "Don't be. I'm not. Call me *ab im kopp*, but it's the best thing that's ever happened to me, next to you and our *sohns*. I used to think blessings came to me because I earned them. Now I know he blessed me in spite of myself."

"Oh, Emmanuel." Tears slipped down her cheeks. "For years I prayed you would realize this. I'm so happy it's happened before . . ."

"Before I die. It's okay. You can say it." His legs started to wobble.

"You need to sit down." Rhoda started to help him to one of the chairs by the table.

"In a minute. I have one more thing to say." He met Rhoda's gaze. "Promise me after I'm gone, you and Loren will marry. You both have *mei* blessing."

"How did you know—"

"I worked for him, remember? I knew last year he had feelings for you. All the changes you've made in the house clued me in too. I'm glad you were going to move on. I don't want to stand in your way."

She took his free hand and pressed it to her cheek. "*Danki*," she whispered.

They both turned at the sound of the back kitchen door opening. "I hope you don't mind a little visit," Irene said as she entered, Solomon and Isaac holding her hands.

"Of course." Rhoda let go of Emmanuel's hand and wiped her cheek. "We were just going to sit down for a snack." She put her arm underneath his elbow. "Weren't we, Emmanuel?"

"*Ya*." He couldn't keep his eyes off his grandsons. He truly believed he would never see them again. Once he was seated at the table, he looked at them. He couldn't stop smiling if he tried.

"*Buwe*," Irene said, bringing her sons over to Emmanuel. "This is your *grossvatter*. He's not feeling well today, so don't be rambunctious."

"Hi," said Isaac, the younger one. Then he went to Rhoda. "Can I have cookie, *Grossmutter*?"

"You sure can."

"Wash up first," Irene said. "You too, Solomon."

But Solomon was still staring at Emmanuel, and Emmanuel couldn't keep his eyes off the boy. The same red hair, green eyes, and wiry body as his father. It was like seeing his Sol again as a little boy.

"Why is he crying?" Solomon said to Irene.

"His eyes are just watering," Irene said, her gaze averted from Emmanuel. "Now, *geh* with Isaac and wash up."

They scampered off, and Irene pulled a handkerchief out of her purse. Without a word, she handed it to Emmanuel.

He wiped his eyes. "I didn't think Sol would let you bring them here," he said.

She lifted her chin. "He doesn't know I did."

Rhoda moved next to her, holding a plate of butterscotch cookies. She exchanged looks with Emmanuel. They both knew the risk Irene was taking. And while Emmanuel's heart ached knowing it was unlikely he would see his oldest son again, he was filled with joy that he could see his children. *My grandchildren. Thank you, Lord.*

Chapter 29

Galen stood in front of Eugene and Iva Miller's door but hesitated to knock. He hadn't been to Katharine's parents' house since he discovered Elsie's hidden letters, honoring Simeon's request not to tell them that their daughter was in Ohio. That was over two weeks ago, and as far as he knew, Simeon hadn't said anything to them. Things were just as they had always been. Simeon continued to work, he never mentioned Katharine to Galen, nor had he said anything to Elsie about not telling him the truth about her. He was also at Katharine's parents' house every evening. Which was why Galen thought they might know where Simeon was, because for the past two days, he hadn't been able to find him. Katharine hadn't responded to Elsie's letter either.

He knocked on the door, and Iva opened it. "Hello, Galen," she said, giving him a big smile that reminded him of Katharine. "What brings you by today?"

"Do you and Eugene have a few minutes? I need to talk to you about something."

"Sure. He's in the living room." She opened the door wider so he could come inside. "Would you like something to drink?"

"*Nee*, but I appreciate the offer." As she shut the door, she gestured to the small hallway behind her that led to the living room, and he followed her there.

"Eugene, Galen Schroeder is here."

Eugene rose to his feet, which was difficult to do because of his crooked back.

"You don't have to get up," Galen said.

"*Ya*, I do." He straightened his back the best he could. "The pain is worse if I sit too long, so don't mind me standing a little while."

"How's Elsie?" Iva asked, gesturing to the couch across from the recliner her husband had just vacated and another, smaller chair next to it. A side table sat between the chairs, and a pile of books and magazines was perched precariously on top of it.

"She's well." He sat down, looking around the room. He hadn't noticed this the last time he was here for church two months ago, since he was busy visiting with other church members, but he could see that the recliners were leather, and looked expensive. The woodstove in the corner of the room appeared to be brand new, and so did other pieces of furniture. Considering Eugene couldn't work anymore, that surprised him. "Have you spoken to Simeon lately?" he asked, knowing he needed to get to the reason he was here and stop evaluating the Millers' furniture.

Iva and Eugene exchanged glances. "Why do you ask?" Eugene said.

"I haven't seen him for a couple of days, which is unusual. I checked the forge yesterday, but he wasn't there, and it was a workday. I stopped by his *haus* on the way home from work and didn't see him there either." He left off the fact that he had been keeping tabs on Simeon. The best he could anyway. He didn't want to raise the man's suspicions.

"We should tell him, Eugene." Iva clasped her hands together, a delighted sparkle appearing in her eyes. "Everyone will know soon enough."

Galen frowned. "Know what?"

"Katharine's coming home." Eugene beamed, then shifted on his feet.

Shock coursed through him. "Sh-she is?"

"Simeon went to get her," Iva said. "He came by day before yesterday and told us everything."

Alarm bells went off in Galen's head. "Everything?"

"About how she had gotten cold feet about the marriage. I knew that she was nervous about getting married—what new bride isn't—but I didn't realize it was that bad. He's on his way to West Kootenai to fetch her back."

He stilled. "Are you sure he said West Kootenai?"

"*Ya*," Katharine's father said. "That's where she ran off to. Turns out she hadn't found another man after all—"

"That was the nerves talking," Iva interjected.

"And they've been writing letters to each other for months. Simeon didn't want to say anything about that in case she wasn't ready to come home. He finally convinced her, though. After all this time, we'll have our *dochder* back."

Galen fell against the back of the chair. Simeon was lying to them. Flat-out lying, and Katharine's parents didn't doubt him for a moment. Even knowing the truth, Simeon's fabricated story didn't make much sense. "Have you talked to her since he left?"

Eugene shook his head. "*Nee*."

"He said he needed to handle things himself." Iva nodded. "Of course he's right. This is between the two of them."

"I gotta admit, though. We're upset that she didn't just tell us she was nervous about the wedding. We would have understood and let her postpone it." He rubbed the back of his neck. "Then there's her refusal to give us her address or phone number."

"Simeon explained all that, dear." Iva patted his knee.

"What did he say?" Galen asked.

"That Katharine didn't want to disappoint us. She doesn't like to see anyone unhappy."

"Simeon told you that."

"*Ya*. Once he explained everything it all made sense." Iva's tone turned somber. "It's *nee* secret she's struggled with her weight. Eugene and I have tried to encourage her."

"We love her *nee* matter what," Eugene said.

"But I could tell she was getting anxious the closer it was to the wedding date. She doesn't like having a lot of attention focused on her. And *nee* matter what we said, she was still nervous."

Or afraid. Galen was starting to realize the signs had been there all along.

"I'm so glad the two of them worked it out," she said. "Simeon's perfect for her."

Did he tell you that too? Galen held his tongue, not wanting his anger to get the best of him. The Millers were a kind, genial couple. Much like Katharine, now that he thought about it. Elsie had reminded him of how she used to be before she and Simeon got together. How she was always willing to help anyone, no matter who they were. He hadn't paid attention, focusing more on work and Elsie and Jason. Katharine was an afterthought.

"We tried to pay his way to West Kootenai," Eugene said. "But he wouldn't hear of it. He said we'd been generous with him enough over the past year."

Iva nodded. "Of course we had to offer, considering business has been so slow for him. Why people would buy their horseshoes in Rapid City when Simeon sells them here in Hulett is beyond me."

Another lie. As long as he'd known Simeon, his business had been thriving. Why did he deceive them? Then he remembered the day he went to the smithy to tell him about Katharine being in Birch Creek. How the forge had looked different, and that Simeon not only had a new anvil but also a new leather apron. Both were high quality, and neither were cheap.

"What's money between in-laws, I told him." Eugene made his way back to the recliner and carefully sat back down. The man was in obvious pain but hadn't uttered a word of complaint. "The settlement will be his and Katharine's eventually."

"What settlement?" Galen blurted.

"The one the roofing company gave us for Eugene's fall." She leaned close to Galen. "We don't like to talk about it."

"I told *mei* boss I didn't need the money, but he insisted," Eugene said. "*Gut* thing we took it too, so we could help out Simeon."

"Does he know about the settlement?"

"*Ya*. Soon after the accident he came by to reshoe *mei* horse."

"He's thoughtful like that," Iva said.

"The representative from the insurance company was here, and Simeon came inside for a drink as we were discussing it."

Galen's stomach churned. "I'm sorry, but I have to ask this. Did you get the settlement before or after Simeon and Katharine started dating?"

"A little before," Eugene said, frowning. "About a month, I'd guess."

Galen leaned back on the couch, the pieces starting to fit together. Elsie had been right, about everything. Did Katharine know that Simeon only dated her because of the money?

"You're looking a little pasty," Iva said, her brow furrowing. "Are you feeling all right?"

"I hope there's *nix* wrong," Eugene added.

Everything was wrong. Not only had Simeon used his relationship with Katharine to get to the Millers' money, but he also lied to them about his business. And then there was the biggest lie of all—that he was going to Montana to bring Katharine home.

He must have gone to Birch Creek instead.

"I have to *geh*," Galen said, jumping up from the chair.

"*Danki* for stopping by." Eugene slowly stood up again. "We enjoy having the company. Simeon has been a godsend in that regard."

"It's still difficult for Eugene to get around," Iva said. "But he'll be up and about soon." She grinned at her husband. "He's worked hard to heal from the accident."

"With your help." He smiled.

"And now that Katharine's coming home, we'll be a *familye* again."

Galen nodded, and tried not to hurry to his buggy. When he got inside and on the road, he urged his horse into a brisk trot all the way home. He brought the buggy to a halt and rushed inside. "Call your *mamm*," he said as soon as he entered the living room.

Elsie was seated on a chair, reading a book to Jason. "Why?"

"I'm pretty sure Simeon went to Birch Creek."

She paled. "What?"

Galen knelt down in front of her. "I have to *geh* after him," he said. "But I know you're due soon."

She nodded. "*Geh*," she said. "*Mamm* can be here in two days. Until then I'll let the Davises know you're gone."

That was a good idea. Their English neighbors, an older couple with grown children, were good friends with him and Elsie. He could count on them to take care of her and Jason if anything happened. "You were right," he said. "You were right about everything. I'll be back as soon as I can." He touched Elsie's belly, then stood.

"What are you going to do?"

"I'm not sure." *But I have to do something.*

In the week following Emmanuel's return to Birch Creek, a solemnity settled over the community. Guests at the inn weren't aware, though. Ezra was impressed with Loren's professionalism and ability to hide his emotions, considering he'd had his heart broken. Delilah was in work mode too, although he'd seen her shoulders slump and heard her sigh heavily a few times, the only sign that anything was amiss.

And then there was Katharine. While he had been disappointed that she didn't invite him to stay for lunch last Sunday, he was more concerned with her headache. On Monday she seemed back to her normal self, although more serious than usual. By Thursday he'd finished up the landscaping, and when he saw her going to the barn, he followed.

She didn't turn around as he walked a few paces behind her, and he figured she must be deep in thought. Not wanting to startle her, he waited until she was seated at her table before softly saying her name. "Katharine."

Her head jerked up, and for a minute he saw a flash of fear in her eyes, something he hadn't seen in a long time. Then she smiled. "Hi, Ezra."

When he saw her smile, his apprehension disappeared. "I finished the flower beds," he said, pulling out the extra chair next to her. He sat down. "That was a job."

"They look wonderful. The flowers and plants are beautiful."

"So are you." He looked at her light-blue dress. "Have I ever told you how much I like you in blue?"

She chuckled. "*Nee*. I guess I'll have to wear it more often."

He stood and held his hand out to her. She slipped hers in his and stood in front of him. He put his arms around her waist. "I've been waiting all week to hold you," he said. "And I have to be honest and tell you that even though I've been working on it, I'm not a patient man. So if you don't want me to kiss you, tell me now."

Her response was a smile.

He bent down and kissed her. His intention was to give her a quick kiss and step away. But once his lips touched hers, he couldn't hold back. He never wanted to let this woman go.

When they broke the kiss, he couldn't hold back his words either. "I love you, Katharine. I know it's probably too soon to say that, but if I wait a month or fifty, my feelings won't change. So I might as well say it now."

Her eyes widened, and he wasn't surprised she was caught off guard. When she didn't say anything, he knew he'd blundered. "You don't have to say it back," he fumbled.

She stared up at him, her mouth opening to speak. Then she closed it. Opened it again, and said, "I—

"Katharine?"

They both turned to see a man standing there gaping at them. Ezra didn't recognize him.

"Galen?" Katharine ran out of his arms and over to the man.

Ezra's stomach plunged to his feet. Was this the guy who had caused her so much pain? He couldn't tell. They both stood apart from each other, neither one of them saying anything.

Finally Galen spoke. "I hardly recognize you," he said.

"I look a little different, *ya*?" She grinned at him.

"You look great."

Ezra thought he was going to throw up. They sure didn't act like they were at odds with each other. Then again, she had never confided in him about her past.

"What are you doing here? How's Elsie?"

"She's fine. Did you get her letter?"

Katharine shook her head. "I haven't heard from her since the last one I sent. Did she have the *boppli*?"

"Not yet."

"Ahem." Ezra cleared his throat.

Katharine turned around. "Oh, I'm sorry." She motioned for Ezra to join them. "This is Galen. His wife is *mei* best friend."

"Nice to meet you," Galen said, holding out his hand. Then he looked at Katharine. "You're happy, *ya*?"

She gazed up at Ezra. "*Ya*. Very happy."

He blew out a breath. "Then Simeon never showed up, did he?"

Ezra felt Katharine stiffen beside him. "Simeon? Here?" Her hand shot to her chest.

"I guess he changed his mind," Galen said with a half grin.

"About what?" Katharine asked.

"It's a long story. Is there somewhere we can talk? I could use a drink too. It's a long ride from Wyoming."

"Of course. We'll *geh* to the inn." She and Galen started to leave.

Ezra stood there, unsure what to do. Obviously, whatever was going on was personal. Something she couldn't or didn't want to share with him. He had to respect that, even if he didn't like it.

Wait . . . Galen was from Wyoming? Not Montana?

She stopped and ran back to him. "Are you coming?"

"I wasn't sure you wanted me to."

Katharine took his hand. "I do. I need to tell you the truth."

As the three of them walked out of the barn, Ezra asked, "The truth about what?"

"About—" She came to a halt. "Oh *nee*."

He immediately put his arm around her waist as a man who looked like he split cement blocks in half for a living approached from the inn's parking lot. He was broad, with the biggest arms and shoulders Ezra had ever seen.

"Oh *nee* is right," Galen muttered.

The man stopped in front of them. Looked at Galen, then at Katharine. Finally he set his sights on Ezra and said, "I'd appreciate it if you'd get your hands off *mei* wife."

Chapter 30

Wife?

Ezra let go of Katharine, unable to comprehend what he'd just heard. His mouth fell open. "You're *married*?"

"*Nee*! I'm not! I promise you I'm not married."

"We are betrothed, though." Simeon walked up to Ezra and held out his hand. "Simeon Kuhns."

Ezra stared at the huge hand extended to him. This guy had to be kidding.

"How did you find me?" Katharine said. Despite the fear in her voice, she stepped between him and Simeon. Ezra moved to stand next to her.

Simeon smiled in an arrogant way. "I guess Elsie isn't the friend you thought she was. Isn't that right, Galen?"

Galen scowled. "And you're not the friend I thought you were."

His jaw jerked, and the innocent expression turned hard. "What are you doing here?"

"Stopping whatever it is you plan to do."

He grinned. "The only thing I'm doing is taking my sweetheart back home to Hulett. Where she belongs."

The color drained from her face.

Ezra was floored. "What are you talking about? She's from Montana."

Simeon laughed, and Galen shook his head.

Turning to Katharine, he said, "You lied to me? To Delilah and Loren? To all of us?"

She gripped his hand so tightly he thought his fingers might snap. "I didn't want to," she said, her voice shaking. "I had to. I couldn't take the chance that anyone here had a connection to Hulett."

"Don't feel bad," Simeon said. "She lied to me too. And to her parents. But I forgive her, and I'm sure they will too."

Ezra was too shocked to move. For the second time, he had fallen for a woman who was involved with someone else. At least Gloria wasn't engaged. But she lied to him too. Why was he such a naive fool?

"It's not like that and you know it, Simeon." Galen stepped between them. "Leave her alone. She's moved on. Time you did too."

Simeon turned, his gaze narrowing. "You're *mei* best friend. How could you turn on me like this?"

"And how could you abuse someone you said you loved?"

Galen's words punched through Ezra's pain. Simeon was the man who had hurt her. The one who put that fear in her eyes, who scared her so much that she flinched anytime a man came close to her. He was so big and strong that Ezra was sure he could take on both him and Galen. Anger rose inside him at the mere thought of Simeon hitting Katharine.

"You don't know what you're talking about," Simeon said, his mouth twitching like a nerve had jangled loose. "What stories did she tell you and Elsie? Don't believe them. She's a liar, as you can see." He spun around and faced her. "But despite that, I love you. I forgive you for leaving me. Come back to Hulett. Your parents miss you."

"Don't listen to him, Katharine," Galen said.

But Ezra could tell she couldn't hear him. She was lost again, frozen with fear as she clutched his hand and stared blankly at Simeon.

Simeon moved toward her. When Galen grabbed his arm, he shook the smaller man off.

Galen staggered backward, almost falling on the gravel.

His gaze traveled up and down Katharine's body. "Glad to see the diet finally worked for you," he said, a slight edge to his tone now. "*Yer* skin has cleared up too. All in time for our wedding."

She didn't move.

As if Simeon finally realized Ezra was still there, he looked at him. "I need to talk to *mei* fiancée, in private." He glanced at their clasped hands, then back at his face. "Let. Her. *Geh*."

Ezra didn't move from her side. "You'll have to make me."

"That won't be a problem." Simeon took a step toward him.

Then Katharine let go of Ezra's hand.

Katharine had never been so afraid in her life. Or so confident. How she could feel both, only God could explain, and she said a quick prayer as she let go of Ezra's hand. She needed to deal with Simeon.

"Katharine," Ezra said, his anger and hurt and confusion evident.

She smiled up at him, hoping that her eyes told him what her heart felt. *I can handle this.* When Ezra nodded and stepped back, she knew he understood.

She turned to Simeon. "I never told Elsie where exactly I was in Birch Creek," she said, staring him down. "How did you know I was here?"

"You told me, when you called your parents. I called the number back, and a man named Levi answered."

Vaguely she remembered hearing the phone ring as she was leaving the Stolls' phone shanty.

"From there it didn't take much to figure out where you were staying."

"You've been gone from Hulett for a week," Galen said, moving toward him again. "Where have you been all this time?"

"Sightseeing. There was *nee* hurry to get here."

"Other than seeing your fiancée who disappeared for a year?" Galen scoffed.

"I'm not going back to Hulett." With Ezra and Galen here she was physically safe from Simeon. He wouldn't dare hit her with a witness present. But she didn't miss the familiar spark of fury in his eyes, or the quick way he hid it, instantly becoming the affable man everyone thought he was.

"I wanted to give you your space," he said, ignoring her declaration.

"I don't love you, Simeon."

"Oh, Katharine." He moved closer to her. "I understand you're confused. You were nervous about getting married, and we had a whirlwind courtship, after all. And now another man is giving you attention. Something you're not used to. But I'm the one who loved you through *thick*," he said, giving her body another perusal, "and thin."

He knew where she was most vulnerable, but his verbal arrow missed the mark. "Ezra isn't a shallow man," she said. "He's *nix* like you."

Simeon's mouth twisted into an ugly snarl. This time it took longer for him to regain his composure. "Think of your parents then. Your father is in immense pain, and your mother is exhausted. They've had to worry about you on top of all their other problems. You don't want to make things *worse* for them, do you?"

She caught his double meaning. If she didn't return with him, he would take his revenge out on her parents. Her resolve started to falter.

"Why don't you tell her the real reason you want to marry her?" Galen said.

"I love her, that's the reason."

"More like you love her parents' money."

Katharine glanced at Galen. His arms were crossed, his expression resolute. He had no reason to lie. Simeon had thousands, it turned out, all with dollar signs in front of them.

I'm so stupid. How had she not seen his real motive before? Shortly before Simeon asked her out, her parents had received their settlement. His attachment to them was making sense. Heartbreaking sense. "It's over," she said to him. "You won't get *mei* parents' money."

"But—"

"You won't get me either."

He stilled. Then the sneer he gave her made her blood run cold. "I never wanted you."

"That's it." Ezra jumped in between them. "She told you to *geh*. Now *geh*."

"It's over, Simeon." Galen went to him. "Don't make it worse."

Simeon glared at Galen, then turned and stalked off.

"*Mei* parents," Katharine said.

"Don't worry about them," Galen reassured her. "I'll call the bishop and let him know what's going on. He'll make sure they're protected. But I don't think Simeon will be a problem anymore."

"What makes you say that?"

"He doesn't like to lose. If he goes back to Hulett, he'll have to admit that he did, and everyone will know he was after your parents' money. I'm sorry, Katharine. I didn't believe Elsie when she first told me." He stared at Simeon, who was at the edge of the inn's driveway. "I thought I knew *mei* best friend. Turns out I didn't know him at all."

"It's all right. He had everyone fooled."

"I saw a phone shanty down the road. I'll *geh* make the call as soon as I'm sure Simeon's gone." Then he pointed behind her. "You should *geh* talk to him."

She turned to see Ezra walking to the Stolls' house. Then she looked at Galen again. "*Danki* for coming here," she said, then hurried after Ezra. Now he knew the truth, at least most of it. He also knew her lies. Was she going to lose him because of it?

Chapter 31

Ezra continued to walk past the Stolls' house to the woods behind their property. He knew Katharine was behind him, but he didn't stop. It wasn't until he entered the cool shade of the sparsely leafed trees that he was able to think straight.

He stopped in front of a long log and sat down, then ran both hands through his hair. Katharine had been engaged, and she wasn't from Montana. Was everything she told him a lie? Believing that would make everything easier. But he couldn't, and now he didn't know what to do.

He heard the sound of leaves rustling behind him.

"Ezra?"

"*Ya*," he said bluntly, keeping his back to her.

"Can we talk?"

For a split second he considered telling her no. But he couldn't. Despite her deception, his feelings for her hadn't changed. He still loved her, and he needed to let her speak. "Okay."

She sat next to him on the log, and he noticed there was plenty of space between them. He stared at the ground, unable to look at her.

Then she spoke. "I'm sorry I lied to you, and to everyone else. I was scared, Ezra. And confused. All I knew was that I had to get away from Simeon, and I didn't want him to find me. I thought if I told people where I was from, there might be someone here who knew about Hulett, or worse, knew him."

He drew in a deep breath. "I understand you keeping that from the rest of the community. And I figured you'd been hurt in the past. I never guessed you'd been engaged, though. Or that you had run away."

She wrung her hands in her lap. "I don't expect you to understand *mei* reasoning."

"Try me."

Katharine turned and faced him. "For so long I wanted to be with someone who wouldn't judge me, either for *mei* weight, *mei* complexion, *mei* abilities . . . everything. I thought Simeon was that person. And he seemed to be, at first. Then he changed, and not only could I not be myself but I was also punished for not being what he wanted me to be."

Ezra shifted on the log and looked at her, his heart aching. He listened while she explained how Galen's wife, Elsie, had told her about the ad in the paper and encouraged her to come to Birch Creek, about Simeon's emotional hold on her parents, about her confusion and worry about their safety.

"The hardest thing about leaving Hulett was leaving them, then having to lie every time I talked to them." Tears filled her eyes. "I didn't know what to do."

"Why didn't you tell me? I wouldn't have said anything to

anyone. I could have helped you too. We could have gone back to Hulett together."

"You would have done that for me?"

He took her hand. "I would have done anything for you, Katharine. I even would have fought Simeon, but I could see you needed to handle him yourself." He gulped. "Did you . . . love him?"

"*Nee*. I loved the idea of being in love, but he killed that too." She released his hand. "I have a new start on life now. I can *geh* back to Hulett and see *mei* parents again. And Elsie, and *mei* community. I don't have to hide or keep secrets from anyone. I don't have to pretend anymore."

He tried to keep his expression blank, but he failed. He turned away from her, feeling like she'd dropped a boulder on top of his heart. Was she talking about pretending with Simeon . . . or him? He was afraid to ask. Afraid he wouldn't like the answer—that all this time he had misread her feelings for him. She didn't respond when he told her he loved her. Had he inadvertently taken advantage of her when she was vulnerable because of her abusive relationship with Simeon?

"Ezra?"

Shoving down his insecurity, he looked at her again. "That's great, Katharine. All great." By some kind of miracle he managed a half smile. "When are you leaving?"

"Leaving?" she asked, her brow furrowing.

"For Hulett."

"I'm not sure. I haven't decided yet."

He rose from the log. "I'm sorry," he said, raking his hand through his hair again. A warm breeze fluttered the fresh green leaves on the trees.

"For what?" She stood and walked over to him. "Ezra, what's going on?"

"If I had known about Simeon, I wouldn't have . . ."

"Wouldn't have what?"

He almost choked on his next words. "I wouldn't have fallen in love with you."

Katharine's knees nearly buckled. After her confrontation with Simeon and then having to explain and apologize for lying to Ezra, she was exhausted. She expected him to be upset. He had a right to be, and so did everyone else she'd lied to, and she intended to apologize to all of them too. But now he was apologizing? Telling her he wouldn't have fallen in love with her if he'd known the truth? "I . . . I don't understand."

His intense gaze held hers. "You came to Birch Creek to escape. Not to be pressured into another relationship."

"Ezra, where is this coming from—"

He held up his hand. "You were vulnerable. I think I might have taken advantage of that."

She didn't respond, trying to figure out what he was talking about. "You didn't take advantage of me. Simeon did."

"And if I'd known about that, I would have kept *mei* distance." His Adam's apple bobbed.

Finally she was starting to comprehend. "I'm glad you didn't," she said, moving closer to him. "Because of you, I was able to confront Simeon myself. I felt a strength and confidence I didn't know I had, and that's because of you."

His gaze softened. "I'm glad I helped you. I mean that, Katharine.

But I don't want you to feel obligated to me, or to make you feel trapped. I love you too much to ever do that."

His words brought more tears to her eyes. He was such an amazing man. She stepped on a nearby stump so they were eye to eye. "*Danki* for that too. I didn't get to finish what I was going to say before Galen showed up." She put her arms around his neck. "I love you, Ezra Bontrager. I understand if you don't believe me, but know this . . . I intend to show you my love until you do." Then she kissed him, her fingers brushing over the ends of his hair resting on his neck. She let out a tiny yelp of delight when he pulled her close.

When they parted, he grinned. "Message received." He kept his hands on her waist. Then he turned serious. "I love you, Katharine. I'll love you *nee* matter what."

"And I'll love you *nee* matter what," she echoed. "That's the truth."

Chapter 32

Sol stood near the barn outside his mother's house and watched as people came and went, paying their respects to Emmanuel, who died three weeks to the day he came back to Birch Creek. Irene was inside helping to serve food, being there for his mother, just like Aden and Sadie were. But he hadn't been able to step foot in that house since Emmanuel returned from the dead. Now that he really was dead, Sol didn't feel anything at all.

Irene was frustrated and disappointed in him, even though she hadn't said so outright. He could tell, though. He'd been distant from her and the boys since the letter, and even more so the past month. And when he found out that she took Isaac and Solomon to see Emmanuel, he came too close to lashing out at her in front of them. Somehow, he'd managed to keep his temper in partial check and he'd stormed out of the house before saying something he would regret.

He was aware that he shouldn't be shutting people out, but he couldn't help himself. *Old habits die hard*. Irene didn't know about the bottle of liquor he purchased the day after he got the letter from Emmanuel. He'd gone to Barton and straight to the liquor store, the worst thing he could have done. He was an alcoholic, and even though he didn't want to go back to drinking, the urge had overwhelmed him. Sol hid the bottle in his workshop, and it was still there. He hadn't given in to temptation yet, but right now he would do anything for a drink.

"Waiting for everyone to leave?"

He almost groaned out loud before turning to Cevilla. This woman. He hadn't paid much attention to her growing up, or when he was struggling with his addiction. But once Emmanuel left, it was as if Cevilla had every finger in the Birch Creek pie. Now she was meddling with his slice. "For what?"

"So you can pay your respects." She tapped her cane against the ground.

Sol almost glared at her. She was small and barely came up to his chest, but she was also a force to be reckoned with. "I'm waiting for this to be over."

"My, aren't we a bitter man."

"Don't you have someone else you can annoy?" He sounded like the surly son he used to be, and he hated himself for it.

"Actually, I don't." She gestured for him to follow her. "We need to talk. But I also need to sit down."

Knowing he'd have to face plenty of wrath if he didn't comply, he trailed behind her. She parked on the first hay bale she found and pointed at the empty space next to her. "Sit."

"I'd rather stand."

"And I'd rather you sit." She peered at him over her glasses. "I'm not going to get a crick in *mei* neck because of your stubbornness."

"Speak for yourself," he muttered and did as he was told.

"Now, tell me what's on *yer* mind."

He glared at her. "*Nix*. There, can I *geh* now?"

"Absolutely not." She used her cane as leverage to angle herself toward him. "I've known you *yer* entire life, Solomon Troyer. I knew a bright little *bu* who, overnight, changed into a sullen, angry one. Who grew up into a teen and a young man filled with anger and hate. Who then worked through his demons with the help of God and became a man who loves the Lord and his *familye*."

She sure did know a lot about him. Then again, he was positive he'd been the object of gossip over the years, particularly during his youth. "And?"

"And that man wouldn't be able to live with himself if he didn't pay his last respects."

Sol stared at his shoes. They were covered with old sawdust and dirt from the floor of his shop. Aden said the same thing when he came over last night and read him the riot act for not seeing Emmanuel before he died. Sol kicked him out of the house and spent the night in his workshop . . . again. He didn't want to admit it to anyone, but Aden and Cevilla were right. But he couldn't face the man who had broken him, instead of loved him.

They sat in silence in the barn. His mother's horse whinnied, and two barn swallows soared back and forth in the rafters.

Cevilla sighed. "Guess you've got to do you, as Meghan says."

"Who?"

"Richard's English granddaughter." Cevilla got up from the hay bale, and when he saw her struggle, he helped her to her feet. "*Danki*. Guess I sat for too long." She looked up at him, sadness in her eyes. "Emmanuel lived with a lot of regrets. Don't be like him."

Her words had knocked a chip in the wall around his heart. "What if I am?"

She touched his arm. "What do you mean?"

Against his will, his voice shook. "What if I'm . . . just like him?"

"Do you really believe that?"

"I don't want to. But I've always been afraid I will be. I haven't felt like myself since he came back." He couldn't believe he was admitting this to her, but now the chip had turned into a crack. "I feel like that scared *kinn* again."

"Oh, Sol. Such a burden you carry. You don't have to carry that alone. And it's all right to admit feeling weak, or unsure, or afraid. God already knows our feelings anyway. You have to let him help you. If Emmanuel had done that sooner, his life would have been different." She patted his arm, then walked out of the barn.

He stood there, her advice sinking in. Aden said that Emmanuel seemed like a different man since he'd come back to Birch Creek. That didn't surprise Sol. The man was eaten up with cancer. Of course he was different. But Aden said he was different inside, and that Sol should see for himself. He refused, up until the bitter end.

He looked at the barn door. He had his own regrets. The way he'd abused Aden, even though his father forced him to do it. The regret that he didn't fight back hard enough when he was old enough to. The regret of alcoholism. Of how he had treated Sadie before she and Aden married. And most of all, how he was pulling away from his wife . . . and from God, when he needed them the most.

Slowly he walked out of the barn. The buggies had thinned out, and the sun was hovering above the horizon, flames of fiery orange and yellow streaking the sky. He stopped in front of the door. Opened it. Ignored Jordan, Richard, Cevilla, Delilah, and Loren, who were seated in the living room. Went downstairs to the basement where his mother and brother were standing in front of Emmanuel's body.

His father's body.

Mamm and Aden turned around. They looked at each other, then moved away from the casket. He heard their footsteps fade as they went upstairs, leaving him alone with his father. Sol moved closer, his eyes blurring. He blinked the tears away and stared down. Then he touched his father's hand. "I forgive you," he whispered. Then more loudly, "I forgive you."

"Sol?"

He spun around to see Irene at the foot of the stairs. His beautiful wife who put up with so much from him, especially lately. They met each other in the middle of the room. Without saying a word, he put his arms around her, buried his face in her neck, and began to sob.

Epilogue

SIX MONTHS LATER

"What a beautiful wedding." Katharine sighed.

"*Ya*," Ezra said. "It was very nice."

They were sitting on the patio, taking a rest from cleaning up after Rhoda and Loren's wedding. Although the day had been overcast, the rain held off, and now a brisk wind was blowing the last of the fall leaves all over the yard. She huddled in her jacket.

"Are you cold?" Ezra asked. "I can give you *mei* coat. Or I'll *geh* inside and get a blanket."

"*Nee*. I'm comfortable here." She smiled. "With you."

He grinned and stuck his hands into the pockets of his navy peacoat. Then his smile faltered. "Are you all packed?"

"*Ya*, except for a few things."

"I wish I could *geh* with you."

"Me too."

Tomorrow morning would start her long trip back to Hulett.

It would be the second time she'd gone back to see her parents and friends since the incident with Simeon. No one knew where he went, although during her first visit, Galen and Elsie told her that they suspected he was in Pennsylvania, where he was originally from. "I'm still angry, but I hope he comes around and realizes how much he's wronged everyone, including you and your parents," Galen told her. "Until then, I'm glad he's gone."

"Now we can all move on with our lives," Elsie said.

Katharine agreed with both of them. There was no reason to shore up bitterness against him, or to wish him harm. He'd stolen her happiness and peace for too long, and she was ready to live her life, free from the past.

"Tell your *mamm* and *daed* hello for me," Ezra said.

"I will. They're disappointed you're not coming with me. They really liked 'meeting'"—she made air quotes—"you on the phone." During her first return to Hulett, she'd introduced them to Ezra. He and *Daed* had especially hit it off, and they were eager to truly meet him when the timing worked out.

"I liked 'meeting' them too," he said, mimicking her gesture. "Hopefully one day soon I can see them in person."

"I'm sure you will. They understand that you're busy helping Levi at the inn while Loren takes some time off to be with his new wife. And I know Levi is grateful for your hard work. As soon as Daed's up to traveling, they want to visit Birch Creek. He's come so far since his accident, I don't think it will be long before he's able to come here."

Ezra tapped his finger on the arm of the patio chair. "Do they ever mention . . . you know?"

"*Nee*. Not since I explained what happened." At first they were so shocked by Simeon's deception they had a hard time believing her. But when Galen and Elsie validated what Katharine said, they were dismayed they'd been taken in by him so completely.

"I'm sure that's for the best."

She nodded. "I think so too."

He took her hand, and they sat in silence for several minutes, both knowing that their time together was winding down until she returned to Birch Creek. "Do you need some help packing?" he eventually asked her.

Running her fingers lightly over the back of his hand, she said, "There's not much more to pack, just a few small toys for Jason and Alice." Elsie and Galen's daughter was almost six months old, and Jason was a great big brother.

Ezra nodded, his hands still in his pockets. "Sounds like you've got everything ready to *geh*."

A wave of sadness washed over her. She was eager to see her parents and friends again, but she would miss Ezra more than anything. They'd talked a lot about their future together, but he hadn't proposed. She was okay with taking things slow. It had given both of them time to get to know each other, the good things and the not so good. She'd jumped into an engagement before, and she refused to do that again. Yet during Rhoda and Loren's wedding, she realized she was more than ready to be Mrs. Ezra Bontrager. But she would be in Hulett for six weeks. That was a long time to be separated from the man she loved.

"Katharine?"

She blinked and looked at him. "Oh, I'm sorry. Lost in *mei* thoughts again."

"I said your name twice before, so I figured that was the case. I'd give you a penny for your thoughts, but with inflation they're probably worth at least a nickel."

Laughing, she said, "Or maybe even a whole dime."

He fished in his pocket, and she thought he was actually going to pull out a dime and give it to her. Instead he handed her a small box wrapped in plain brown paper and tied with a green ribbon.

"What's this?" she said, taking the box.

"Open it and see."

She untied the ribbon and ripped open the paper, then lifted the lid of the box. "Oh, Ezra." Inside was the powder jar she'd been so enamored with at Schlabach's Antiques on their first trip to Barton. She and Ezra had been there several times since, and each time the jar was still there, looking as lovely as ever. Now it was hers. "*Danki*," she said, holding the jar against her. "I love it."

"Consider it an engagement gift." His eyes were full of anticipation and the love she knew he felt for her.

Katharine met his gaze. "Seriously?"

"*Ya*." He got up from his chair and knelt in front of her. "You know how much I love you. And not to sound presumptuous, but I know how much you love me."

She cradled his cheek in her hand as a drop of rain fell. "I do."

"Then it's time to make it official." The drop of rain turned into sprinkles, but that didn't stop him from taking her hand. "Will you marry me?"

"*Ya,*" she said, without a second of hesitation. "I'll marry you." She put her arms around his neck and kissed him. Then she whispered in his ear, "It's about time you asked me."

He laughed and kissed her again. "Now you can plan the wedding with your *mamm* and Elsie. We can get married in Hulett if you want."

She shook her head. "Birch Creek is *mei* home. I want to get married here."

Suddenly the sky opened up and rain gushed down. Ezra grabbed her hand and they hurried to the Stolls' kitchen. Even though the patio was right off the house, they were nearly drenched.

Delilah entered the kitchen. "*Mei* goodness, that's a gully washer . . ." She tilted her head at Kathrine and Ezra.

"I know, we're soaking wet," Katharine said.

"*Gut* thing the rain held off until we finished cleaning up," Ezra added.

Delilah nodded, her expression turning sly. "True, but what's going on with you two?'

Katharine giggled. "We can't hide anything from her, can we?" she said to Ezra.

"Nope." He put his arm around her waist. "And in this case, I don't want to."

"You're engaged!" Delilah clasped her hands together. "Finally. I didn't think you'd ever get around to it." She grinned. "Ah, love. It happens when you least expect it."

Katharine leaned her head on Ezra's chest, happier than she'd ever imagined she could be. She loved this man who noticed her when she wanted to be unnoticeable, encouraged her when she was discouraged, and loved her when she believed she was unlovable. He was in plain sight all along.

Jesse plunged the axe into the stump near Cevilla and Richard's house. It was his turn to chop wood for the Thompsons, a job he and his single brothers started doing years ago to help Cevilla out. He didn't mind the task and actually enjoyed chopping wood. He was also glad to get out of his house. His mother was giddy about another one of her sons getting married. That was fine. No, it was good. He was glad Ezra was happy, and he liked Katharine. What wasn't good was that Malachi and Judah, his best friends, were also caught up in their girlfriends. And Nelson was sweet on a new girl who had arrived in Birch Creek two days ago. It was like love had become a contagious disease around here—and he didn't want to catch it.

Although the weather was damp and chilly, he'd worked up a sweat. He slipped off his jacket and hat and continued to split wood until there was a good-sized pile ready to be stacked on the Thompsons' porch. He finished that task, then knocked on the door. It took a few minutes, but Cevilla opened it.

"Land sakes, Jesse. Where's your coat?"

"Over there." He gestured with a nod to the stump. His axe was sticking out of the center of the stump again and his coat hung off it. "I'm ready to bring some of this wood inside."

"*Danki.*" She opened the door. "I made some hot cocoa for you."

"Sounds *gut*, thank you." He picked up an armful of wood and brought it into the small living room. He had just placed it in the bin next to the stove when he heard Cevilla speak.

"Did everything work out the way you planned?"

He whirled around. What a strange question. "I got all the wood cut, if that's what you mean. I didn't need a plan for that."

"I'm not talking about cutting wood." She paused, as if for dramatic effect. "You put the bachelor ad in the paper, didn't you?"

His mouth dropped open. "How did you know?"

She walked over to the couch. "I didn't, not until recently." She sat down and gave him a sly grin. "I thought Delilah did it, and she thought it was me. Each of us assuming the other was responsible made perfect sense. We are the Birch Creek matchmakers . . . much to the chagrin of just about everyone."

Jesse walked over and sat down on the chair next to her. A mug of cocoa sat on the end table between his chair and hers. He should have known his secret would come out eventually. "How did you figure it out?"

"One thing about being old, you get to observe a lot. I can't do much, but I can people watch. You'd be amazed at what you learn just by paying attention. And once I knew that your *mamm*, Delilah, and Mary Yoder didn't have anything to do with the ad, I started wondering . . . Who would get the biggest kick out of the bachelors in this town being overrun with women? And which family has the most bachelors?" She leaned forward and peered at him over her glasses. "And which Bontrager *bu* is the biggest troublemaker? Am I on the right track?"

He leaned back in the chair, unable to look at her. "Yeah," he grumbled. "I did it."

Cevilla clucked her tongue. "That's quite the scheme, Jesse."

He couldn't help but smile. He did enjoy teasing his brothers, especially Zeb, Zeke, and Owen. Even Ezra, although the shine was starting to wear off the apple. But for a while, watching his siblings try to deal with the barrage of single women was entertaining. And all it took was one tiny, inexpensive ad that he thought might bring one or two women. Maybe five or six at the most. Instead more than a dozen showed up from all over the country, and they were still coming. "Things are getting a little out of hand."

Her smile disappeared. "What you did was wrong, Jesse."

"It seemed funny at the time. Honest, I didn't think a little prank ad would travel so far. I doubted anyone would even notice. And if they did, they would realize it was a joke."

"Interfering in other people's lives isn't appropriate."

Jesse smirked. "Oh, *really*."

She rolled her eyes. "You're impudent, you know that?" But her smile was back. "God has obviously used your mischief for *gut*. Your older *bruders* are happy, and almost all of them are wed or will be soon."

"Then *nee* harm done, *ya*?"

"Not yet. And hopefully there won't be. There's a few more Bontrager *buwe* that are going to need wives in the future."

"*Ya*, but I'm not one of them."

"Oh, *really*?" she said in a decent imitation of him.

He laughed and stood. "*Ya*, really. Not everyone is interested in getting married."

"That's true. For years I believed that about myself. Then Richard came along."

"Well, if God wills me to get married, then so be it. Until then, I'm in *nee* hurry. I plan to be single for a long, long, *long* time."

Cevilla smiled and picked up her teacup. She peered at him over the brim. "We'll see."

Acknowledgments

It's been a nine-year journey since I wrote the first Birch Creek book, *A Reluctant Bride*, and two people have been by my side during the entire process—my editor, Becky Monds, and my agent, Natasha Kern. Thank you both for your knowledge, support, and encouragement. I say it all the time, but I can never say it enough.

Another thank you to Karli Jackson, who also edited this book. Thank you for finding my mistakes and keeping me on track.

And thanks to you, dear reader, for joining me on another adventure in Birch Creek. Stay tuned for my next series, set in Birch Creek's "sister" town of Marigold. You'll recognize some old favorites, along with some new characters that I hope you'll love. Will Jesse's practical joke backfire on him? Wait and see . . .

Discussion Questions

1. At the beginning of the story, Katharine hopes she will eventually be comfortable with herself. What advice would you give her to help her see her own value?
2. Katharine has to be deceptive in order to escape Simeon. Do you think her lying was justified? Why or why not?
3. When Aden and Sadie are talking about Rhoda, Sadie thinks, "There's a fine line between worry and concern, and he was crossing that more and more." Was there ever a time when your concern turned to worry? How did you handle it?
4. Why is asking for forgiveness from God and from those we've wronged so important?
5. Rhoda had lots of mixed emotions after she received Emmanuel's "death" letter—confusion, guilt, shame, and relief. Do you think these feelings are normal? How would you encourage Rhoda?
6. Rhoda didn't feel God's comfort or presence after

receiving Emmanuel's letter. What are some practical ways we can nurture our faith in God when he feels far away?

7. If you were Jordan, how would you have handled helping Emmanuel return home?
8. What—or who—do you think softened Emmanuel's heart enough for him to return home?

The Maple Falls Romance Novels

Enjoy Kathleen Fuller's sweet and delightful small-town romances!

USA TODAY BESTSELLING AUTHOR
KATHLEEN FULLER
Hooked on You
A MAPLE FALLS ROMANCE

USA TODAY BESTSELLING AUTHOR
KATHLEEN FULLER
Much Ado About a Latte
A MAPLE FALLS ROMANCE

USA TODAY BESTSELLING AUTHOR
KATHLEEN FULLER
Sold On Love
A MAPLE FALLS ROMANCE

Available in print, e-book, and audio

THOMAS NELSON
Since 1798

About the Author

With over a million copies sold, Kathleen Fuller is the *USA TODAY* bestselling author of several novels, including the Hearts of Middlefield novels, the Middlefield Family novels, the Amish of Birch Creek series, and the Amish Letters series, as well as a middle-grade Amish series, the Mysteries of Middlefield.

Visit her online at KathleenFuller.com
Instagram: @kf_booksandhooks
Facebook: @WriterKathleenFuller